on magnolia lane

Center Point
Large Print

Also by Denise Hunter and available from Center Point Large Print:

The Wishing Season
Married 'til Monday
The Goodbye Bride
Just a Kiss
Sweetbriar Cottage
Blue Ridge Sunrise
Honeysuckle Dreams

This Large Print Book carries the Seal of Approval of N.A.V.H.

on magnolia lane

A Blue Ridge Romance

DENISE HUNTER

CENTER POINT LARGE PRINT
THORNDIKE, MAINE

This Center Point Large Print edition
is published in the year 2019 by arrangement with
Thomas Nelson.

The text of this Large Print edition is unabridged.
In other aspects, this book may vary
from the original edition.
Printed in the United States of America
on permanent paper.
Set in 16-point Times New Roman type.

ISBN: 978-1-64358-054-8

Library of Congress Cataloging-in-Publication Data

Names: Hunter, Denise, 1968- author.
Title: On Magnolia Lane / Denise Hunter.
Description: Center Point Large Print edition. | Thorndike, Maine :
    Center Point Large Print, 2019. | Series: A Blue Ridge romance
Identifiers: LCCN 2018046113 | ISBN 9781643580548
    (hardcover : alk. paper)
Subjects: LCSH: Love stories. | Large type books.
Classification: LCC PS3608.U5925 O52 2019 | DDC 813/.6—dc23
LC record available at https://lccn.loc.gov/2018046113

on magnolia lane

ONE

Jack McReady had fallen in love with Daisy in one-hour increments. How many men could claim that? he thought as he swung his Mazda into the diagonal slot in front of her flower shop, his palms sweaty against the leather steering wheel.

This wasn't his ordinary way of seeing her. Usually she came into his office to talk—hence the one-hour increments. It was the reason he knew more about Daisy than most, even their mutual friends.

But today he was getting flowers for his secretary, Gloria, as tomorrow was Administrative Professionals' Day. Sure, he could've phoned the order in, but then he would have missed a prime opportunity to see Daisy.

Entering the shop was always a full sensory experience. The bells tinkled out a welcome as the cool, bright fragrance of flowers rose to his nostrils. The colorful array of flowers and knick-knacks, so artfully arranged, begged the shopper to stop and touch and appreciate.

"Be with you in a minute!" Daisy called from the back.

The sweet sound of her voice made Jack's heart thump harder. He knew she'd be working alone because today was Tuesday. Her mom was out delivering flowers, and her grandma only worked half days on Tuesdays and Thursdays. He knew—and retained—way too much about Daisy, he thought with a rueful shake of his head.

Jack stuffed his hands into his Docker pockets and perused the shop. When he was inside Oopsy Daisy he always felt as though he were meandering through the garden of Eden. Everything was arranged so perfectly, displayed so creatively. Who but Daisy would think to use an antique bicycle basket or a mailbox to display a lovely bouquet of flowers? Or an outdoor fountain to showcase a cascading arrangement of flowering vines? Everywhere he looked was another inspired idea.

"Pastor Jack!"

He'd given up on getting her to drop the title. Her appointments had started two years ago, rarely scheduled but always delightful. He loved that she was a little overly sensitive, and he knew no one more conscientious than she. It was one of her finest qualities.

His heart fluttered at the sight of her silky blond hair and the faint spray of freckles that dotted her nose.

"Hello, Daisy. How are you this afternoon?" His tongue felt thick and uncoordinated.

"Just fine. I'm working on an order for a Cinco de Mayo party, believe it or not."

"Sounds intriguing." Was it just him, or was it hot in here? He tugged at his collar.

"I can't believe we're almost to May," she said.

"Step out onto the sidewalk; you'll believe it soon enough."

Her laughter was like a melody that plucked the strings of his heart. "I hear you." He let his gaze drift around the shop. "It's beautiful in here, Daisy. Every time I come in I'm just astounded by your displays."

"Oh, it's nothing really." She waved a hand as she reached the glass counter that separated them.

She was the worst at accepting a compliment. He gave her a long, steady look, as he was in the habit of doing when she tried to sell herself short.

"What? Oh, right. I'm supposed to be working on that." She pasted on a sweet smile. "Thank you ever so much, Pastor Jack. That is so nice of you to say."

"There, was that so hard?"

"You'll never know." She tilted a smile up at him. "So let me guess—you're here for Secretaries' Day."

"Got it in one."

"I'll fix Gloria up with a nice bouquet. Maybe some roses and daisy poms, some asters and

9

purple delphinium? I have a large blue mason jar she'd just love. I can tie a nice big bow around it."

He loved the way her green eyes sparkled when she talked flowers. He fought their magnetic pull and was grateful for the umpteenth time that his olive skin wasn't prone to blushing. "Whatever you come up with will be perfect."

Daisy wrote up the order as Jack signed a card for Gloria. His secretary had been with him since he'd taken the job seven years ago. He'd be adrift without her, and they both knew it.

"You want to wait while I make it up or should we deliver it for you tomorrow?" Daisy asked after he'd swiped his credit card.

"Whatever's easiest for you."

The bell tinkled as the door opened, allowing the entrance of a tall, slender woman with straight brown hair. She was well dressed and looked to be in her early thirties.

"Welcome!" Daisy said, peering past Jack with a friendly smile. "Let me know if I can help you with anything."

"Actually, I'm just looking for a bouquet. Maybe you can point me in the right direction."

Jack stepped back from the counter, nodding at the woman before turning back to Daisy. "Go ahead and help her. You can just deliver the flowers tomorrow."

"Sounds great. Thanks, Pastor Jack."

• • •

"Sorry if I butted in line," the woman said.

Daisy's eyes slid from Pastor Jack to her new customer. She looked as if she'd stepped straight out of a Dove soap commercial with her creamy complexion and natural beauty. Intelligence flashed in her blue eyes as she took in the small shop.

Daisy smiled. "Not at all. We were finished. Would you like to look at our fresh bouquets, or did you have something specific in mind? I'm Daisy, by the way—one of the owners."

The woman gave her a crooked smile. "Ah, Daisy . . . hence the name of the shop. I'm Julia."

"Nice to meet you. The name wasn't my idea, believe me. My grandma started the place when I was young enough to think having a store named after me was the best thing since sliced bread. Can I help you find something?"

"I'm not really sure what I want. Let me look a minute, I guess."

Julia wandered over to the floral display case, grace in her movements. She wore quality black slacks and a trendy top. The bag and shoes looked like designer wear. In other words, she wasn't from around here.

Daisy wiped the lacquered counter and restocked the floral cards and envelopes. When she was finished, the woman was still perusing the case.

11

Daisy stepped out from behind the counter. "What's the occasion, Julia? Maybe I can help."

"Well . . . I guess you could say they're for an old friend."

"Man or woman?"

"Man, but . . ."

"Hmm. Something cheery, maybe? Spring's a great time for colorful blooms." Daisy slid open the case and pulled out a cellophane-wrapped arrangement of yellow roses, white lilies, and blue delphinium. "What do you think? This one isn't too feminine. I love the lemon leaf with the roses."

"That's the very one I was eyeing."

She smiled. "You have great taste."

"Let's do it then."

Daisy carried the bouquet to the counter and began ringing up the purchase. The cellophane crinkled as Julia picked up the bouquet and took a whiff.

"What brings you to Copper Creek? Just visiting your friend?"

"Kind of. I'm just passing through. I've never been to Georgia before. To be honest, I didn't even know there were mountains here."

"It's all we have up north. The Appalachian Trail starts not far from here. We get a lot of people passing through town, especially in the summer."

"It's a lovely town."

"Well, it's small, but it's home. I love the people and the familiarity of it all. You know how it is . . . Everybody knows everybody."

"And their business?" Julia gave her a wan smile as she pulled a bill from her wallet.

"Sometimes." Daisy laughed. "Okay, most of the time. But the pros outweigh the cons, to my way of thinking. Where are you from?"

"North Carolina, the Winston-Salem area."

"You're a ways from home then. Well, I hope you enjoy your visit." Daisy made change and counted it back to Julia. "And I hope he enjoys the flowers."

Julia blinked before giving a smile that didn't quite reach her eyes. "Thank you."

Just as Daisy's customer left the shop, a series of thumps sounded on the staircase at the back of the store. She got there in time to hold the door open for Ava Morgan, who was carrying a box of old junk from the upstairs apartment.

"Thanks." Ava edged past Daisy on her way to the Dumpster out back.

The eighteen-year-old had added a subtle auburn rinse of some kind to her dark hair. The color was a striking contrast with her pale skin and blue eyes. Today she wore it back in a messy bun, exposing her long, slender neck. She was lovely, inside and out, so it had been no surprise when she was crowned Miss Georgia Peach at last year's Peachfest.

A longtime resident of the Hope House, a local girls home, Ava was graduating from high school in a month and had asked about renting the small apartment above the shop. It was full of junk the old owner had left behind and had been sitting empty for years. The deal was, if Ava cleaned it out, it was all hers. The girl had jumped on the offer.

"I'll help you after the shop closes," Daisy said when Ava returned from the Dumpster.

The girl wiped her hands on her black yoga pants. "Believe it or not, I should be done by then."

"Wow, you've really put in the hours. I don't know how you've had time with school and work."

"They kind of go easy on the seniors. They know we're seriously burnt out." Ava looked up the stairwell, smiling. "The place just needs a good cleaning now, and it'll be ready to move into. I can't wait."

Daisy remembered the stained grout in the bathroom and the thick layer of dirt on the windowsills. Ava still had a huge job ahead of her.

"It'll probably be great having a place of your own, huh?"

Ava rolled her eyes. "You have no idea. I share my room with a twelve- and fourteen-year-old."

Daisy laughed. "No wonder you're in such

a hurry. A young woman needs her privacy. What are your plans going forward? Will you be working full-time at the Peach Barn once school's out?"

"For the summer, yes. Then I start classes part-time at Dalton State."

"I thought I heard you got a full scholarship to UGA."

Zoe, Ava's boss at the Peach Barn and Daisy's good friend, had mentioned it a few months ago.

"I did. But I don't want to leave my little sister." Millie was nine and also a Hope House resident. Their mom had passed several years ago, and their dad was in prison. "My plan is to get my degree as quickly as possible, then save up so she can go to college. I don't think she's going to be getting an academic scholarship at this point."

"Ah, that makes sense."

The girl was making a big sacrifice for her sister. There was nothing wrong with Dalton State, but Ava would shine even at a big school like UGA.

"What's your major going to be, do you know?"

"Not sure yet. I'll just take gen eds at first and see how it goes. I really liked my marketing class last year, so maybe business."

"I'm sure you'll do great no matter what you choose."

"Thanks. I don't suppose you have a vacuum

cleaner I can use? The carpet's a wreck up there."

"Oh, honey, I've seen it. You need a carpet cleaner. My grandma has one. How about I bring it over after I close up, and we'll do it together?"

Ava gave a grateful smile. "Sweet. To be honest, it was kind of grossing me out."

Daisy laughed. "It's nasty. I'll be back around five thirty, and we'll get it cleaned right up."

TWO

Daisy's childhood home was nestled at the base of the north Georgia mountains. The clapboard farmhouse with a wraparound porch was like something from a storybook. The rolling green land begged for horses—just as she'd done as a child, but her pleas had gone unheard. A fact she never let her mother forget.

"Knock-knock!" she called before slipping through the screen door. It slapped into place behind her as a delicious aroma mingled with the familiar smell of home. Thursday nights were for supper with her mama, and after a long day at the shop, Daisy was happy to skip out on cooking.

"Come on in, honey."

Daisy dropped the newspaper on the end table and entered the kitchen just as her mom was pulling a pot from the stovetop. Daisy grabbed the strainer and set it in the old farm sink just in time for her mom to empty the pasta and water into it.

"Thanks."

Once the pasta was drained, Daisy kissed her mom's cheek. Karen Pendleton was still attractive at almost fifty-five and kept a tight rein on her figure. Her shoulder-length hair curled under the steam of the boiling water, and her green eyes, so like Daisy's, sparked whenever she got bent out of shape, which was often.

Daisy began setting out the silverware. "Deliveries go all right today?"

"Mostly. Mrs. Forsythe refused her flowers, though."

Daisy sighed, thinking of the lovely bouquet of blue and white hydrangeas. "He must've really blown it this time."

"No doubt. I put the arrangement in the case. Maybe it'll sell."

"I'll refund his credit card tomorrow."

"You shouldn't. It's not our fault his wife didn't want them."

"I know, but . . . he's a steady customer."

"Which only speaks to the man's poor behavior."

Daisy shrugged. Part of her didn't know why Mrs. Forsythe put up with her husband's shenanigans. The other part—the one who'd been on a dozen first dates in the past few months—understood perfectly well.

They finished putting the food on the table and sat down in front of the bay window facing the backyard. It was a beautiful view—the vegetable garden her mother lovingly tended, the copse of evergreens from Christmases past, and the white fence she'd helped her father put up when she was twelve.

"Daisy."

Daisy looked over to realize her mom was ready for grace, had maybe even said her name a time or two.

"Sorry. Lost in thought. Go ahead."

After the prayer they tucked in. The food was healthy but a little bland. A chicken breast with a light lemon sauce and whole-wheat pasta topped with her mom's homemade marinara.

"How's Ava coming along with the apartment?" her mom asked. "Gram said she's been quite the busy bee the past couple weeks."

"She's up there cleaning every spare minute. But between school and her job she can't have many of those. The carpets were so disgusting. We worked until after midnight Tuesday and still didn't get finished."

"I hope this isn't a mistake. She's so young to be living on her own."

"She can take care of herself. She seems years older than most eighteen-year-olds."

"Isn't that the truth. Poor thing, her and those other girls. I'm glad you do that Spring Fling dress drive for them."

"We've gotten quite a few donations. I just picked them up from the cleaners today."

"Was the shop busy?"

"Pretty steady. The insurance forms came in the mail, and I worked on them between customers."

"Oh, don't worry about those," her mom said. "I can fill them out this weekend."

"That's all right. I've already got a good start."

"I don't mind, honey. I know how you struggle with—"

Daisy gave her mom a look. "I've got it, Mama."

A long pause ensued, then Karen gave a tiny nod, her mouth tightening. "Of course you do. I was only trying to help."

Daisy's fork scraped the plate as she stabbed at the grilled chicken.

"How did your coffee date go with that gentleman friend?" her mom asked.

Daisy's fork paused on its way to her mouth. "How did you know about that?"

"You must've mentioned it to me."

"I'm sure I didn't." Daisy told her mom as little as possible about her love life—or lack thereof. Including the fact that she'd recently branched out with a dating app.

"Well, maybe someone else mentioned it to me. So how did it go? Was he nice?"

"He was just fine." For a thirty-year-old man still living at home with his parents and working at the Dairy Freeze. He'd had beady little brown eyes that never left hers, not even for a moment. He'd talked about his motorcycle (Sasha) like she was the love of his life—and blew his nose repeatedly at the table. *Allergies,* he'd said.

"You're too picky, honey. You'll never find a perfect man, you know."

"I'm not talking about this with you, Mama. I'm fine just as I am. I don't even need a man." She simply *wanted* one. Rather badly. Okay, desperately.

"Now stop that foolish talk. Of course you do. You could wear a little lipstick now and again. You're not getting any younger, you know."

Nor was she likely to forget it, with her mom reminding her every five minutes.

Daisy reached for the serving spoon. "Would you like more pasta? It's very good."

"Of course not. I'm watching my weight." Her quick assessment of Daisy's figure didn't go unnoticed.

Daisy scooped a heaping spoonful of pasta and dumped it on her own plate. "Well, I'm starving."

"I always make too much pasta. Are you still jogging, dear? It's so healthy for you."

"You know I'm not, Mama."

"You were so mellow when you were jogging."

"It's called exhaustion. I couldn't move for days." She'd tried jogging for a week last fall. If there were a second wind, she'd never found it. Maybe she'd take up walking now that the weather was warmer again.

"You should walk with me in the mornings. I'd love the company."

"I'll think about it."

She would definitely not think about it.

Her mom began listing the benefits of aerobic exercise while Daisy finished her food. When she was done, she took her plate to the sink and rinsed it off. She was sliding it into the dishwasher when she noticed a form on the counter by her mom's purse. She couldn't miss the large bold print at the top.

Her stomach shrank two sizes as her breath tumbled from her lungs. She turned and gaped at her mom. "You're selling the house?"

It took her mom two seconds to notice the form on the counter. Her eyes widened and lips parted. Then her gaze slid away, and she traced the eyelet trim on the tablecloth.

"I was going to tell you tonight."

Betrayal whipped through Daisy. It was irrational, she knew. The house belonged to her mother, and she had every right to sell it.

But . . .

"Honey, it's just a house—and a big one at that. It's too much to take care of. Too much property. I'd rather be closer to town, closer to the store."

"Do you need more help around here? I can mow every week, I don't mind. And if it's the cleaning—"

"Honey, you do enough. You have your own house and yard to take care of. I just don't want this big responsibility anymore."

Daisy's heart had taken flight, and her lungs

struggled to keep up. Her eyes darted to her dad's seat at the kitchen table, to the bay window he'd installed, and out to the yard where he'd sometimes camped out with her on mild summer nights.

Losing this house would be like losing another piece of him. The last piece. This was where all her best memories with him were. She blinked against the burn in her eyes.

Her mom approached, taking her hand. "Honey . . ."

"Please don't sell it, Mama."

"It's only a house, Daisy."

She pulled her hand away and turned back to the sink. "No, it's not."

She could still picture her dad on the recliner in the living room after he came home from the office. Could still hear the squawk of the porch swing as he listened to her prattle on about her school day.

"I know this is difficult, honey, but it's been seven years."

"I know how long it's been." The day after tomorrow was the very anniversary of his death. That only made things worse. Made the feelings so raw.

"There's a cute little bungalow on Katydid Lane, just the perfect size for me. The yard has room for a nice garden, and the neighborhood will be a great place to walk."

She blinked at her mom. "You've already found a place?"

"I haven't put in a bid yet. I haven't even put the house on the market." She brushed Daisy's hair over her shoulder and resolutely met her daughter's gaze. "But I'm going to, honey. I have to move on with my life. It's time."

Daisy shrugged her mom away. She couldn't believe this. She'd imagined always having this place to come home to. Sure, her mom had complained a time or two about the upkeep, but she'd never once mentioned selling it. And coming at the anniversary of her daddy's death, it just all seemed like too much.

"I have to go now."

"Honey . . . don't be like this," Karen said as Daisy gathered her purse and fought the rise of emotion.

She paused on the way out the door and gave her mom a weak smile. "Thanks for supper, Mama. I'll see you at work tomorrow."

THREE

Jack tried not to fixate on Daisy at the other end of the table as she conversed with her girlfriends, Hope and Josephine. Last Chance, the local country band, was gearing up to play, and it was standing room only at the Rusty Nail. Music blared through the speakers, and the smell of grilled burgers and french fries made his stomach rumble.

A crack of thunder sounded over the music, and rain pounded the metal roof overhead.

"It's really coming down out there," Jack said to his friend Brady—the only other male still sitting at the row of tables they'd strung together.

Brady ran a hand through his short dark hair, his blue eyes flickering to the nearest window. "There's a thunderstorm warning. Looked pretty nasty on the radar."

"Well, we need the rain."

"True enough."

Daisy suddenly appeared across the table from Jack, jump-starting his heart. "How'd Gloria like the flowers?"

Her green eyes were laser-focused on him, her sweet perfume filling his senses. She wore a little makeup tonight, and her lips looked especially lush.

He pulled his eyes away, ignoring the way his heart punished his ribs. "Um, she liked them. She really liked them."

"Oh. Great." She nodded, waiting for him to expound on the thought.

Jack searched for something else to say but got distracted by the way the light reflected off her hair, making it glitter like spun gold.

Say something. Heat rose from the collar of his button-down shirt as his mind spun like tires in a snowbank.

Traction. He just needed a little traction. "Um . . . She really loves flowers." There was that master's degree at work.

Daisy blinked. "Right. Well. I'm glad she liked them."

Another awkward pause ensued. Jack filled it with a plastic smile.

"I'm just gonna"—Daisy gestured toward the bar—"go get something to drink."

"Sure, sure."

"You want anything?"

He reached for his Coke. "That's okay, I've got"—he bumped his glass, and soda sloshed over the side—"plenty." He grabbed his napkin and began mopping up the mess.

Really, Jack? Really?

"Right," she said. "Okay. I'll be back."

He closed his eyes in a long blink, half hoping he'd vanish. Or she'd vanish. Or he'd suddenly know what the heck he was doing. He was such an idiot. His palms were damp, and the back of his neck had broken out in a sweat.

Brady leaned closer, smelling faintly of car grease and brake dust. "How can someone so eloquent in the pulpit turn into *that* when a woman comes around?"

Jack glared at him. Brady had caught on to his unrequited feelings for Daisy last fall. That made two enlightened people, as their friend Noah had known almost from the beginning.

"You're well-dressed, well-spoken, and you're a nice-looking guy—not my type, honey, but you know."

Jack hated being tongue-tied around Daisy. It was more manageable in his office when she was doing most of the talking. All he had to do was nod and ask how she felt about that and offer to close in prayer. Basically, put on his pastor's cap. But away from church, when casual conversation was supposed to be a two-way street . . .

He just wasn't good with women. He never had been. He'd been such a dork in high school. He had these horrendous thick-framed glasses and a scrawny build. And the acne . . . There wasn't a girl in high school who would've given him the time of day.

"Seriously, man," Brady said. "You've gotta get it together. She's just a woman."

Easy for Brady to say. He and their friend Hope had fallen in love and were currently living in wedded bliss. All of their friends had paired off. Noah and Josephine, Cruz and Zoe, and most recently, Brady and Hope. They all made it look so easy.

That's not really fair, he thought. They'd each had their own share of troubles. It was easy to forget, though, seeing them now.

"I don't know what you're waiting for," Brady said. "Are you ever going to do anything about it or what?"

Cruz appeared in the seat beside Jack. He had good looks that turned the ladies' heads, but he'd only ever had eyes for Zoe. The two had a beautiful little girl named Gracie and worked the peach orchard Zoe had inherited from her grandma.

Cruz was looking between Brady and Jack. "Do anything about what?"

"Jack has a crush on Daisy," Brady said.

Jack gave Brady a withering look. "Seriously?"

Cruz raised his hands, palms out. "Hey, that's cool. Daisy's great. You should go for it."

"I'm not going for anything." He narrowed his eyes at Cruz. "And you didn't hear any of this. Daisy's a friend. Just a friend. End of conversation. Let's talk about something else."

"He doesn't think she wants to be a pastor's wife," Brady said.

Jack scowled at him.

"Also he thinks he's too old for her," Brady said.

"Really?" Cruz eyed Jack speculatively. "What are you, thirty-four, thirty-five? Not exactly a card-carrying member of AARP."

"Plus she's a member of his congregation," Brady said. "I don't know why that matters, but he seems to think it does."

"What part of 'end of conversation' didn't you understand?"

"I don't see why that should matter," Cruz said. "It's not like you're her boss or something."

Brady set down his drink. "And, dude, she's meeting a lot of men right now. She's going to get snatched up, and then it'll be too late. Trust me, you don't want to have regrets. Regrets are the worst."

A weight settled in Jack's chest. "What do you mean, meeting a lot of men?"

"She's using that new dating app," Brady said. "Butterfly or something like that. Hope was telling me about it. It limits the pool geographically so you're only meeting singles in your area."

"You mean Flutter," Cruz said. "My buddy's using it. He loves it. Daisy's on that? I should tell him about her."

Jack stiffened. "Hey."

Cruz shrugged. "Sorry. Just thinking out loud."

Jack's heart had gone into overdrive at the thought of losing Daisy. Losing. As if he could lose something—someone—he'd never even had.

"So what's up with this app?" he said. "Is she dating strangers? How can that be safe?"

"You chat on the app first and see if you want to meet up," Brady said. "She's met guys from all over the region, but I'm sure she meets them in public. She's a smart woman."

Brady leaned forward on his elbows, his blue eyes intense. "She's had a ton of dates in the past few months, man. According to Hope she's pretty serious about finding someone, and she's not wasting any time."

Jack's mood had taken a nosedive. "Terrific."

Bad enough seeing Daisy all the time and knowing he couldn't have her. Watching her dance with other men. How much worse would it be when she found someone and started bringing him around the group every Saturday night? Started bringing him to church on Sundays? How would he even be able to focus on his sermon as he watched her fall in love with another man right in his own pew?

A new thought occurred, this one stabbing like a knife in his gut.

What if she asked him to officiate her wedding?

His breath left his lungs, and he closed his eyes. Took a long sip of his Coke. Unrequited love was awful. No wonder there were so many country songs about it.

God, please. Take it away. I don't want to love someone who doesn't love me back. Do You know how awful this feels?

Jack winced as he realized what he'd just asked the Creator of humankind, who'd been rejected by the same over and over again.

"So why don't you just ask her out or something?" Cruz said. "What do you have to lose?"

It wasn't as if he hadn't fantasized about that very thing. But that's all it was. A fantasy. "She doesn't see me that way."

All he had to do was imagine the look that would come over her face. The way her eyes would widen in shock, then tighten at the corners as pity rolled over her features. She'd wonder what she'd done to lead him on. She'd be consumed by guilt.

"Hope didn't see me that way either, at first," Brady said. "Sometimes feelings evolve, you know."

"Don't you think that would've happened by now? We've spent countless hours together." Movement behind Brady caught Jack's eye. The ladies were returning to the table. "Just drop it. They're coming back."

Cruz pulled out his phone and checked the screen. "Hey, looks like that storm's really moving in. There's a tornado watch."

31

"Well, that would be the third one in as many weeks." Jack drained his soda, unfazed.

Last Chance kicked up their first song, and before Daisy made it back to the table, Bryce Carter intercepted her. Jack tried not to watch as she joined him on the dance floor.

He tried to focus on the conversation at the table, but instead he followed Bryce and Daisy, who were two-stepping, in his peripheral vision. The song seemed to last an eternity, going into an extended instrumental, followed by another chorus.

Just end it already.

The song finally came to a close with a crash of the drums and thunderous applause. When the cacophony faded away, another sound rose up in the distance.

"Is that a siren?" Josephine asked as all conversation came to a halt.

Cruz pulled out his phone. "Uh-oh. There was a tornado sighted just outside of town."

FOUR

The storm clouds of last night had given way to a pink-washed sunrise. The sun peeked out from the clouds, its rays stretching upward like spokes of light.

Daisy drew in a deep breath of pine-scented air and blew it out. After the previous night, the beautiful sunrise was a much-needed reminder of new beginnings. But she couldn't think about that right now.

She stepped from her car, a bouquet of irises clutched against her chest, and stared across the cemetery. Her eyes locked on her dad's marble tombstone, perched at the top of a hill beneath a sturdy oak tree. It was brown and grand, befitting his position as Copper Creek's former mayor.

She'd only been seven when he'd announced his intention to run. She thought it was so cool, but she was too young to know the kind of scrutiny the office would bring. Once he became mayor, he was only hers when they were in the confines of their home. Whenever they left, he was public property, subject to the whims of his constituents. And she was forever expected to be on her best behavior, always smiling, always polite, always sitting up straight.

She'd resented the pretense during her teenage years, and she made sure he knew it. Even to this day she didn't like being the center of attention. She admired her dad's desire to serve the people, but she'd had enough of living in a glass house.

A bird tweeted from one of the many mature trees shading the property. The grass was spring green from last night's storm, and the loamy smell of earth filled her nostrils.

She'd been dreading this day all week. Why was it still so hard? Why did she still miss him as much today as she had seven years ago when the aneurysm had stolen him from them so suddenly?

A car's engine sounded nearby, and she turned to see Gram pulling up beside her. Daisy gave her a wave. Though Gram was her mom's mother, she'd loved Paul Pendleton as though he were her own son, and she accompanied Daisy to his grave sometimes.

Her mom didn't come here as often. "He's not there anyway," Karen always said.

But Daisy found comfort in coming here. In tending the grave. Every spring she planted colorful annuals. She kept up the landscaping year-round and decorated for the holidays: flags on the Fourth of July and wreaths at Easter and Christmas. Today she'd take down the lily wreath she'd put up over a week ago and leave the irises in its place.

Gram's door fell shut, and she came around the front of the car. Her white-blond hair was swept back into a low ponytail, and she wore bright pink capris with a flowy white top.

"Did you hear?" Gram asked as she hugged Daisy.

"I did. I still can't believe it. Thank God no one was hurt." They started up the gentle slope together.

The Hope House had been damaged by last night's tornado. The corner of the roof had been ripped off, and a tree had fallen on the house. If the girls hadn't been on an outing, some of them probably would've died.

"It's a miracle." Daisy's heels sank into the spongy ground. "They were on their way home from the bowling alley. Did you know that?"

"What a blessing. I don't know what's going to happen to those girls now, though."

"They all bedded down in the church basement last night. They were so shaken."

She and her friends had helped Pastor Jack and the Hope House staff get them settled with fresh blankets and pillows. Some of them had lost everything they owned—and they hadn't had much to begin with.

"Well, that's no long-term solution. What are they going to do?"

"I think the house is livable for most of the girls, but the one wing will be off-limits for a while. They'll need places to stay until the damage is fixed. I wish I could take one of them in."

"Me too."

"You don't have the room either." Her grandma lived in a nice one-bedroom apartment on the edge of town. It was perfect for her, as she had no maintenance to worry about.

Daisy thought of her mom's house and her decision to sell it. No. She didn't want to think about that today. Today she was going to remember her wonderful father.

"Look," Gram said as they came over the ridge. "Someone left flowers. How nice."

Daisy followed her grandma's gaze to the grave site. Her eyes homed in on the bouquet of flowers at the foot of her dad's headstone next to the wilting lily wreath. The cellophane was rain-speckled and familiar, as if it had come from their shop.

But it was the arrangement itself that caught Daisy's attention. Yellow roses and white lilies and lemon leaf. It was familiar because she'd arranged it herself two days ago. Right before she'd sold it to a woman from North Carolina. A woman she'd never seen before.

FIVE

Daisy was at a good spot in the latest Debbie Macomber novel when a knock sounded at her door. She paused the audio book on her phone, stopping the narrator's voice midsentence.

When she opened the door, she was surprised to see Ava standing on her porch. Her long hair looked as if it needed a good brushing, and her blue eyes looked troubled.

"Ava, honey, come on in." Daisy opened the screen door and met the girl with a hug. "How are you doing? Did you get any sleep last night?"

"Not much. This has been such a nightmare."

"I know." Both Ava's and her sister's rooms had been in the wing that had been damaged by the tornado. Daisy gave a final squeeze before letting go.

"I'm sorry to just drop by, but it's kind of an emergency, and I don't have your cell number."

"We'll have to rectify that. Have a seat. Can I get you something to drink? Iced tea, Coke?"

"No, thanks." Ava sank onto Daisy's sofa and clutched her purse to her stomach, twisting the straps.

Daisy sat opposite her in the armchair. "What can I do for you, hon?"

"I was hoping to move into the apartment early. Like, tomorrow if at all possible."

"Oh, Ava, we haven't finished cleaning. And the walls are in desperate need of paint."

"The paint will have to wait—we're more desperate than the walls. And I've been over there cleaning all morning. It's much better than it was."

Daisy had wondered why the girl hadn't been at church. "You should've told me you were over there today. I can help you now. I don't have any plans the rest of the day. I'll call my mom and grandma too. We'll get the place in order lickety-split."

Ava's shoulders sank. "Oh, that would be so great. Are you sure you wouldn't mind?"

"Not at all. I should've thought of it sooner." If only she hadn't had her mind on her own troubles. "Do you need any cleaning supplies?"

"I have bathroom cleaner, window cleaner, and sponges . . ."

"I'll round up the rest of what we need." She made a mental note to add rubber gloves to her list.

Ava shifted in her seat, and Daisy could tell there was more. "What else is on your mind, Ava?"

Clear blue eyes met Daisy's. "It's Millie. She

doesn't have a place to stay yet, and I asked if she could stay with me until they rebuild the wing."

"Oh . . . well, that makes sense, I guess. Are they going to let you?" Ava was only eighteen, after all, and had never even lived on her own, much less been fully responsible for a child.

"Mrs. Murdock got through to the social service lady this morning and explained the situation. Things are pretty topsy-turvy with all the girls having to be placed so quickly. They said I have to be able to support her financially, which I can. I've saved up quite a bit, and I'm working part-time until school's out. I also have to provide care for her after school, and Zoe already said I can bring her to the Peach Barn with me. But . . ."

"What is it, hon?"

"It's just . . . They want to know there's an adult—an older adult—to kind of oversee things. And since you're right downstairs most of the time, I was hoping . . ."

"I'll be glad to help out, Ava. I'll meet with Millie's social worker and sign whatever documents I need to sign. Let's get this done as soon as possible so she can move in with you."

"Oh, Daisy, you don't know what a relief that is."

The girl had more weight on her than was right. Daisy wanted to shake Ava's dad for leaving her with all this responsibility.

"It's no trouble. What about furniture and bedding and such?"

"I bought a secondhand bedroom suite with some of the money I saved up. I'll let Millie sleep in the bedroom, and I'll take the couch—just as soon as I get one." She gave Daisy a wry smile.

"I'm sure we can round up a few pieces of furniture plus some towels and bedding."

Her mom was downsizing, after all. She'd probably be happy to part with a few things.

"For now . . ." Daisy stood up and headed toward the kitchen. "Let me get a few cleaning supplies together. Then I'll text my mom and grandma, and we'll whip that apartment right into shape."

SIX

Daisy shifted the armload of gowns and knocked quietly on Hope's screen door just in case Sammy was down for his nap. Hope and Brady Collins lived in a farmhouse just outside of town. He worked on sports cars in the big metal barn at the back of the property, and Hope was currently pursuing her master's in psychology.

"Come in," Hope called.

The cool air brushed Daisy's skin as she slipped inside the kitchen, the clean scent of lemon hitting her nose.

Hope was spooning a bite of something green and goopy into Sam's mouth. She was a natural beauty with her creamy complexion and dark, wavy hair. Her Rachel McAdams smile was aimed at the one-year-old. Though Hope wasn't his biological mom, it was clear no one could love him more.

Sam smacked his lips and banged the high-chair tray with his hands.

Daisy couldn't help but smile at the chubby-cheeked baby. "Hey, little guy."

"Day-Day!" He waved backward, his blue eyes brightening at the visitor.

41

"Yes, it's Day-Day," Daisy said. "How's my favorite little buddy?"

"Let me help you." Hope jumped up and grabbed some of the gowns, and they carried them to the living room couch. "Wow, there must be twenty more here. That's super."

"At least. Some nice ones too, and in various sizes."

The dress drive was just part of their efforts to make sure the Hope House girls had a night to remember at the high school's Spring Fling dance. Oopsy Daisy also provided boutonnieres, and Josephine transformed her barbershop into a day spa for the afternoon, pampering the girls within an inch of their lives.

"With the dozen or so I have upstairs, everyone should be able to find something they like. And Donna Lewis offered alterations if they're needed."

"That's so nice of her. Do we have a final count of who's going?"

"Twelve right now." Hope shelved her hands on her hips, staring sadly at the dresses. "I still can't believe their house was hit by a tornado. Of all places."

"I know. I wish there was something more I could do."

"Well, let's just focus on the dance. It's more important than ever now. One of the girls told Josephine yesterday that it's the only thing she

42

has to look forward to. We'll help them make it a really special night."

"That's something, I guess. Ida Mae Simmons told me this morning they'd already found homes for most of the girls who'd been displaced."

"That was quick. Brady and I were talking about offering up our spare room."

"Pastor Jack made a plea at church yesterday. You should've heard him. I was ready to take them all home with me—even if I have no place to put them."

"He's got a way with words, all right." Hope gave her a speculative look, then headed back to the kitchen, where Sammy was getting impatient for his next bite.

Daisy followed her, wondering about that look. The speculation ended as she spotted a bouquet of wildflowers on the kitchen counter. They instantly reminded her of those flowers at her father's grave yesterday. Gram had assumed they'd been left by one of his many friends, and Daisy hadn't corrected her. Something had stopped her. She had a bad feeling about those flowers and the woman who'd left them there.

"So how's the dating scene?" Hope asked. "I heard you met someone for coffee over in Dalton."

"Good grief, are there no secrets in this town?"

"Nope." Hope cleaned off Sam's hands with a wet wipe and set him on the floor. "So how'd it go?"

"It was a bust. Just like the previous ten." Daisy sank into a chair, watching Hope clean up the high-chair tray. "I think I'm giving up on that app. It's been a disaster."

"It can't be that bad."

"Really? Let's see . . ." Daisy began to tick them off on her fingers. "So far I've been out with a thirty-year-old who lives with his parents, a podiatrist whose *fiancée* showed up halfway through our meal, a man who tried to pay the student rate for me at the theater to save two bucks and let the door fall in my face twice, a guy who invited me back to his place five minutes after meeting me, an engineer who insisted on ordering for me and told me I should never wear white—it washes me out apparently, a guy who cried—literally cried—about his ex-wife all through supper, and a man who hardly gave me a chance to say two words. He was fifty years old, Hope. *Fifty.*"

Just listing her dating failures brought Daisy down to a whole new level of low. How had it come to this? She was not unattractive. She was more or less normal. She had a job and a place of her own.

Hope grimaced. "Fifty? Are you sure?"

"Oh, he was fifty all right. He rambled on all

night about his routine colonoscopy—in pain-staking detail." At the memory of his tale of horrors, Daisy whimpered. "I don't ever want to turn fifty."

Hope laughed as she replaced the high-chair tray. "Couldn't you tell he was, uh, more mature, by his picture?"

"He used an old photo apparently. Hard to believe he used to be good-looking. I just have to face it. There's simply no one out there who's single and available and *normal*."

"Of course there is. Maybe you just need a new strategy."

"Like what? And don't say blind dates. I've already been set up by everyone I know, including my mother—her friend's son. And in case you're wondering, he didn't make eye contact once or crack a smile all night, and he was obsessed with Marvel comics. You know what? You really find out what people think of you when you see who they set you up with. It's not pretty, let me tell you."

"I'm not talking about blind dates." Hope helped Sam with a sorting toy, then sank into the chair next to Daisy. "I'm just saying . . . You kind of plunged into this whole dating app thing. You got on there and just started meeting anyone and everyone. What about taking a little more time? Getting to know a guy online a little before you actually meet in person."

Daisy sighed as she considered. "I don't know. I think I've just about had it with dating."

Hope took her hand. "Then don't date. Chat with them awhile, get to know them as friends, and then, if you decide you really like someone, set up a time to meet."

"But what if I really like someone online but then I meet him and there's no chemistry?"

"I guess that's a possibility. But Brady and I were just friends for a long time before we liked each other in that way. The attraction grew out of the friendship."

"Ha! You're gorgeous, and Brady looks like an Acqua Di Gio model. The real miracle is that you didn't fall for each other sooner."

Hope squeezed her hand. "Try and be patient. God'll bring you the right guy at the right time, just like He did for me. And sometimes that guy can be someone completely unexpected."

"Well, I sure wish He'd hurry. I'm running out of hope here."

SEVEN

Jack clicked on a link on his laptop, and it took him to an article about the Dead Sea Scrolls. It was only Monday, but he was supposed to be preparing for next Sunday's sermon on the inerrancy of Scripture. But he'd gotten caught up in the research, as he was prone to doing when history factored in.

Gloria was clacking away on her keyboard in the office across from his. The phone rang every now and then, but he was mostly immune to the extraneous noises. The afternoons tended to be quiet.

His office was on the small side, though it boasted a high ceiling and ornate paneling. An oriental rug hugged the wood floor, and the pleasant smell of pine cleaner lingered in the air.

On the screen he browsed the photos of the Qumran Caves, where 90 percent of the scrolls had been discovered. Bedouin shepherds found the initial seven scrolls in jars when one of the shepherds fell into a cave in 1946. The scrolls eventually found their way into the hands of a researcher who identified them a year later.

"Pastor Jack?" Gloria stood in his doorway, her

red glasses perched at the end of her small nose. "Yes?"

"Lucille Murdock is here to see you. Do you have a moment?"

Jack closed his laptop. "Of course. Send her on in."

Lucille was a member of the church and the CEO of the Hope House. She was the one who'd asked him to make an appeal to the church for help in finding temporary housing for the girls. He hoped there wasn't an issue with one of the placements. He'd personally vouched for each of the families.

"Thank you for seeing me spur of the moment, Pastor Jack." Lucille strode into the room looking more tired than he'd ever seen her. She was around sixty, slight of frame with cropped gray hair and large hazel eyes. Her usual smile was nowhere to be seen.

Jack stood and took her hand in both of his. "Of course. I've been praying for you and the girls. How's it going?"

Lucille sank into the chair across from his desk, clutching her purse to her stomach. "Not so well, I'm afraid."

"Are the girls having trouble adjusting? You know I'm happy to counsel anyone who—" He stopped at her raised hand.

"The girls are doing as well as can be expected. It's a more practical matter that brought me here today." She gave him a pained expression. "I received some very bad news yesterday. I'm afraid that Jillian, my previous office manager, let the insurance on our building lapse. We've been limping along financially for a while, and she—well, I have to take partial responsibility. With my mother going through chemo, I wasn't as on top of things as I should've been."

Jack sat back in his chair. "Are you telling me you have no way of paying for repairs?"

"I'm afraid so. We have no real reserves. We had all kinds of expenditures over the winter. One of our furnaces gave out. There was that minor kitchen fire that ruined the flooring, and a leaky roof that had to be repaired. It drained our funds."

"I'm so sorry. What will you do? How can I help?"

She shook her head. "I don't know. The roof is covered with a tarp, but obviously it can't stay that way indefinitely. I've thought of relocating, but I don't know who'd buy the old place, especially in its current condition. And where am I going to find a home that can house twenty-seven girls even if we could afford it? Besides, all that would take a lot of time. Time we don't have."

"What about foster homes?"

"There aren't enough of them—that's why I started a residential home to begin with. The families who took in the girls were very clear that this is a temporary solution. If I don't find a way to get that house fixed, those girls will have no place to go."

Jack rubbed his forehead. "Then we'll just have to figure out a way to get it fixed. We have some contractors in our membership."

"Even if they donated the labor, there's still the matter of materials. Thousands of dollars." Her eyes glazed over. "Oh, Pastor Jack, you have to help me. I can't let those girls down. I'm all some of them have."

He reached across the desk and settled his hand over hers. "You're not *all* they have, Lucille. They have a loving heavenly Father, a church family, and a supportive community. Don't lose hope. Let me give it some thought, and I'll get back to you before the week's end."

A few minutes later Jack hugged a teary Lucille good-bye, his mind already at work on solving this weighty problem. His buddy Noah owned Mitchell Home Improvement. He was pretty sure he could get him to provide labor free of charge. But Lucille was right. The materials were going to be costly. He'd been at the house twice since the tornado. The damage was of disastrous proportion. It was going to cost a lot of money that the church didn't have.

He called Noah and asked if they could meet. Noah had just finished lunch and offered to stop by the church on his way to his next job.

Jack hung up and sank into his chair, rubbing his chin. They needed a fundraiser and fast—and he had an ace in the hole. Nobody organized an event like Daisy. Last year she'd put on an auction benefit for a youth member with leukemia and raised almost five thousand dollars. She already headed up the dress drive and corresponding activities for the Hope House girls. She had a soft heart and a willing spirit. He was pretty sure he could get her on board.

But even if she agreed, she'd need help, and lots of it. The church had a handful of industrious volunteers, but they were all tied up with Vacation Bible School preparations at the moment.

Well, there was nothing he could really do until he talked to Noah. He went back to his sermon preparation but only had time to jot a few notes before his friend appeared in the doorway.

Just a few years Jack's junior, Noah could've been mistaken for his brother, with his dark hair and olive skin. But while Jack earned his physique at the high school weight room, Noah's lean muscles were a product of his occupation.

"Your office always smells like old hymnals," Noah said.

Jack stood and shook his hand. "I've gone numb to it. You've got drywall dust in your hair."

Noah ruffled his hair. "Occupational hazard.

I've also got mud on my jeans, so I won't sit down in your froufrou chair."

"Take a load off. It'll clean up. How's work going?"

Noah took him up on his offer. "It's the busy season. Everyone wants new windows and siding in the spring."

"I'll probably be hitting you up before winter. My windows have about had it."

"I'll give you the pastor discount."

"Is that better than the friend discount?"

"One and the same."

"Sounds promising." Jack came around the desk and perched on its edge. "Listen, Noah . . . I've got a favor to ask."

"Okay . . ."

"It's the Hope House. Lucille Murdock was in to see me a while ago. I'm afraid they let the insurance on their building lapse."

Noah's face fell. "You've got to be kidding me. They're missing half a roof."

"I know. It's bad. They need help, Noah. Those girls have been placed temporarily, but they have no place else to go. And selling the building isn't a real option."

"No, it's way too big for a single family— even if it were in good condition." Noah's brows pinched together. "You're asking if we can provide the labor. Absolutely. We can do that."

A portion of the weight lifted from Jack's

shoulders. "That's great, buddy. I was hoping you'd say that."

"Like I said, though, we're very busy. Scheduling is pretty tight for the next eight weeks or so."

"That's okay. It's going to take a while to raise money for materials anyway."

"Raise money? The Hope House doesn't have it?"

"Not even close."

"How are they going to pull that off? I haven't been inside, but they're probably looking at twenty grand, easy."

"Just for materials?"

"Afraid so."

Jack winced. "Well, I have an angle on that too. We'll figure something out." He wondered what kind of event could raise that much money. Hopefully Daisy would have some ideas.

"Thanks for being willing to help, man. Lucille will be so grateful."

"No problem." Noah shifted uneasily. "Say, listen, Jack. I'm actually glad you called. I've, uh, been wanting to talk to you about something."

Jack took in Noah's unsettled look. "What's that?"

The air-conditioning kicked on, filling the office with a quiet hum.

"Well . . ." Noah measured Jack with a look.

"You know I had the guys over to watch the Braves last night."

"Yeah, you invited me, remember?" He'd hated to miss it, but he had to visit one of their youth in the hospital. Emergency appendectomy.

"Right. Well, the guys and I got to talking . . ."

"About . . . ," he prompted when Noah paused.

Noah stood and walked over to the wall, where he straightened a painting of Jesus with a flock of sheep—a gift from the church.

"About Daisy, actually."

Jack's guard went up. He didn't even like the fact that his friends knew about his feelings, much less that they talked about them behind his back.

"Really."

"We know how you feel about her. We've all been there, you know?"

"Have you, now?"

Best Jack recalled, it had been love at first sight for Noah, and Josephine had followed quickly behind. Sure, they'd almost divorced, but love had never been the issue. Brady and Hope had married last year, and Cruz and Zoe, in love since high school, had followed soon after.

"We hate to see you like this, man. And we don't want to see you lose Daisy to some other guy." His eyes flickered away. "Bear in mind we have the best of intentions."

Jack narrowed his gaze on Noah, noticing the

way he shifted, rubbed the back of his neck, and avoided eye contact.

"Did you tell your wives? Please tell me you didn't tell your wives." They were all friends with Daisy. Good friends.

"No, we didn't. And it's not like you really have to follow up on this or do anything if you really don't want to."

"What did you do?" His words were clipped. If they'd told Daisy . . . if they'd let her know in any way that he had feelings for her, he was going to—

"You know that app she's on? Flutter or whatever?"

Dread crept up his spine like two skeletal fingers. The flush climbing Noah's neck wasn't making Jack feel any better.

"Ye-es . . ."

"Well . . . you're kind of on there now too."

"I'm what?"

"Look, we just started a profile for you. It's very basic."

Jack crossed his arms and locked his jaw. A pastor on a dating site. Very nice. Something like this would not go unnoticed. His members were going to have a field day with it.

And what about the single women in his congregation, none of whom he wanted to date—other than Daisy. Some of them viewed a pastor as some kind of challenge. Others were infatuated with the idea of becoming a pastor's wife. He envisioned enduring months of not-so-subtle come-ons from women he'd been so carefully polite to. Not to mention the long line of blind dates he'd have once the older ladies in the congregation found out he was actively seeking to date.

He nailed Noah with a look. "Must've been a very boring game, Noah."

"Extra innings."

Jack rounded his desk and opened his laptop. "You're going to take it down. Right now. What's the website?"

"Uh, wait. You don't want to do that."

"Yes, I do. Preferably before every member of my congregation gets wind of this."

"They won't. It's first name only and—and you really don't have to do anything if you don't want to. But . . ."

Jack leaned on the desk, studying Noah's face. He knew that look. "Why do I get the feeling there's something more here? What aren't you telling me? Just spit it out, Noah."

"We may have, uh . . . nudged her. On your behalf."

Jack gave his head a shake. "Nudged her? What does that even mean?"

"It's the way you get someone's attention on the site. Once you nudge someone, they have twenty-four hours to nudge you back."

Jack shot upright. "She knows I'm interested? Great, Noah. Why didn't you just hand her a note with boxes to check? Are we back in sixth grade or something?"

"Just calm down—"

"You had no right to do that. None of you. I'm a grown man. Don't you think I would've made my feelings clear to Daisy if that's what I—"

"She doesn't know it's you, Jack. You're completely anonymous. Well. Sort of. Let me show you."

Jack made room for Noah as he took over the laptop, hunting and pecking on the keyboard.

Jack tapped his toe and clenched his jaw. His blood pressure had skyrocketed, and his throat was tight from all the words he was holding back. He couldn't believe the guys had done this. At least it was anonymous. He could delete the profile and make this all go away.

"There." Noah turned the laptop his way. "See. You're totally incognito."

There were two photos of Jack, taken during one of his camping trips with Noah. He wore a ball cap in both and had a week's worth of stubble on his face. In the closer shot he wore sunglasses and was looking over his bare shoulder at the camera. The other was taken from a distance. He was standing in the middle of a stream, holding up his catch. His ball cap shaded his face.

"No way will anyone recognize you from these

pictures. We only see you clean-cut around here, in khakis and button-downs, every hair in place."

He grimaced at how square Noah made him sound. But he was right. The camping trip was the one week of the year he completely let himself go. Thank God the photos didn't capture smells.

He skimmed the text and gave Noah a look. "TJ? That's what you're calling me?"

Noah shrugged. "Thomas Jackson, right? And we thought Daisy might know your first name, so we went with TJ."

Since his dad was Thomas, he'd always gone by Jack. He continued reading. The bio was vague enough. At least no one, especially Daisy, would've recognized him if she'd stumbled upon his profile.

"Great job," Jack said, straightening. "Very eloquent. Now get it off there."

"You don't want to do that, Jack."

"Yes, I do." He spied the Delete Profile button and reached for the keyboard.

Noah caught his hand. "Wait. Look. She nudged you back. Yesterday. She's interested, Jack—as are seven other women, but I assume you don't care about that."

His eyes locked on the screen where Daisy's profile picture appeared.

"She nudged a guy who doesn't even resemble me."

"She didn't just nudge you. She left you a message. Look."

Noah clicked on something, and her comment appeared.

> Hi there! You seem like an interesting guy. Great pictures. I love the one with the trout. I used to fish with my dad, but I haven't gone in years. To be honest, I've become a little gun-shy lately about this app. I'm interested in getting to know people slowly before meeting up. If that's agreeable, I hope to hear back from you.

There was a smiley face and her first name.

"See . . . she's interested."

Jack swallowed hard, staring at the message. It was a legitimate response from Daisy. She *was* interested. She wanted to get to know him. The notion was heady and oh so tempting.

But where could this go anyway? She already knew the real him. If she were interested in Pastor Jack, surely he'd know it by now.

"You can't just ignore her response, Jack."

He crossed his arms. "Yes, I can. I have my reasons for not pursuing her, Noah."

"What? The age thing?" He pointed to the screen. "Look. Your real age is right there. It didn't stop her from responding to your nudge."

Jack blinked at his statistics, some of the wind

going from his sails. Well, what about that. He'd always assumed . . .

"And that excuse about her being a member of your congregation? So what? Is there some rule I don't know about?"

"Not a rule, exactly—"

Jack pressed his lips together. Although some churches forbade single pastors from dating members of their congregations, his own denomination had no such rule. Maybe that was just an excuse. Something he'd told himself because he'd never received any encouragement from her. Because he was afraid of being rejected.

Besides, Daisy didn't want to be a pastor's wife. Didn't want a glass-house life like she'd had when her dad was mayor. She fully understood what it was like to be watched so closely. It was one of the things they'd connected over initially.

He looked at her profile picture. At her big green eyes and sweet smile. He remembered all the times she'd been in his office—door open, Gloria nearby, nice and proper—unloading her burdens. She trusted him, and he took that seriously.

"No. This is wrong. It's not honest."

"There's not a single dishonest statement in that bio. And those are your pictures. What's dishonest about it? She wants to get to know you before meeting up. She'll get to see you outside your role as pastor. Get to know *you,* and this is the perfect way to make that happen. Once that happens, you can shoot straight with her."

"Pastor Jack?" Gloria had appeared in the doorway. "You have that town council meeting in fifteen minutes."

"Right. Thank you, Gloria," he said distractedly, his mind still mulling over everything he'd just learned.

"Just think about it," Noah said. He'd exited from the website, conveniently preventing Jack from deleting the profile. "Give it a day or two. If you still want to, you can delete it, no harm done. But I think you'd be missing a great opportunity."

Noah jotted something down on a Post-it note and handed it to Jack. "Here's your log-in information. We've done all we can, buddy. The rest is up to you."

EIGHT

Daisy arranged the long-stemmed lilies in the wicker basket, her hands working quickly, her mind someplace else entirely. Her mom was at the front counter ringing up a purchase.

This was the longest Monday ever. Those flowers on her father's grave had haunted her all day yesterday while they'd cleaned Ava's apartment. It had occurred to her late last night that she could check the credit card records to find out Julia's last name. But when she'd done so first thing this morning, she'd realized Julia had paid with cash.

"Lillian bought the little wagon with the peonies," her mom said as she returned to the back of the shop. "A gift for her daughter-in-law's birthday."

"Oh good. Hannah will love that."

"Are they all settled upstairs?" Karen asked, looking at the ceiling. They'd moved Ava and Millie in first thing that morning.

"As settled as they can be with only four pieces of furniture."

"At least it's clean now. We'll move some of my things over later this week. I have your grandma's dinette that's just collecting dust in the attic, and we have a few spare pieces in the basement. We'll fix them right up."

Her mom took her seat in the office at the metal desk and began punching the calculator. She was a whiz with that thing. Though she was a retired attorney, she was also skilled with numbers, so she did the books for the shop. Gram had opened the flower shop when Daisy was fourteen, and it had been a team effort ever since.

Karen had seemed to weather the anniversary of her husband's death pretty well. Staying busy yesterday had helped them all.

"You've been awfully quiet today," she said, her fingers still punching numbers. "Are you still upset about my selling the house?"

"I'm trying not to think about it. I've found denial to be a legitimate coping mechanism."

"Daisy . . ."

"I don't want to talk about it today, Mama. I'm sure I'll be fine. Life does go on."

"Well, I don't want you angry with me."

"I'm not angry. It's just been a stressful weekend."

A truck roared by on the road outside. Daisy fussed with the white roses and eucalyptus on a funeral arrangement.

"I know. I'm sorry about the timing, I truly am. That was poor planning on my part. But I've been keeping the place up for a long time. Your dad would understand."

"I know." Her dad's feelings weren't the issue. That probably made her selfish.

She thought of that woman . . . Julia, from North Carolina. What kind of connection had she had with Daisy's dad? She was afraid to carry the thought any further.

She kept going back to their brief conversation. The woman hadn't seemed to know Daisy or realize that she was Paul Pendleton's daughter. She hadn't seemed evasive or curious or peculiar. It was quite possible she'd just wanted to visit his grave and stopped in for flowers not knowing the shop belonged to Paul's family.

But that didn't answer the question of how she knew him.

"Mama . . . Daddy didn't travel much, did he? I remember him being gone on a trip or two, but that was a long time ago."

"When he worked as a sales rep, he traveled quite a bit, but that was in the earlier years of our marriage. He only made the occasional trip when he was mayor. Why do you ask?"

Daisy lifted a shoulder. "No reason. I've just been thinking about him a lot recently."

She needed to put this from her mind. Julia was probably just an acquaintance of her father's or a family friend. But she was too young to have been a childhood friend. She was at least thirty,

Daisy speculated, but no more than thirty-five. Surely too young to be—

No, she wouldn't let her mind go there. Her dad had been a good man. He'd loved her mother and never would've cheated on her.

She tried to remember what Julia had said. That she was just passing through. Had she said that the flowers were for an old friend or that she was in town visiting an old friend?

"Well, something's on your mind. You're much too quiet."

She needed another angle. Something more specific. She had to solve this for her own peace of mind.

Her heart thumped as she worked the words around in her head. "I forgot to mention someone dropped by the flower shop last week. Someone who knew Daddy."

"Oh? Who's that?"

"Her name was Julia, I believe she said."

"Julia?" Her mom stopped punching the keys and looked at Daisy, her bifocals halfway down her nose. "I don't think I know a Julia." She went back to work.

"Well, I don't think she was from around here." Daisy trimmed a lily-of-the-valley stem and tucked it into the arrangement. She couldn't quite get up the nerve to mention North Carolina. Last thing she wanted was to worry her mother or cause her to speculate as Daisy was now doing.

"Well, honey, your daddy never met a stranger. And he touched so many lives. How nice that she stopped in to say hello."

"Yeah, it was . . . very nice of her."

Murphy's Park spread out, green and lush, at the edge of town. Jack passed the shaded play area and walked toward the baseball diamond beyond it. The late-afternoon sun dappled the rolling lawn, and the squeals of children rang out from the playground. The earthy scent of spring mingled with the smell of freshly cut grass.

The crack of a bat rent the air, and a cheer rose up from the wooden bleachers on one side of the dugout. The community had four co-ed teams that faced off on Monday nights from spring to midsummer. The competition was all in good fun.

He knew Daisy would be in the stands. It was a little sad that he knew her daily schedule so well. There was a fine line between interested and obsessed; he sometimes wondered if he was on the wrong side of it.

He spotted her in the nearest stand, on her feet and clapping, all but jumping up and down. She wore a pair of white shorts and a bright pink top with fluttery sleeves. Her blond ponytail was threaded through a white baseball cap, making her look about eighteen. It reminded him once again of the disparity in their ages, but this time the thought was blunted by what he'd learned on that dating app.

She doesn't even mind that you're nearly ten years her senior.

Correction: she didn't mind that TJ was nearly ten years her senior. It was a minor distinction, but an important one nonetheless.

"You got this, Zoe!" Daisy called as she took her seat again.

Jack greeted his neighbors as he sidled down the row toward Daisy. Among the T-shirts and tennis shoes, he felt out of place in his khakis and collared shirt.

When he reached the middle of the row, he sank down next to Daisy, taking care to keep a respectable distance. "Looks like a close game."

When she saw Jack her eyes lit up. And there was that smile that pulled him right under. "Pastor Jack . . . what are you doing here?"

"Well, I, uh, needed a word with you, Daisy." He lifted a shoulder. "And I figured you'd be over here, cheering on your friends."

Great. Now she'd think he was stalking her. But no, she wasn't thinking about him at all. Her eyes were trained on Zoe Huntley, who was waggling the bat as she awaited a pitch.

"Maybe this isn't the best time," Jack said. "I could stop by the shop tomorrow if you're free in the morning."

A crack sounded. It was a hard grounder

between short and second, but Zoe made it in plenty of time to beat the throw.

"Whooo!" Daisy screamed, clapping along with everyone in the stands. "That's my girl!"

The crowd quieted as the next batter came up— no one Jack knew.

Daisy turned her attention back to him. "Sorry about that. I'm rooting for Buddy's Hardware. They haven't won a game yet. You were saying?"

He could hardly think with those green eyes trained on him. With that distracting spray of freckles dotting her nose.

He looked away. "Um, Lucille Murdock came in to see me today. I'm afraid she had some bad news about the Hope House." He went on to explain the situation, only pausing when a triple brought Zoe across home plate in a close play.

"Safe!" the umpire called, and the crowd cheered.

Daisy's reaction to the run scored was noticeably subdued, no doubt in light of the news he'd just delivered.

When the crowd quieted, he went on to explain the Hope House's financial problems and Noah's contribution to the project. He didn't even have to ask what he'd come prepared to beg for.

"What can I do?" she said. "I can plan a fundraiser—would that help?"

A smile formed helplessly on his lips. "You

have such a giving heart, Daisy. Here you are, still neck-deep in the Spring Fling benefit, and you're already prepared to jump headfirst into another project."

She waved him off. "Oh, it's nothing. I'll have plenty of—"

She stopped, probably at the look he was giving her.

"Right." She lowered her head in a grateful nod. "Thank you very much, Pastor Jack. That's awfully kind of you to say."

"Much better." They shared a smile. "I know your hands are full right now . . ."

"The Spring Fling is this Saturday. I'll be freed up after that. How much do we need to raise?"

"Noah hasn't gotten over there to do a bid yet. But he speculates at least twenty grand." He couldn't help but wince at the number.

Daisy's brows disappeared under the brim of her cap. "Oh my goodness."

"I know. It's a little daunting. But I have faith in you, Daisy. And I'm willing to help however I can."

"Don't be silly. You have your hands full with the church. I'm sure we can scare up some volunteers."

"Well . . . that's just it. Most of the people I count on for these things are busy gearing up for VBS. I'm sure we can round up some extra hands for whatever event you plan—but not until after

VBS. In the meantime, however, I'm at your disposal."

"How long do we have to raise the money?"

"Well, Noah can't even fit in the repairs until mid-June, so we have at least till then. It's not much time to raise that much money, though. I don't have any idea where to start, but I hoped you might."

"I'll give it some thought, do some research, and get back with—" Her gaze shifted over his shoulder, and she went still. Her eyes widened and her lips parted.

"Daisy?"

She popped to her feet. " 'Scuse me," she said distractedly, edging her way down the row. At the end of the row she hopped from the stand.

"Daisy!" Jack called.

But when she hit the ground, she took off at a run toward town.

Jack stood and followed, excusing his way across feet and purses and water bottles. He leaped off the end and started across the lawn. The slippery soles of his dress shoes made running hazardous, and by the time he reached Daisy she was standing in the gravel parking lot of the Clip 'n' Curl, bent over, hands on knees, huffing and puffing.

"Daisy, what's wrong? Are you all right?"

Her cheeks were flushed and perspiration dotted her forehead. But it was the expression on her face that worried him. There was a hopeless look shadowing her eyes, and sadness tugged at the corners of her lips.

"She's gone," she whispered between breaths.

"Who's gone?"

She straightened, shoulders drooping. She looked down the street toward the west, but Jack saw nothing save the normal evening traffic and a few pedestrians.

His gaze returned to Daisy. She'd placed her hands on her hips. Her chest rose and fell with her breaths.

"What's wrong?" he asked. "What's going on, Daisy?"

After a long moment her gaze flickered off him, then her face closed down like a curtain falling at the end of a play. "Nothing. I just . . . I thought I saw someone I knew."

NINE

It had taken ten minutes to get rid of Pastor Jack. He was noticeably concerned about her, and no wonder, the way she'd taken off out of the stands midsentence.

She could've spilled her guts to him. Heaven knew she'd already done plenty of that. But she couldn't talk to him about this. Just the thought of verbalizing her suspicions made her feel guilty—disloyal to her dad.

And yet when she'd spied Julia leaving the Clip 'n' Curl, she'd been propelled toward her like an arrow from a bow. She'd assumed the woman would be gone by now. "Just passing through" meant a day or two at most to Daisy. It had been four days since Julia stopped in at the shop.

Daisy entered the hair salon, the cool air a welcoming reprieve. A bamboo ceiling fan whirled lazily overhead, and the chemical odor of hair dye lingered heavily in the air.

Three of the stylists were busy with clients, but Shirley Evans was at the last chair sweeping up hair. Dark hair that very well could have belonged to Julia.

It had only been several weeks since Daisy'd

had a trim, but she approached the counter anyway.

"Just come on back, hon," Shirley called.

Daisy walked back to the chair and sank into it. She pulled off her ball cap and tugged at the rubber band, meeting Shirley's eyes in the mirror.

"How's it going, Shirley?"

The woman was in her midfifties with a slight wave in her shoulder-length hair that was more natural than the almost-black color. She wore no makeup, but that only made her brown eyes seem friendlier somehow.

"Oh, you know. Not too bad." She set the broom aside and grabbed a black cape. "What can I do for you today? Just trim you up?"

"Yeah, that's fine."

The cape floated around Daisy's shoulders, and Shirley fastened the Velcro, then ran her fingers through Daisy's hair. "You have the prettiest hair. People pay a lot of money for this shade of blond. Weren't you just in a few weeks ago?"

"Yeah, but I just, uh, had some time to kill and felt like being pampered a little."

Shirley laughed as she tilted the chair toward the bowl. "Well, you just sit right on back then, sugar. I'll give you an extra-long scalp massage."

Five minutes later Shirley dragged the towel from Daisy's hair. The massage had been heavenly, but her mind had been full of Julia. Why was she still in town? Where was she staying?

The phone began ringing at the front desk.

Shirley spritzed on a detangler and began working a comb through Daisy's locks. "It's sure been a busy Monday around here. We've been tied up all afternoon."

Daisy cleared her throat. "I think I passed your last client on my way in. Tall, pretty lady, dark hair . . . ?" She tried for a casual tone.

"Yes, her name's Julia. She really liked what I did with her hair, though with those cheekbones, I could hardly go wrong."

"Did she recently move to the area? I don't think I know her."

"Just passing through, she said." Shirley paused, a thoughtful look on her face. "Actually, now that I think on it, your name came up in conversation."

Daisy's eyes shot to Shirley's, but the stylist was now staring toward the front of the shop.

She set down the comb. "Excuse me. I have to get the phone." She raised her voice, a teasing note in her voice. "Since no one else around here seems to hear it ringing off the hook."

Charlotte held up her messy gloved hands, and Marylou blinked innocently. "We're knee-deep in some good gossip over here. You can't expect me to just walk away from that now, can you?"

Daisy met her own gaze in the mirror, her heart thumping from Shirley's last words. Why had Daisy's name come up? Had Julia asked about her or just mentioned she'd stopped by the shop for flowers?

Her mind spun with all the possibilities, her foot tapping the metal bar impatiently. The phone call seemed to be taking forever.

Finally Shirley returned, grabbing the comb and dragging it through Daisy's hair. She seemed to have forgotten they'd been in the middle of a conversation. Her eyes were locked on Daisy's hair as she raked out a length of it and began snipping the ends.

"So . . . ," Daisy said. "You were saying my name came up in conversation with, uh, your client."

"Oh! Right. Julia. Heavens to Betsy, I'd forget my own name if not for this nametag. She was asking after your dad, and I mentioned that you and your family were running the flower shop nowadays. You use any special conditioner on your hair? It's so soft and not a split end in sight."

"Just something store-bought. She mentioned my dad?"

Shirley fussed with Daisy's hair, then combed out another length. "Yeah, just in passing. Said she knew him or knew someone who knew him or something. I was a little distracted because that handsome contractor came in to give us a bid on a new back room. Noah or Seth? I can never remember which brother is which, they're both so darned cute."

And half Shirley's age, but Daisy didn't mention that.

"It's the one who married Josephine, the barber. Boy, he sure has some biceps on him. Whooee."

"That'd be Noah."

"That's right, y'all are friends. Well, that is one lucky lady, I'll tell you that. Handsome as sin and all those muscles besides."

Daisy shifted in her chair as Shirley switched combs. "So you don't remember how that client, Julia, knew my daddy?"

"Sorry, hon, I can't rightly recall. Or maybe she didn't even bring it up. Maybe it was me. I can't really say. Why are you asking?"

"Oh, I was just wondering. I love talking to people who knew my dad, you know? Sometimes they have stories I've never heard and whatnot. It helps." She finished with a shrug. "Did she say how long she was in the area? Or where she's staying?"

Shirley ruffled Daisy's damp hair. "I don't think so. Probably a rental cabin, though. Seems too classy for the motel. This short enough for you, hon?"

Daisy gave it a quick look. "Perfect."

"Want me to cut in some bangs?" Shirley asked with hopeful eyes. She was always trying to give Daisy bangs.

"No, thanks. I like it all one length."

"Let me just dry you up then, and you'll be

good to go. Unless you want some curls . . . Got a fun evening ahead? I could fix you right up."

Daisy thought of the baseball game, but somehow her heart just wasn't in it anymore. "Go ahead and dry it; I'm only going home."

"You're too young and pretty to be spending your nights home alone. Hey, I have a nice nephew I could fix you up with . . ."

Daisy quickly put the kibosh on that idea, sighing with relief when the hair dryer came on, ending the conversation. The last thing she needed was another disastrous blind date.

Jack rolled over and faced the window for the dozenth time. He had to get some sleep. He had to be up early for a VBS planning meeting, and he'd really hoped to run at the high school track prior to that.

But it was going on midnight, and he just couldn't get Daisy from his mind. He kept seeing that look on her face in the Clip 'n' Curl parking lot. That lost, vulnerable look that made him want to move heaven and earth to help her.

He'd thought she might open up to him. She always had before. One thing Daisy had no problem doing was divulging her secrets to him. But that was in the church office, when he was behind his big official desk, talking in his patient pastor voice.

Out in the wild he was apparently not the

confidant he'd hoped to be. She'd shut down immediately, and it had smarted. Though they hung with the same group most weekends, she obviously didn't consider him much of a friend. He was simply Pastor Jack.

Frowning, Jack rolled back over and scowled at the red numbers on his clock. Maybe Noah was right. Maybe if she viewed him as an ordinary man she might warm up to him. Might even develop feelings for him. It wasn't completely implausible, was it?

He lay there, the covers pushed down to his knees, his feet tangled up in them. Across the house, the air-conditioning kicked on, and a cool breeze drifted over his bare chest.

Outside his window a cricket chirped, and a few doors down a dog barked. It was nights he felt the loneliest. During the day there were people. Lots of people. Friends, neighbors, members of his congregation. His life kept him busy helping and serving, and he wouldn't change it for anything.

But the long nights were, at least, conducive to quiet conversations with God. He wondered— aloud sometimes—if he was destined to live like the apostle Paul, a life of service without a mate to share it.

But merciful heavens, he sure hoped not. He prayed for a woman, a wife, who'd serve along-side him. For someone to share meaningful conversation with, someone to laugh with, and yes, someone to warm his bed at night. He was a man, after all.

And sometimes he despaired of ever having those things.

His mind flashed back to his conversation with Noah. To the website and profile and Daisy's sweet little note. He wanted to read it again. Just to see her words and feel her interest, he told himself. He'd never even clicked on her picture to look at her photos or read her profile. He wondered how she'd described herself. If she'd mentioned her guilt complex or her soft heart or the adorable way her nose wrinkled up when she laughed. No doubt there was no mention of the way she loved, so openly and freely, or her uncanny ability to bring beauty into the lives of others.

Unable to tamp down his curiosity, he kicked the covers from his feet and went to the living room, where his laptop was charging on the end table. He pulled up the website and got to the log-in page before he remembered the slip of paper Noah had given him. After returning to his bedroom to retrieve it from the pants in his hamper, he came back and keyed in the information.

A few seconds later his profile opened, and his eyes darted straight to Daisy's note. He read it again, his heart giving a little stutter.

He clicked on her picture, and her profile

appeared. It was much longer than his, and he found himself smiling at the modest way she described herself: a florist who enjoyed good conversation, herbal teas, and leisurely scenic walks. She talked about her faith, admitted to a weakness for reality TV and chocolate-covered cherries, and said she was close to her family and enjoyed small-town life.

It was simple and honest, and yet it didn't begin to capture the essence of Daisy. He could only be glad, since he couldn't help but hope no one else would pursue her.

His eyes danced over her photos, over her sparkling eyes and that long blond hair that begged to be touched. Who was he kidding? Every man on the app had probably already contacted her or nudged her or whatever.

But she wrote to you.

He tucked that little fact into the empty space beneath his heart, letting it warm and comfort him. Letting it lift the corners of his lips. Maybe she wasn't interested in Jack, the pastor. But she was interested in TJ, the guy on Flutter. At least interested enough to respond to his nudge. And after all, weren't TJ and Pastor Jack one and the same?

Could this, in fact, be the very answer to his prayers? A chance for Daisy to get to know the real Jack McReady? His heart thudded heavily in his chest even as he lifted his hands and set his fingers over the keyboard.

TEN

Daisy ran Mr. Francis's credit card and had him sign for the purchase. He'd ordered a peony arrangement this week, and her mom had selected only the brightest and freshest of the bunch.

Mr. Francis was an artist, perhaps in his mid-fifties, and the shop kept him in supply of still-life material. Physically, he was trim and fit, on the short side, with salt-and-pepper hair. But it was his George Clooney eyes that stole the show. That and his adorable bashfulness.

Daisy handed him the vase of flowers. "I hope you'll show us your masterpiece when it's finished, Mr. Francis. We're itching to see your work, you know."

The man blushed, his eyes darting toward the back of the shop, where her mom was studiously ignoring him. "Oh, I just paint for pleasure, Daisy. I'm really not that good."

"I'm sure that's not true. Right, Mama? Wouldn't you love to see one of Mr. Francis's paintings?"

Her mom, elbow deep in a funeral arrangement, flashed her a look. "Leave the man alone, Daisy.

I'm sure he has better things to do than hang around here."

Daisy shot her a look in return before turning back to Mr. Francis. "Well, you enjoy your painting time. We have some lovely purple hydrangeas coming in at the end of the week. You might keep that in mind for next week."

"I'll do that." He gave Daisy a nod. "Thank you for the lovely arrangement."

"Oh, that was all Mama. She did a beautiful job, didn't she?"

"That she did." His cheeks turned a deeper shade of pink as he looked Karen's way. "Such beauty is sure to inspire."

Aw. Daisy wondered if he was talking about her mom or the flowers.

Karen tucked a strand of hair behind her ear, visibly flustered. "Thank you kindly."

Mr. Francis gave a nod. "Well . . . have a nice day, ladies."

"Bye, Mr. Francis," Daisy said.

The bell was still tinkling when Daisy turned toward her mom, crossing her arms over her chest. "Really, Mama. Would it be so hard to give the man a kind word?"

Her mom pursed her lips. "I said thank you."

"He is completely smitten with you."

"Oh, *pshaw*. He is not."

"He comes in here every week like clockwork,

making eyes at you and blushing like a school-boy. What else could it mean?"

"You've been watching too many Hallmark movies. He's only after the flowers."

Daisy laughed. "You're so in denial. How can you resist those puppy-dog eyes? I just want to wrap my arms around him and feed him a good meal."

"Well, go right ahead. The last thing I need is a man to feed."

She'd never complained about feeding Daisy's dad. They'd been quite happily married. Daisy had never heard a single argument. Having a front-row seat to the loving marriage had been both inspiring and daunting—especially in light of the recent dates she'd had. She despaired of ever having that kind of marriage.

Daisy started to respond to her mother, but the bell on the door tinkled again. She turned, hoping Mr. Francis had returned with the gumption to finally ask her mom on a date. That line about being inspired by beauty had been surprisingly romantic, and Daisy was more than happy to make herself scarce.

But it wasn't the older gentleman who wan-dered in. It was Julia.

Daisy's heart stuttered at the sight of the woman. Her brown hair was somehow sleek and straight, despite the day's humidity. The sun-light shining through the window revealed its mahogany highlights. She wore a pair of trendy jeans and a lacy ivory top with cap sleeves.

There was a moment of connection when their eyes collided. Or maybe it was only Daisy's imagination.

Daisy offered a bright smile. "Hello . . . How are you?"

She refrained from using Julia's name in case it jogged her mom's memory. Besides, it would be odd, wouldn't it, if she remembered the name of a new customer from almost a week ago?

"Hi there." Their eyes held for a long moment, and something like curiosity flickered in Julia's eyes before she looked away and began browsing the displays. "It's looking like rain out there."

"Maybe it'll cool things off a bit." Daisy's heart was pounding against her ribs. Had Julia come with a purpose? She had so many questions, but she couldn't ask them, not with her mom nearby.

"Can I help you find something?"

"I think I'll just look a minute if that's okay."

"Of course. Let me know if I can help you with anything."

Daisy made herself busy, straightening the florist cards and moving displays around. Julia knew now that Daisy was Paul Pendleton's daughter. What were the chances the woman only needed more flowers? And why was she still in town?

Daisy kept an eye on the stranger from beneath

her lashes. Julia meandered around the store, touching this and that, but otherwise seemed distracted. Their eyes met twice, and both times Julia simply gave her a polite smile and went on about her browsing.

Daisy's nerves rattled as the wait lengthened. Part of her wanted to grab the woman and demand to know how she'd known her father. Another part of her wanted to rush her from the store. What if she said something in front of her mother? Something that stirred up all the awful suspicions Daisy had been having since she'd seen those graveside flowers.

"Thank you," Julia called over her shoulder as she reached for the door.

"Have a nice day." The words flew automatically from Daisy's mouth.

But now that the door was swinging shut behind the woman, a jolt of alarm shot through Daisy. What if Julia was leaving town now? She could go back to North Carolina, and Daisy would never see her again. Could she live the rest of her life with these niggling doubts?

No, she could not. They'd kept her awake for hours this week, and this could be her last chance.

Daisy skirted the counter. "I'll be right back, Mama," she called.

"Where are you going?"

"To lunch."

"But it's only ten thirty!"

Daisy was already pushing out the door. Once on the sidewalk, she looked both ways and spotted Julia getting into her red car a few shops down. Daisy rushed toward her.

"Julia!"

The woman stopped, her door open, her manicured fingers resting on the frame. Her eyes had gone a little wide, her features frozen in a "caught" look.

Indecision and something else—wariness—flashed in her eyes. "Yes?"

Daisy stopped on the sidewalk at the front of the car, her heart beating up into her throat. Her mom couldn't overhear now, and it might be her last opportunity to learn the truth—whatever it was.

Was she sure she wanted to know? She stared at the woman, all her feelings for her dad rising up in her. Love and respect. Once the truth came out, there was no putting it back. Did she want the truth, or would it be easier to live with fabricated lies?

"I—I should go." Julia moved to slip into the driver's seat.

"Wait!"

The woman paused again, and the look on her face sucked the moisture from Daisy's mouth. Yes, it was wariness in the tightened corners of her eyes. In the firm line of her mouth. Julia was hiding something.

And Daisy realized with sudden clarity: regardless of the cost, she had to know what it was. She swallowed hard, bracing herself. "What was your relationship with my father?"

Julia blinked. Once, then twice. Her hand came off the doorframe and fluttered around her chest. "What—what do you mean?" Her eyes darted away, and her wan smile wobbled.

She was a very bad liar.

Daisy straightened to her full five feet four inches. No sense backing down now. "I saw the flowers at the grave, Julia. I know you knew him somehow."

Julia looked down at her hands, now clutching her purse. Her knuckles went white as she squeezed.

"You've been asking questions, and it's a small town." No reason to throw Shirley under the bus. "You already know I'm his daughter."

Julia's lashes lifted as she met Daisy's gaze. Something else was swimming in those blue depths besides wariness . . . Regret? Pity? Whatever it was, Daisy didn't like it.

"Look . . . Daisy . . . I don't want to cause any trouble."

Daisy huffed. "Well, it's a little late for that. I need to know how you knew him."

Julia shifted. She looked over to the east where the Blue Ridge Mountains stood sentinel over the valley. Dark clouds had gathered on the horizon, covering the sun, and the air was thick with the smell of rain.

"I need to know," Daisy reiterated. Her illusions that this was a little bit of nothing had dissipated like morning fog.

Finally Julia looked back at her, but the look in her eyes did nothing to assuage Daisy's fears. "Can we get a cup of coffee somewhere?"

ELEVEN

The Mellow Mug was half empty midmorning on a Tuesday. The robust aroma of java filled the rustic shop, and the espresso machine screeched loudly behind the counter.

Daisy had ridden with Julia the two and a half blocks down Magnolia Lane, but, as if by mutual agreement, they'd put their conversation on hold during the drive and while they ordered drinks. Once they collected their teas, Daisy wove through the wooden tables and chairs to the sofa and armchairs set up in the back along the brick wall. They'd have some privacy back here, and Daisy had a feeling they were going to need it.

A Rascal Flatts song played quietly from a nearby speaker, which should have been soothing. But her stomach was churning, and the mint tea wasn't going to do a thing for the acid rising at the back of her throat. She should've ordered a nice calming chamomile, but she'd been distracted by her spinning thoughts.

She prayed she wasn't making a terrible mistake. She wished she'd opened up to Pastor Jack in the parking lot last night. He would've had some words of wisdom on whether or not to pursue this. But it was too late for that now.

Maybe she'd completely miscalculated. Maybe this only had to do with business or something. Maybe her dad had owned some piece of property that hadn't been included in his will. Or maybe Julia was the daughter of a childhood friend here to mend fences on his or her behalf. It could be anything.

But no, if it were that simple, why all the cloak-and-dagger stuff? And why was Julia sitting across from her right now, wearing that wary look again?

Daisy's white mug clattered in the saucer as she set it on the table between them. Julia had yet to sample her drink. Her eyes were fastened onto the cup as she dipped the tea bag repeatedly, her fingers trembling.

Daisy sat back against the sofa and crossed her arms, a flimsy barrier against the imminent disclosure. "So . . . go ahead. Tell me how you knew my father."

Julia's eyes flickered off Daisy, shifting over to the left before returning to her tea. "I actually didn't know your father. I never even met him."

Daisy tilted her head. If there was anything she couldn't abide, it was a liar. "Try again."

Big blue eyes met hers. "It's true. I—I only knew of him."

"You're some distant fan of the former mayor of Copper Creek, Georgia?" She wasn't normally sarcastic and found it didn't become her. But the woman was trying her patience.

Julia's eyes flashed. "Of course not. He was a friend of my mother's." She gave up on the tea and set it on the coffee table, clutching her mani-cured hands in her lap. "I never intended for us to meet at all. I was just going to slip quietly in and out of town."

"Just spit it out, Julia." Daisy couldn't let go of the first thing she'd said. Couldn't stop won-dering what kind of friend Julia's mother was to her dad. An awful dread bloomed inside like dark thunderclouds.

"Years ago . . . ," Julia continued, her eyes now locked on Daisy's. "Years ago, my mom and your dad were in love. They had an affair."

Daisy's throat tightened, locking down on words, on her very breath.

"I was hoping maybe you already knew. That this wouldn't come as a shock." Pity shone from blue eyes that looked an awful lot like her dad's.

A cold shiver passed through her.

"Daisy . . . the last thing I want to do is hurt you. When I initially came into your shop, I didn't know who you were. I was only after the flowers. And I didn't intend to stay here, but seeing the place where he lived roused my curiosity about him. I couldn't seem to help myself."

"How long ago?" Daisy asked.

"It was thirty-two years ago."

Daisy did the math. What would've been her parents' thirty-fifth anniversary was coming up. "My dad would've already been married, and he wouldn't have cheated on my mom. You didn't know him. He was a good Christian man and a devoted husband. He never would've done such a thing."

"It was a long time ago . . ."

"I don't care. You have no right coming here and saying such terrible things about him. What are you going to tell me next? That you're his daughter?"

Julia's dark lashes fell as she studied her clenched fingers. A flush filled her cheeks as a long moment stretched between them like a tight wire.

"Is that what you were going to say?" Daisy prodded. Her breath suddenly felt stuffed in her lungs, hot and heavy, as if they'd forgotten how to expand and contract. How dare this woman show up, saying such audacious things.

"He wouldn't do what you're accusing him of." But the whispered assertion lacked confidence, and the backs of her eyes stung as dread settled in.

Oh, Daddy. Tell me you didn't. Please tell me you didn't.

"This was a bad idea." Julia's brows pinched as she gathered her purse. "I think maybe I should just go."

Daisy nailed her with a look. "You can't just

drop something like that in my lap and leave."

The woman seemed to waver, her purse perched on her lap, her tea forgotten on the table.

Despite Daisy's vehement denial, Julia's declaration was settling in with a disturbing ring of truth. Wasn't this what she'd been fearing since seeing those flowers at her dad's grave site? But she could hardly believe her dad would do something so despicable. It went against everything she'd known and respected about him. Against everything he'd taught her about love and loyalty. She couldn't envision him being so deceitful and hurtful.

Maybe he'd been a politician in his latter years, but he wasn't the usual kind. He was forthright, well respected, and completely devoted to his family. He was widely known for his integrity and had an ability to see two sides of an issue and bring people together.

"How do you know it was my dad? Maybe you're wrong. Maybe your mom was wrong."

"She wasn't. She had pictures of the two of them together."

"That doesn't prove anything."

"They met when he was traveling to North Carolina regularly. He came into the restaurant where my mom worked at the time, and they started talking. One thing led to another, and she fell in love with him. She believed he loved her too."

"No." Daisy closed her eyes, hating the picture that was forming. A picture that was so at odds with the father she knew. "That's ridiculous. My dad loved *my mom*."

"Love is complicated sometimes."

"Love is loyal, always," Daisy said firmly.

A long silence followed while Daisy tried to digest what Julia was saying. She'd never heard either of her parents mention so much as a whiff of trouble between them in their early days, much less a full-blown affair that had produced a child, for heaven's sake.

Still, if it weren't the truth, why else would Julia be here, telling some outrageous story? What reason could she possibly have to—?

Suspicion churned in her mind. She thought of her dad's considerable success. Before he'd been mayor, he'd made a name for himself as a sales rep in the medical equipment business. The money he'd earned there had set up her parents quite nicely for retirement.

And if there was anything Daisy had learned from her front-seat view of the political world, it was that most people were only out for themselves. How many times had wealthy constituents and businessmen wormed their way into her dad's life only to gain some political advantage? Maybe Julia was after something.

She gave the woman a hard look. "How do I

know you're not just trying to blackmail me or something?"

Julia's chin tipped forward. "Blackmail you? You're the one who cornered me. I wasn't even going to tell you about any of this."

Was that true? Or had Julia only been cleverly stringing her along? "So you say."

Julia's eyes turned cold and flinty. She shoved her purse straps onto her shoulder. "Look. You're the one who wanted to know who I am. And now you do. I'll just be going now. You can forget I ever came here if that's how you want it."

Daisy felt a prick of guilt as those familiar blue eyes turned glassy. The unexpected emotion softened her tone. "All I know is what you believe to be true. There's no proof of what you're saying."

Julia stood, back ramrod straight. "My mom was telling me the truth. She only told me just before she passed because she wanted me to know. My life is perfectly full as it is; I have a dad who raised me and a brother I love. I just wanted some closure. If you need a DNA test to prove what I'm saying is true, I'm happy to oblige. I'll be at the Starlight Motel for one more night. Otherwise . . . have a nice life, Daisy."

There was a note of regret in the last bit that sharpened Daisy's sting of guilt. But Julia was already weaving through the tables, her slender form silhouetted against the picture windows.

Daisy sat immobile, her tea forgotten as the conversation whirled in her head. Julia seemed sincere enough, but could she be trusted? What should Daisy do with this unwelcome news? Did she want a DNA test? What if Julia's assertion proved to be true? Was it possible her dad had actually done this?

She needed answers to these questions. She needed to make a decision and fast—one that could change her life, not to mention her mom's. But she didn't know if she should travel down this path. Maybe she should forget the whole thing and go on as if Julia had never come to town.

Suddenly twitchy, Daisy left the shop, emerging into the sultry afternoon. The clouds threatened rain, but so far the sidewalks remained dry. She began walking, her mind still whirling. She didn't even know where she was going until she reached the corner of Magnolia and Peachtree.

TWELVE

Jack listened on the phone as one of his elders updated him on a maintenance issue. The water pump on the outdoor fountain had quit working, and Donald Warren was collecting bids on its repair. Jack authorized Donald to contract with the lowest bidder and hung up, running a hand over his face.

His sermon preparation was slow going today with a million interruptions. Gloria was out sick so he was fielding calls, and he felt he needed to answer them all. It wouldn't do to have one of his congregation in need and no one responding. As it happened, though, he'd only found himself dealing with inquiries about VBS, youth camp forms, bulletin announcements, and maintenance issues.

His eyes locked onto the computer, where he'd barely begun his notes. He minimized the document and clicked on Safari instead—what was one more distraction?—going to the Flutter website. His pulse skittered as he logged in. He'd had many second thoughts about his response to Daisy last night. When his profile opened, his eyes flittered across the page and he saw a notification.

She'd already read his message. It was too late for second thoughts now.

Had she written back? He gave the page a good hard look—he was new to the site, after all. There. By an envelope icon there was a bright red number one.

Bingo. He couldn't help the smile tugging at his lips. He could hardly wait to see how she'd responded.

He clicked on the icon and his smile fell. The note was from some other woman. It was brief and gracious, but disappointment sliced through him. Wasn't she required to nudge him first? Weren't those the rules? He didn't want to hurt anyone's feelings, but he wasn't interested in anyone but Daisy.

A knock sounded on his door and he jumped. He promptly closed the website, mortification filling him at the thought of being caught on a dating website in the middle of a workday. This was so unlike him.

"Yes?" he called as he moved around his desk and approached the door.

"Pastor Jack? It's me. Daisy."

Daisy. His hand paused on the doorknob at the distress in her voice.

Oh, dear God in heaven, he thought as a possibility presented itself. What if she'd somehow found out he was TJ? What if she knew that letter was from him? Her pastor?

There was a filigree window cutout in the old wooden door, but it was above Daisy's line of sight. He glimpsed the top of her blond head, panic setting in.

Another knock sounded. "Pastor Jack? Please, I have to talk to you. Do you have a minute?"

The rising alarm in her voice did nothing to assuage his fears. It was true. He'd made some kind of error on the app, and somehow she knew. He closed his eyes and swallowed hard.

You've really done it now, McReady. Time to face the music.

He forced himself to open the door. Her hair was windblown, and she still wore her pink Oopsy Daisy apron, but it was the look on her face that hit him like a sucker punch. Her eyes were bloodshot, worry pinched her brows, and she was looking at him oddly.

Of course she's looking at you oddly, you imbecile. You're her pastor and you hit on her.

You hit on a member of your own flock.

"I'm sorry to stop in unannounced. Gloria's not in her office. Do you have a minute?"

"Of course." He ushered her in, leaving the door wide open as he always did, even though today there was no one else in the church. He vaguely thought of their cars, just the two of them, out in the parking lot for anyone to see. A pastor had to be careful with his reputation. But he had bigger, more immediate fish to fry.

As he rounded his desk, he mentally punched himself in the face. Twice, because he deserved it. How could he have let Noah talk him into that ridiculous dating site? How could he have participated? He'd jeopardized their friend-ship—if that was even what they had. More important, he'd undermined his position as her pastor.

Our Father, who art in heaven, hallowed be Thy name—

"Pastor Jack, are you all right?"

He realized he'd been sitting across from her with his eyes closed—maybe because he'd been praying, or maybe he just was attempting that whole ostrich-with-its-head-in-the-sand thing. Obviously not working.

"I'm fine." He had to address this head-on. Apologize profusely and hope their relationship, such as it was, could survive this awkward blip.

"I— Listen, Daisy . . . I can explain."

She gave him a perplexed look. "You're over-worked and tired, there's nothing to explain. Plus Gloria's not here, so the phones are probably ringing off the hook. Is she on vacation this week?"

"What?"

"Gloria . . . She usually visits the grandchildren in May, right?"

"Ah . . . yes. But not till the end of the month. She's home sick today."

Jack gave Daisy a speculative look. Was it possible she was here on some other issue? The Hope House fundraiser perhaps? He was no idiot. He was going to find out before he shot off his big mouth. Then tonight he was going to get on that website and delete his account for good.

"Oh, Pastor Jack . . ." Daisy's eyes teared up, glossing over as she stared so pitifully at him.

His chest ached at the sight. She opened up to him a lot, it was true, but she wasn't given to weeping. Whatever this was—*please, please let it not be my fault*—her heart was breaking before his eyes.

"I don't even know where to start."

He unconsciously pulled a tissue from the box on his desk and handed it to her. Now he was in his element. Sitting in his office chair, a big, safe desk between them.

"How about at the beginning? That's usually a good place."

"Thanks." She took the tissue and dabbed at her eyes. Then it all began to spill out: a woman who'd purchased flowers, Daisy finding the bouquet at her father's grave site, the conversation with Shirley from the Clip 'n' Curl, and finally today's run-in with Julia.

At first Jack's shoulders had sunk in relief as he realized he wasn't responsible for Daisy's distress. But then, as the story unfolded, he scolded himself. This was so much bigger, so much more hurtful than his lapse in judgment. She'd potentially discovered the terrible indiscretion of someone she loved dearly.

He leaned forward, wishing he could pull her into his arms and comfort her. "I'm so sorry this is happening, Daisy."

She was questioning Julia's motives and the truth of what she'd said. But it sounded to him as if the woman had no reason to lie. However, it might take Daisy a while to come to grips with reality.

"It can't be true, right?" she asked with a sniffle. "You knew my dad. He was a good man."

Jack gave her a compassionate smile. "From everything I saw, he was a devoted husband and father."

"Exactly! He'd never do this to my mom."

A long pause ensued as she locked onto Jack's eyes, searching for something. Hope, maybe. The moment stretched, and he watched as uncertainty flared in her eyes. Then her chin slowly crumpled, her forehead furrowed, and tears sprang to her eyes again.

"But she was so . . . sincere. And she didn't seek me out—I had to press her to tell me who she was. And once she did tell me, she seemed almost . . . hurt about the way I responded. What if it's true, Pastor Jack? What if my dad really did do this? What if I have a sister I didn't even know about?"

He folded his hands on his desk. "Well, let's say you knew for sure that what she's saying is true. How would you feel about that?"

A tear tumbled down her cheek. "I don't know! It's not just me I have to worry about, it's my mom. There's no way she knows about this . . . this affair, if it really happened at all. She'd never stay with a man who—did that. And if I explore this further and find out it is true, it would only hurt her. I couldn't do that to her. She shouldn't have to find out something like this, especially not after he's gone and it's too late to even confront him."

"It's also possible that it's not true at all. That Julia's mom lied to her about all of this. Or maybe your dad did have the affair but isn't really Julia's father."

Daisy sniffled. "I guess that's possible. She seemed so sure though."

"Let's talk about you, Daisy. How would it be, finding out so suddenly that you have a sister?"

She shook her head. "I don't know. I've been an only child so long I can hardly even imagine it. And an older sister, besides."

"That would be quite a change and quite a challenge I would think, with the family dynamics."

"It would upset the apple cart in so many ways."

"The question is, can you live without knowing one way or another? How do you feel about letting Julia leave and never having your questions answered?"

Daisy stared back. She was leaning forward, her elbows propped on the desk, her fingers shredding the tissue. "I don't know if I can do that. But I don't know if I can hurt my mom either."

"And yourself." This would be a tough truth for Daisy to swallow. She looked up to her father so much. Perhaps had him on a pedestal. It was easy to do, especially after the death of a loved one.

"Yes, and myself."

"But the test could also be negative."

"That's true. But what if it's not? What if she really is my half sister?"

"Would you like to pray about it?"

"Yes, please." The words came as a sigh of relief.

Jack took her hand and led them in a heartfelt prayer, asking for God's wisdom and guidance. Asking for Him to comfort Daisy during this confusing time. Daisy sniffled throughout, and when he finished she squeezed his hand before drawing away.

"Pastor Jack, if I take the DNA test . . ." Her sad green eyes just about did him in. "How will I know if I'll be able to live with the repercussions?"

He wished he could tell her what she should do. But that wasn't his call to make. "Only you can answer that question, Daisy."

THIRTEEN

Daisy blew out a breath and rapped on the freshly painted red door. The Starlight Motel wasn't the Ritz, but it was Copper Creek's only hotel. Owned by Lurline Reynolds, it was a U-shaped two-story structure with exterior doors. The building flanked a well-lit pool—heavily chlorinated, based on the strong smell wafting her way. Though vacation cabins were the more popular choice, the motel and its property were well maintained and had a reputation for being kept scrupulously clean.

The door swung open and Julia appeared in the opening wearing yoga pants and a purple V-neck T-shirt. She looked five years younger without her makeup, but her skin was so flawless, her eyes so blue, that she was still very attractive.

Daisy could tell by the lack of surprise on her face that she'd checked the peephole before answering.

"I hope it isn't too late to stop by." It was after nine, and Julia's expression and body language weren't exactly welcoming.

Julia crossed her arms. "Would you like to come in?"

"We could sit out by the pool if you'd rather."

"The chlorine burns my eyes." Julia opened the door wider and stepped aside.

Daisy followed her into a room that smelled faintly of the citrusy scent she recognized as Julia's perfume. A table for two sat in front of the picture window, and a king-size bed, its floral spread slightly rumpled, dominated the room. The television was tuned to one of Daisy's favorite reality TV shows.

Julia muted the set and gestured to the round table. "Have a seat. I'd offer you something to drink, but I'm out of vending machine change."

"That's okay. I just came from the diner."

Julia lowered herself across the table from Daisy. "They have good food. I've eaten more than my share of meals there the last week—as is apparent by my expanding waistline."

"Louisa's a great cook, but she's not happy if it hasn't been rolled in flour and fried twice over."

"Back home they put the calories on the menus."

Daisy gave a rueful laugh. "That will never happen here."

An awkward silence ensued. Julia looked down at her slender fingers, laced on the lacquered wood table.

Daisy squirmed in the chair. "Listen, Julia . . . I'm sorry about how I responded at the coffee shop. This is all just . . . a complete surprise to me."

Julia made a face. "And not a good one—I get it. My stepdad warned me it could be stirring up a hornets' nest to come here. But I really didn't intend to stay. I was just going to lay some flowers by his grave—I was just after some closure. Then, being here where he lived, I got curious about who he was. What his life was like, what kind of person he was."

"I'd like to take that test," Daisy blurted out, her heart hammering.

She hadn't actually made up her mind until that moment. She'd only planned to talk more with Julia and apologize for her response. After talking with Pastor Jack and praying about it, she knew she needed to do that much.

But seeing Julia this way—in her comfy clothes, her face stripped of makeup—she knew she couldn't let this woman walk away not knowing if she was her half sister.

Julia stared back, unblinking, her lips parted.

"I'll be honest," Daisy said. "Even though it was a long time ago, I don't want to believe my father could've done this. And I don't want to bring any hurt on my mother. But the truth matters to me. I need to know."

Julia's shoulders sank on an exhale. "I understand. I don't want to cause any trouble for you or your mom."

There was something in her eyes, something

sweet and vulnerable that made Daisy hope—just for a split second—that Julia really was her sister.

Daisy flipped the channel on the remote control. There was nothing on. She was bored and restless and couldn't get Julia out of her mind.

She'd tried to stay busy since she'd left the motel. She'd done some research on fund-raisers—she had a meeting with Jack tomorrow to discuss their options. And she'd already paid the bills, something she'd been putting off for three days. Facing pages of numbers was not her favorite thing to do.

She flipped off the TV and tossed the remote aside. She thought of Julia again and wondered if the woman had inherited her dad's intelligence—if she really was her dad's daughter. She seemed pretty smart, and she was certainly confident. Daisy bet she had a college degree and a few letters behind her name besides. Brains apparently ran in the family—except for Daisy, of course. She'd barely made it through high school.

But unfortunately she'd have to wait on any answers. Somehow she'd figured that, once she made the decision to do the DNA test, Julia would whip the kit out of her purse, and they could be done with it.

But Julia had been as caught off guard by all

of this as Daisy, and a DNA test wasn't exactly something they could pick up from the Piggly Wiggly. They'd searched on Julia's laptop and found a reputable business that would ship a DNA kit via express mail. They'd get results two days after the company received the completed test. All told it would take about a week.

How in the world was she going to wait a whole week? How could she face her mother every day, knowing she was keeping this secret from her? But what good would it do to tell her when nothing might come of it?

She was just going to have to stay busy and hope time passed quickly. She needed a distraction. She couldn't get any further with the fundraiser until she talked to Pastor Jack.

Her eyes lit on her phone, sitting on her end table. Daisy grabbed it and opened the Flutter app. She'd gotten a nice note from that man she'd written. When she'd explained she wanted to go slowly, she figured she wouldn't hear back. She'd written something similar to two other men who'd never responded. It seemed most guys weren't interested in taking things slowly.

Maybe she'd write him back tonight.

FOURTEEN

Jack needed a second cup of coffee just to make it out the door of his home. He shoved a Keurig pod into the machine, set it to strong, then gathered the things he'd need at the office today.

Grabbing his laptop case, he remembered his Flutter profile, which he'd never gotten around to deleting. All hell had broken loose after Daisy had left his office yesterday. First a conflict had erupted between the strong-willed VBS co-directors, and he'd had to mediate the disagreement. Then he'd counseled a couple from his church who were on the brink of divorce.

After that he'd been notified via phone that a sprinkler on the west lawn had been damaged by a lawn mower and was now spraying directly onto their neighbor's front porch—a fact Mrs. Willow had discovered because she'd been on said porch reading her paper, minding her own business. It had taken over an hour to rectify the problem and calm her down. It wasn't the first run-in they'd had with Mrs. Willow, and he didn't imagine it would be the last.

After that he'd intercepted at least a dozen

calls—trivial queries that could've been answered by simply clicking on the church's website.

Then, just when he was ready to leave for the day, he received a call that one of his congregation had been taken to the ER with chest pains and was being admitted to the hospital. Jack spent the rest of the evening awaiting test results and praying with the family. By the time he left, the patient had been scheduled for a triple bypass.

Jack had rolled into his driveway after one in the morning and dropped into bed, exhausted. So far he had exactly five lines of notes on Sunday's sermon and another full schedule today. He thought of Gloria, home sick and in bed, and reminded himself to send her more flowers. The woman deserved her own botanical garden.

At the thought of flowers, his favorite flower-named woman came to mind. He glanced at the clock. If he skipped his regular morning muffin stop at the Mellow Mug, he'd have time to delete his Flutter profile before his nine o'clock appointment with the director of missions.

He wasn't especially fond of muffins any-way . . . He stopped there mainly to minister. Lindsey, one of the young baristas, was depressed about her parents' divorce and opened up to him easily. Gage, the owner, seemed the personification of chill, but the shadows in his eyes hinted at hidden pain.

The Keurig completed its brewing, and Jack grabbed the steaming mug of coffee. Yes, he'd delete that ridiculous profile now, before the entire day got away from him again. He pulled out his laptop and sat at the rustic pine table in his kitchen.

It was all rustic, his cabin. A former vacation rental, the place had been furnished and priced to sell, deer head and bear rug included. But it looked to Jack as if a pine forest had exploded, and perhaps the deer and bear had been collateral damage. Oh well. He'd get around to redecorating eventually.

He opened the website and logged on to his profile. He was doing the right thing. That much was clear after experiencing so much anxiety yesterday when he thought he'd been caught.

Nothing like being caught red-handed to—

His eyes locked on the envelope icon and the red numeral one on it. It was probably from some poor, unsuspecting woman, maybe the one who'd written him before. He'd just check, maybe write her a polite response before deleting his account. He didn't want to hurt anyone's feelings. The dating world could be such a harsh environment.

But when he clicked on the envelope, he saw the letter was not from a stranger. It was from Daisy. The Second Coming couldn't have stopped him from reading it.

Hi TJ,

Thanks for writing back. I appreciate your willingness to take things slow.

So tell me something about yourself. You mention in your profile that you do counseling and teaching. I'm all right with keeping things general. You don't have to share the particulars or anything else you're not comfortable with. Can I ask what drew you into those fields?

As I mentioned in my profile, I'm a florist in a small town. Needless to say I love flowers, but mostly I love the creativity. I love a blank canvas, whether it's a vase or a display window, and getting to fill it with things from my imagination. Don't tell anyone, but I kind of have a black thumb when it comes to growing things!

All in all I love my quiet little life with my flower shop, cute bungalow, and handful of good friends. I'd love to hear back from you if you're so inclined.

Warmly,
Daisy

Jack didn't know he'd been holding his breath until he released the lungful of oxygen. She'd written him back. He scanned the letter again. It was open and honest, positive and nonthreatening. So very like Daisy.

She didn't mention the recent upset in her life, but then why would she? TJ was a stranger to her. He felt a moment's pride that she'd opened up to him, Pastor Jack, about such a delicate matter. At least he'd earned her respect and trust.

But maybe TJ could earn that too, given enough time. Maybe he could even earn her affection, her love.

His gaze dropped to the Delete Profile button, and he wavered. He couldn't do it now, could he? What would Daisy think if he never even responded to her note? He could write her back with apologies and then delete his account.

But he knew Daisy; she'd take it personally no matter what excuse he gave. She'd pick apart her sweet note, trying to ascertain where she'd gone wrong. The last thing he'd ever do was hurt her.

He sat back, staring at the screen, and took a sip of the hot brew, thinking. His choices were pretty straightforward. He could respond as TJ and keep the charade going, but that was dishonest. He could respond to Daisy's message and let her down easy, but that would hurt her feelings. Or he could write back and tell her the whole hairy truth, but that would only embarrass them both. Not to mention destroy their relationship, such as it was. There was no perfect solution.

He had that meeting with Daisy this evening. He'd purposely asked to meet at the Mellow Mug instead of the church. He deduced that the more she saw him out of his office the better.

He wouldn't do anything hasty with his profile for now, he decided. He'd think about it, pray about it, and see how he felt after their meeting. But he just had to read Daisy's letter one more time.

Locating an empty table at the Mellow Mug that evening proved to be a challenge. The shop buzzed with conversation and laughter. The staff darted around behind the counter, too busy to make small talk, and the espresso machine screeched intermittently. In the far corner Rawley Watkins, lead singer of Last Chance, competed with the noise, strumming a mellow tune on his guitar.

Jack collected his mug of decaf and carried it to a recently vacated table for two back along the brick wall. He'd almost ordered Daisy's favorite drink—Darjeeling tea with a splash of milk—but he didn't want to admit to remembering something she'd only mentioned in passing.

He opened his laptop so he wouldn't look lame waiting for her when she arrived. His sermon document opened on the screen—he'd added three whole lines today. Great progress.

Gloria, come back!

He winced at the selfish thought and soothed his conscience with a prayer for her recovery, repenting of his self-centeredness for good measure.

It turned out he didn't have time to add more thoughts to his sermon. A neighbor stopped by to chat, followed by a member of his congregation who was at the coffee shop with her daughter-in-law. Before he knew it, Daisy was dropping into the seat across from him, a delightful smile stretching across her face as she set a manila folder on the table.

"Hey, Pastor Jack. Man, this place is hopping tonight."

"Sure is. We were lucky to get a table."

Daisy dunked her tea bag several times before taking a sip. Her gaze connected somewhere over his shoulder, and her eyes lit up. She gave a friendly wave.

Rawley Watkins. He knew without looking that the good-looking musician had probably given her one of his low-key nods in the middle of his acoustic set.

Jack felt a pinch of jealousy. He forbade the scowl that wanted to form and smiled at Daisy instead. "So how are you doing, Daisy? You were pretty shaken up when you stopped by my office yesterday, understandably so."

She blinked as her gaze came back to him, a look of alarm on her face.

He realized they'd never once discussed her personal matters outside his office. He guessed that was off-limits and probably unprofessional.

He cleared his throat. "Sorry to bring up a personal matter. If you don't want to talk about it here, that's fine."

"Oh, no . . . It's okay. I could actually still use your prayers about that. I did go to see her last night—Julia. We're going to do the DNA test." She gave a firm nod, but he saw the worry in her eyes.

"Well, no matter what, Daisy, just continue to seek God's guidance. I'm confident He'll steer you in the right direction."

It took an act of God to keep his eyes from roving over her beautiful features: the cute nose with the sprinkle of freckles, the curve of her cheek, the fullness of her lower lip.

Don't look at her lips. Do not look.

Daisy took a sip of tea. "You're right, of course. And I do feel I'm doing the right thing. But I still feel kind of bad, keeping all this from my mom. We won't have the results for about a week."

"Waiting is hard. What will you do if Julia turns out to be your half sister?"

She gave a self-deprecating laugh. "I guess I'll show up at your office and whine and complain until you tell me what to do."

He gave a gentle smile. "You never whine and complain."

"And you never tell me what to do." She narrowed her eyes in a speculative look that came across as delightfully flirty. "Which only makes me wonder why I keep spilling my guts to you. Is there some kind of truth serum in that iced tea you serve me?"

If only. He chuckled. "Most people have the right answers they need. I just remind them what the Scriptures say, pray, and talk it out of them."

"Hmm. Well, you're very good at it."

His cheeks warmed, and he picked up his coffee, giving a grateful nod. "Thank you for saying so."

She gave him a speculative look. "You're much better at accepting compliments than I am."

"You're getting better at it every day."

"Well, you give me plenty of opportunities for improvement." Daisy opened the folder and pulled out her notes. "So . . . I've been doing some research on fundraisers. I've never had to raise so much money before. I confess, it's a little daunting."

"I have complete faith in you."

"That's very kind of you to say." She bit her lip. "So, I've been looking around online to see what's been most profitable for other organizations."

"Makes sense."

"We have lots of choices. We could do one major event or do a handful of smaller things like crowd funding, restaurant fundraisers, or a walk-a-thon . . . The list is endless."

"What do you think would be best?"

"I'm thinking one big event would be more impactful. This is a caring community. If we all come together at one time and place, I think people would rally around the Hope House in a bigger way."

"That's a good point. Okay, what kind of event, do you think?"

"Well, auctions can be very successful. A lot of local businesses would donate generously. We could even offer some Blue Ridge getaways, open the bidding online and involve people from all over the region. I'm sure we could get locals to donate some cabin rentals."

"I like that. That could be very profitable."

"Or we could hold an event of some kind. A barbecue or one of those expensive galas that charge by the plate. My dad used to do those to raise money for his campaigns."

"That might eliminate people who want to help but don't have much to give."

"That's true. And besides planning the event, whatever it ends up being, we also have to get the word out quickly. And timing-wise we have to schedule this within the next eight weeks and yet work around Peachfest in June."

Peachfest . . . Jack's thoughts spun. "Could we capitalize on that in some way? Peachfest draws a huge crowd."

She tilted her head. "You're right. Hmm. That's not a bad idea."

"What kind of event would make a lot of money? A booth of some kind? A featured dinner?"

"I can't imagine that either of those things would be profitable enough on its own. But maybe we could do multiple booths."

They discussed ideas for booths and talked about asking restaurants to donate food for a big supper. Daisy didn't seem convinced that the fundraiser would raise enough money, but they both promised to give it some more thought.

An hour had passed when Daisy closed her folder. "We don't have much time. I'm going to need a lot of help to pull something like this off."

"Once VBS is over you'll have plenty of help. You'll see. Until then, I'm all yours."

Someone shuffled to a stop beside their table, and Jack's gaze climbed the taut plaid-shirted torso all the way to Rawley's stubbled neck and crooked smile, aimed straight at Daisy.

"Hey, girl."

"Hey, Rawley. You sound great tonight. I love your acoustic set."

"Thanks. I prefer playing with the full band, but the extra money's nice." He gave Jack a nod. "Pastor Jack. How you doing?"

"Nice to see you, Rawley."

The guy had that scruffy-look thing going for him and long hair that flopped over his brow. The ladies went crazy for him when he was onstage, and he'd danced with Daisy more times than Jack could count.

Not that he was keeping track.

Rawley had turned his attention back to Daisy. "So looks like your meeting's all done, and I'm on break. Wanna hang out awhile?"

"Sure." Daisy beamed at Rawley, then glanced back at Jack. "We're all done here, right, Pastor Jack?"

"Um, yes. Absolutely."

Rawley hovered over their table, obviously waiting for Jack to vacate the chair.

Don't mind me or anything. Jack gathered his mug and laptop and stood, dredging up a smile. "Thanks for your help, Daisy. Y'all have a good evening."

Y'all have a good evening? Heat climbed the back of Jack's neck as he left the shop. He couldn't pull off the Southern-charm thing like Rawley did, and it sounded ridiculous when he tried.

He grimaced at the way Rawley had just inserted himself so casually between him and Daisy. What if they'd actually been on a date? Was that so preposterous? After all, Daisy was a young single woman, and Jack was a semi-young single man.

Why had Rawley just assumed they were there for a meeting? Because of a folder? And Daisy had ended their meeting quickly enough to socialize with another man. Was there some reason she couldn't socialize with Jack?

He opened his car door, giving his head a hard shake. Okay, so it really had only been a meeting, but it was disheartening to have Daisy abandon him so quickly. And downright emasculating to be so thoroughly dismissed as nonthreatening.

The same way Daisy had been dismissing him for months.

He settled into the driver's seat, growing still as the thought sank in, going deep into a place that ached. It was probably only his pride talking, but was it too much to want Daisy to view him as an ordinary man? To her he was only a pastor, a convenient sounding board. She probably hadn't thought of him as a real man one single time.

Well, he was done with that. He put his car in reverse and backed from the parking space. This Flutter thing gave him a way in the back door. Maybe Daisy wasn't interested in Pastor Jack, but she *was* interested—at least a little bit—in TJ. And there was no way on God's green earth Jack was going to surrender that advantage now.

FIFTEEN

From the moment Ava and Millie entered the shop after school, Daisy knew something was wrong. Even if it weren't for Ava's absent smile and tense shoulders, her red-rimmed eyes would've given her away.

Daisy hadn't seen much of her since the Spring Fling on Saturday, but she knew the girl had had a great time. All the high school girls had looked so pretty after their afternoon at Josephine's shop. Daisy wondered if something had happened today between her and the boy who'd taken her to the dance.

Little Millie seemed just fine, strolling through the store with her purple backpack, smile in place. She had long dark hair like Ava's, but hers was curly, and her eyes were deep brown instead of blue.

"Hi, Miss Daisy," Millie called on her way to the back stairs.

"Hello, Millie. How was school today?"

"Miss Walker made me class leader, and we had mac and cheese for lunch."

"Well, it sounds like you had a great day." She looked at Ava. "You all right, Ava?"

Ava gave a wan smile as Millie scampered on ahead. "I'm fine."

"Hey." Daisy caught her arm on the way past. "You're not fine. What's wrong? Did something happen with Jason?"

"No. We're fine. Just friends." Ava wavered, shifting her purse higher on her shoulder. "It was just a long day, that's all."

Ava was very mature for her age, but she had a lot of responsibility right now: school, childcare, a part-time job. Maybe she needed a girls' night. She'd been in charge of Millie for over a week now, and the younger girl was pretty spirited.

"How about if I hang with Millie tonight while you go out with your friends?" Daisy said. "I can come over as soon as we close up, and we'll order pizza."

Ava finally looked Daisy in the eye.

Daisy wilted at the hopelessness she saw there. "What is it, Ava? You can tell me, whatever it is."

She teared up. "Miss Walker asked me to come by after school. She said Millie's fallen behind. I knew she was struggling, but I didn't know how much. She's suggesting we hold her back a grade."

"Oh, honey." Daisy understood what that was like. Watching all your friends move ahead while you stayed behind with the "babies." Being teased by both former classmates and the new, younger ones.

"She said she didn't see any other way," Ava said.

"I'm so sorry. That's really a hard thing for a child to understand." And Millie had already been through so much.

"She's going to be so upset. How do I tell her this without making her feel stupid?" Ava swiped the tears from her cheeks. "And she's not! She's a smart girl. She just struggles with school-work."

Daisy squeezed Ava's hand. "One step at a time. Let's give you a chance to catch your breath first. Why don't you call a friend and make plans for after work? I'm on babysitting detail tonight, remember?"

"You've already done so much for us."

"Hey, I love you guys. Millie and I will have a great time, *and* get her homework done. I'll be up a little after six if that's okay with you."

"That would be so great. A friend from school's been asking me to come over for weeks. Thank you, Daisy."

Millie was already in her pj's when she opened the door to Daisy's knock. Her curls were still damp from her bath.

"Hi, Miss Daisy!" Millie hugged Daisy as if she hadn't just seen her a few hours earlier.

"Hello, Millie-Banillie."

Millie rolled her eyes, looking more like a

preteen than a nine-year-old. "That's not my name."

Daisy laughed at the girl's indignant expression. "It's not? I thought you were Millie-Banillie Morgan."

"Millie *Renee* Morgan."

"Are you sure? You look like a Millie-Banillie to me."

"Millie . . . ," Ava chided as she emerged from the apartment's short hall, still buttoning her sleeveless blouse. "You are not to answer the door without me."

"It's only Miss Daisy," Millie said, letting Daisy in.

"But you didn't know that before you opened the door."

"How am I supposed to know who it is unless I open it?"

"That's *my* job."

"Well, how are *you* supposed to know?"

Ava gave a deep growl.

"Can we order pizza now?" Millie asked Daisy. "Ava said you were going to order pizza and we were going to play games."

"That's exactly right. I'll order pizza—but while we're waiting for it . . . homework."

"Uuugh! I knew there was a catch."

Daisy laughed. "Smart girl."

Ava grabbed her purse from the kitchenette counter. "Her bedtime is nine o'clock, and don't let her con you into extra time. She's a bear to get up in the morning."

"But it's a special occasion!" Millie said.

Ava gave her a stern look. "It's a school night. You have a reading paper and a spelling test to study for." She tousled Millie's hair. "Be good for Miss Daisy."

After Ava left, Daisy ordered the pizza and settled Millie at the kitchen table to do homework. They started with the reading paper. There was a story paragraph to read aloud and then questions to answer.

Daisy tried not to wince as Millie struggled through the paragraph, mispronouncing many of the words. By the time she finally finished, Daisy knew the child couldn't have comprehended much of it. She looked frustrated and ready to quit and, judging by the pink tinge to her cheeks, more than a little embarrassed.

Just as Daisy suspected, Millie couldn't answer any of the basic questions about the plot. "Let me read the paragraph this time, and you just listen, okay?"

Millie huffed. "Fine."

Daisy read slowly and carefully, her own reading issues making it harder than it should've been. When she asked the first question, Millie answered it correctly. The same for the next four questions. But she struggled to write the answers on the paper.

Daisy praised her efforts, and by the time they moved on to spelling, the girl was in a better mood. But spelling was also an effort. The pizza arrived when they were only halfway through the words.

Daisy declared it break time, and they devoured the cheese pizza. After supper, Millie was reluctant to settle back into homework. Daisy could hardly blame her. She knew exactly how Millie felt.

Daisy grabbed a Scrabble game from a box of stuff in the kitchen. "Come on, let's work on your spelling words."

Millie looked at her skeptically. "That's a game."

"I know. We're going to use it for practice." Daisy sorted the letters on the table and let Millie spell the spelling words with the tiles, praising her success and encouraging her when she got something wrong.

"Very good, Millie! Now let's write them on paper and we'll be done."

Millie grumbled but took out her sheet of paper. She only missed four out of the twenty—a huge improvement.

"Bravo!" Daisy said. "We're all done, and now you get to pick a game to play."

"Yay!" Millie chose Yahtzee and proceeded to soundly beat Daisy three games in a row.

"All right, Millie-Banillie," Daisy said after the last round took them a few minutes past nine o'clock. "You're the official Yahtzee champion . . . but it's bedtime. Go brush your teeth and get into bed. I'll be there in a few minutes."

"Aw, just one more game?"

"Next time. I made your sister a promise, and we're already five minutes late."

Millie went off to brush her teeth while Daisy put away the game. A few minutes later she listened as the girl said her prayers, including her sister, the other girls at the Hope House, and her daddy in prison.

Daisy turned out the light and went to the living room where she listened to her Debbie Macomber book until Ava returned home at ten.

Daisy touched the pause button on her phone and pulled out her earbuds. "Hey, how was your night?"

"I had a great time. I really needed that. I don't even remember the last time I just hung out at a friend's house."

Daisy wound the cord around her phone. "Aw, I'm so glad, Ava. Millie was great. Her homework is all done—and you didn't warn me she was the Yahtzee Queen! She killed me."

Ava laughed. "Yeah, I never play that with her."

Daisy hated to ruin Ava's good mood, but she had to talk to her about Millie's struggle with the schoolwork. "Can we talk a few minutes?"

"Uh-oh, that doesn't sound good." Ava sank down beside Daisy.

"I understand Millie's struggles, Ava. I had difficulty in school too. In fact, I was held back in fourth grade, so I completely get it."

Ava's brows popped upward. "You?"

Daisy nodded. "School was pretty awful. I was diagnosed with dyslexia in the sixth grade. Do you know what that is?"

"It's where you mix up letters, right?"

"That's part of it. There's actually a lot more to it than that, and there are all different types of dyslexia too."

Ava's expression was guarded. "Why are you telling me this?"

"Ava, I'm not a professional . . . but after working on homework with Millie, I'm wondering if she might be dyslexic too."

Ava blinked, then her eyes began filling with tears.

"It's not the end of the world. In fact, if she does have dyslexia, that would explain her struggles. There are tools and coping methods to help her, and the school would make accommodations for her."

Ava closed her eyes. "This feels so overwhelming. I don't know anything about all that."

"You're not alone. And I could be completely wrong, but I don't think so. Talk to her teacher, and make sure Millie gets the testing she needs. I'm sure the school has resources for a professional evaluation."

"Okay. I guess I'll talk to Miss Walker tomorrow."

Daisy set her hand on Ava's arm. "It's going to be all right. I promise."

The next evening Daisy smiled as she finished reading TJ's latest note, sent at 7:23 this morning. Was it too soon to write back? She got settled at her dining room table. They'd been writing back and forth all week, on alternating days. TJ had a self-deprecating sense of humor that made her laugh out loud, and he was such an eloquent writer.

Since writing wasn't her strength, she mostly used voice-to-text and checked and double-checked the spelling and punctuation. He must be well-educated if he was a teacher and counselor. She hadn't yet mentioned that her higher education had ended with her high school diploma, and she was grateful he hadn't asked.

Maybe she should play it cool and wait till tomorrow to respond . . . but then she'd have to wait another whole day for his response. She started a new note, conscious of the little smile on her lips. She'd found herself increasingly eager for his responses. Truth be told, she'd checked her phone app several times today, her heart giving a little flutter each time.

It was silly, really. She hardly even knew the man. But she was having fun with their communication. She touched the microphone button on her phone.

Hello friend,
I just got home from work and saw your note on my phone app. Your friends sound great and so do your camping adventures. I have to say, though, that my idea of camping involves the Holiday Inn.

You mentioned the importance of your faith in your profile—a bold and respectable move. So tell me a little about that. My faith is important to me too. I'm not hung up on denominations, just doctrine. So tell me more about your beliefs and ask me anything you like—I reserve the right to plead the fifth! (And so do you!)

You must miss your family. Thank God for FaceTime, right? The Midwest seems so far away, but I'm glad they come and visit you sometimes and you get to go home for the holidays. I'm very blessed to have my family—small as it is—right here in town.

Daisy read the note, stopping to correct errors along the way and hoping she'd caught them all. Her stomach gave a hefty growl just as her phone buzzed in her hand.

She clicked over to see that Julia had texted her.

Just got an email saying the results are up on the website. Want to come over and check it together?

Daisy's breath caught in her throat. In a matter of minutes she was going to find out if her dad had had an affair. If Julia was her sister. Her thumbs hovered over the phone.

She had discovered over the last week that she actually liked Julia. They'd even found it in themselves to poke fun at each other as they did the mouth swabs. That night Daisy had ended up sticking around for a movie and a pizza in Julia's hotel room. Daisy had mailed off the package herself the next morning before work. The whole process seemed to have built a bridge of trust between the two of them.

They'd texted on and off, both eager for the results. They avoided talking about Daisy's dad and instead focused on the test. There did seem to be a connection of some type between them.

And now Daisy found herself confused. Did she *want* Julia to be her half sister? If she was, it would change everything . . . some of it not for the better. But her hopes had no bearing on the truth anyway. It would turn out however it turned out, and she'd just have to deal with the fallout.

She sent a text saying she'd be over shortly. Her mind a million miles away, she sent the note she'd written TJ, pocketed her phone, and grabbed her purse.

SIXTEEN

Daisy's heart was pounding like a jackhammer by the time she knocked on Julia's hotel door. She'd prayed her heart out on the short drive over, and now there was nothing to do but let the truth unfold.

The truth . . . Was she ready for it?

The door opened, and Julia appeared in yoga pants and a grass-green T-shirt, her damp locks hanging over her shoulders. She smiled nervously. "Come on in."

Daisy gave her a speculative look as she crossed the threshold. Had Julia sneaked a peek already? Somehow she didn't like that idea. "You haven't checked yet, have you?"

"I told you I wouldn't. We're in this together, for better or for worse."

It was a nice thought, but Daisy couldn't decide which result would be better and which would be worse. She wondered how they'd both feel five minutes from now. The thought sent a shot of adrenaline through her system. She sucked in a lungful of oxygen, finding the air laced with pine cleaner and the fruity scent of Julia's shampoo.

Julia held up a bottle of whiskey in one hand

and a bottle of champagne in the other, looking a little uncertain. "I wasn't sure which would be more needful—or appropriate."

Daisy huffed a laugh. "You can decide for yourself, but I'd just as soon have some chamomile tea either way."

"Actually . . . I think that might be an option." Julia headed toward the coffee setup on the dresser.

"No, please, that can wait. Let's just get this over with, if it's all the same to you."

Julia's shoulders fell as she did an about-face. "Oh good. I feel the same. I've been so antsy since I got the email."

Daisy settled at the table, her purse cradled in her lap. Julia pulled up her chair so they could both see the screen.

"They gave me a link." Julia opened the email and clicked on it. "I just have to put in our access code and password . . ."

Daisy twisted her purse straps. Her mouth was as dry as August dirt. She bit her lip as Julia took out her phone and pulled up the code and password that had come with the test. It seemed Daisy no more than blinked and Julia had it all typed in.

She leveled a look at Daisy, a flicker of anxiety in her blue eyes. "Okay . . . are you ready?"

"As I'll ever be."

Their gaze held for a long moment, then Julia

spoke. "Daisy . . . whatever happens, I just want you to know I'm grateful you were willing to take the test with me. I hope . . . Well, let's just see what we have, and we'll go from there."

Daisy gave a nod. "All right."

Her eyes moved to the screen, and Daisy watched as the arrow moved to the Get Results button and hovered there. Her stomach clenched as her breath caught in her throat.

The click of the trackpad seemed loud in the dead stillness of the room. The screen began loading. Text and images appeared, as did the image of a loading circle. Daisy couldn't even blink. Then the content appeared. She skimmed over their names and came to the pertinent paragraph. But her dyslexia interfered, making the reading slow and tedious.

Finally the last line registered, and her heart galloped off. She blinked and read it again just in case her brain had jumbled things up.

Julia sat back in her chair, looking at Daisy wide-eyed for a long, stunned moment. "We're sisters."

Oh, dear God . . . The prayer petered out as words jumbled in her head and emotions raced through her too fast for any to take hold. She had a sister. There was no going back now. What had she done?

"Are you okay?" Julia asked. "You're looking a little pale."

"I—I don't know." A terrible dread had filled her. Had she made a horrible mistake? Now she *knew*. There was no way she could keep this from her mother now.

Right?

"Daisy?" Julia's softly spoken question drew her gaze. There was a world of vulnerability in the woman's eyes.

No, not "the woman." Her sister.

Daisy had a sister.

Her chest tightened until it ached painfully. The expectant look on Julia's face was too much. She couldn't deal with Julia yet. She couldn't even process her feelings. She had to—

She couldn't—

All of this just—

She gasped for breath, her lungs seemingly unable to keep up with her heart rate.

Her chair nearly toppled as she popped to her feet. "I—I have to go."

"Daisy . . ."

Her legs trembled as she edged around Julia. "I'm sorry. I just—need some time, okay?"

"Don't go. Let's talk about it."

"I can't do that right now."

"Daisy."

Daisy didn't look back. She didn't want to see the hurt look on Julia's face. As she left the room, her chest felt hollow and white dots speckled her vision.

She was so deep in thought she didn't even remember walking to her car or getting in. Didn't remember starting the ignition or pulling from the motel parking lot. She didn't even know where she was going until five minutes later when she pulled into a gravel drive off Old Mill Road.

Jack smiled at the laptop screen. Daisy had written him back so quickly. That was good, right? They'd previously set an every-other-day pace, but tonight she'd broken that practice by responding sooner.

He liked that she'd inquired about his faith. He should've already asked about hers, but he kept forgetting to query about things he already knew. He wasn't very good at subterfuge—which, he supposed, wasn't an altogether bad thing.

He started a note back.

> Hi Daisy,
> What? There's a Flutter phone app? Now you tell me. I'm not very adept at all this technology stuff, but I'll figure out how to download it. It would be convenient to be able to check for messages on the go.
> I admit I miss my family, though we talk at least once a week. I miss my mom's cooking and her enveloping hugs. I miss watching baseball with my dad and

arguing with my sisters over who's the favorite—me obviously.

He started writing about his faith, keeping it general, trying not to delve too deeply into theology. That had been his major, after all, and he was passionate about it. But laypeople's eyes tended to glaze over at words like *ecclesiology* and *theodicy*.

He moved on from there to ask about her work.

Do you ever have crazy things happen at your shop? I did a funeral one time—

Whoops. He backspaced.

I was at a funeral one time where there was a huge arrangement from the daughter of the deceased woman. It had a big ribbon reading "Bon Voyage!" I thought it must've been a terrible mistake on the florist's part, then I learned that the deceased had always referred to her passing as "going on her final cruise." I guess it's all a matter of perspective!
    So . . . any good stories to tell me?

He reread his message. It was a little verbose, but that was all right, wasn't it? He'd be elated to receive a long letter from Daisy.

He heard the popping of gravel out front and leaned back to peek out the picture window, but there was no view from where he sat.

He set his laptop on the coffee table and went to the front door. He wasn't expecting anyone, and people rarely stopped by unannounced.

His jaw slackened at the sight of Daisy's bright yellow Ford Focus, and his heart leapt. But then he spied her expression through the windshield and concern filled the empty spaces in his chest.

She'd never come to his house before. Well, except for the one time when she retrieved the canned goods for the Thanksgiving baskets from his garage.

His worry only escalated as he watched her step from her car and rush to his front door. She stopped short when she saw he was already standing behind the screen door.

She placed a hand on her chest. "Pastor Jack. I'm sorry to just stop by like this, but—"

"It's all right. Take a deep breath, Daisy." He opened the patio door to let her in as two thoughts collided: his neighbor had stopped weeding her flower beds to stare, and his laptop was on the coffee table, open to the Flutter website.

He stepped in front of Daisy, causing her to bump into him on her way in. His face warmed at the brief contact. "Um, let's talk on the porch, shall we?"

She quickly scanned the room, her gaze coming back to him. She didn't seem to have noticed the laptop.

Please, Lord.

"Oh . . ." She stepped hesitantly out the door. "Sure. That's fine."

"Can I get you some iced tea?"

"No, thank you."

Letting the screen door fall between them, he darted across the living room, pushed his laptop closed, and followed Daisy onto the porch.

She was perched on the edge of one of the chairs, arms straight, palms digging into her slender thighs. Her cheeks were flushed, and she stared off somewhere much farther away than his front yard. She must've gotten the results of that DNA test. They'd been due any day now.

The squawk of his chair as he seated himself seemed to snap her out of her reverie. Her gaze toggled around the porch. "You know, your place isn't really what I pictured."

"You've been here once before . . ."

"I mean the inside, mostly."

"What did you expect?" he asked lightly. "Thomas Kinkade paintings . . . crucifixes . . . an altar or two?"

She gave a raw laugh. "Very funny. It just kind of . . . I don't know. I didn't expect it to be so . . . Early Hunter."

His lips twitched. "In my defense, it was this

way when I bought it. I just haven't gotten around to redecorating."

"Maybe I can help you with that one of these days. I'm not bad at interior design, you know."

"I do know. The fellowship hall turned out wonderfully."

She was stalling. He leaned back in his chair. "But you didn't come here to talk about my cabin's decor."

Worry crumpled her forehead, and a long pause ensued. "I don't know, Pastor Jack. Maybe I shouldn't even be here at all. I know this isn't . . . professional or whatever, but—"

"No, Daisy. It's fine. I know I'm your pastor, but I'd like to think we're friends as well."

Daisy blinked as if that might be a new thought.

Oh, good gravy, it probably was. Nothing like putting it right out there. He swallowed hard, glad once again he wasn't prone to blushing. So much for all those casual outings with their friends at the Rusty Nail. Or all those lame excuses to stop in at the flower shop.

But then the corners of her lips turned up. "Sure. Of course we are."

"Then having you stop by is perfectly fine."

"That's good . . ." She turned those moss-green eyes, all wounded and troubled, on him. "Because I'm just about to burst, Pastor Jack."

He leaned forward, setting his elbows on his

knees. "What happened, Daisy? Did you get the test results back?"

"Yes. And it's all true, everything Julia said. She really is my half sister. I just found out. We found out together."

He nodded slowly. "And how are you feeling about that?"

"I don't know! I'm having so many conflicting emotions, I can't make sense of anything. But I have this horrible dread inside. Now I'll have to tell my mom, right? I mean, I can't keep a secret like this from her. But how can I tell her the truth when it'll hurt her so much?"

"That puts you in a difficult position, Daisy. I'm so sorry you're going through this."

She punched her leg. "And my father! I'm so angry at him. *He* did this, not only to my mom, but to me, and to Julia. How could he be so selfish?"

"I've been counseling long enough to know that good people can make some pretty terrible decisions. Sin comes with repercussions, and sometimes those repercussions go far and wide. It's always difficult to learn that someone we look up to can be so fallible."

"Fallible? He *cheated* on my mom. He had a baby—a child he turned his back on."

"So your father did know about Julia?"

Daisy squirmed in her chair. "I—I don't really know that for sure, I guess. Julia and I have been avoiding talking about my dad this week. It's been the proverbial elephant in the room. I just kept thinking the DNA results would be negative, and then none of this would even matter."

"How did Julia take the news?"

Daisy sank back into the chair, giving Jack a rueful look. "I kind of rushed out on her. I was just so overwhelmed. I feel bad about that, especially when I remember the look on her face. I think I hurt her feelings."

"This likely wasn't such a surprise to her. From what you say, she seemed certain of what her mother told her."

"Well, she was right. My dad was a first-class jerk."

Her eyes had gone glassy, and Jack's heart squeezed at the pain she was going through. He wished he could take it all away. He couldn't, but he knew someone who could. He took a moment to say a little prayer for her, letting the silence stretch between them.

"How am I going to tell my mom, Pastor Jack?" She turned her gaze on him. "*Do* I have to tell her?"

He let that question sit for a moment. "What do you think you should do, Daisy?"

"I think I couldn't possibly carry this secret for the rest of my life. Wouldn't that make me as bad as him?"

"Do you think you and Julia will have a relationship going forward?"

"I don't know. I guess that's something we'll need to talk about. I do like her . . . and she is my half sister." She gave him a wry smile. "I've always wanted a sister—I just never expected to get one like this."

He sat back in his chair, letting the pause lengthen. Mrs. Farber kept sneaking peeks at them as if she expected something untoward to happen any second. And so what if it did? So what if Daisy was his girl and he felt like giving her a kiss on his front porch? Was there something wrong with that?

He gave his head a shake. He was letting his imagination run away from him. She'd only just barely agreed they were friends. But he did have some promising messages from her sitting inside on his laptop.

"It must get very old—always being onstage. You're 'Pastor Jack' everywhere you go. The Rusty Nail, the coffee shop, the grocery store . . ." Her gaze shifted to Mrs. Farber and back to him. "Even on your own front porch."

He gave a good-natured shrug. They'd discussed this more than once, since Daisy's father had also been a public figure. "I love ministering to people, and if that means I'm under a little extra scrutiny . . . that's all right by me."

She didn't have a response, so he let the

tweeting of a robin, the nattering of squirrels fill the silence.

A moment later she nodded her head sadly. "I'm going to have to find a way to tell my mom."

"Would you like me to help? I could be present when you break the news if you want."

She turned her look on him, surprise flickering in her eyes. The flare died down as resolution settled in. "That's really nice of you to offer . . . and very tempting. But I can't imagine this is something she'd want to hear in front of someone else—even you."

"You're probably right. But if there's anything I can do, just let me know, Daisy. I'm here for you."

Daisy felt more at peace after talking to Pastor Jack. He had such a calm presence about him. He was wise and kind and so patient. She pulled into the motel parking lot and slid into a vacant slot. The sun had gone down and lights twinkled over the pool area and beside each doorway.

She still had a mess to sort out, but she had to talk to Julia first. She left her car, approached the red door, and gave a soft tap. A few long seconds later, the door swept open.

Julia stood on the threshold, looking just the same as she had a while earlier. Only now her eyes were bloodshot, and she had that guarded look back in place again.

Guilt pricked hard as Daisy remembered her sudden departure. "Can I come in?"

There was only a brief pause before Julia opened the door wider.

Daisy turned a few feet into the room, waiting for the other woman to shut the door. She noticed the laptop, closed on the table, and a tissue wadded up on the nightstand.

"I'm so sorry I left like that. I didn't mean to hurt your feelings, but I know I did."

Julia stared back, seemingly weighing her sincerity.

"I'll be honest, my feelings are kind of bouncing all over the place right now. I'm so disappointed in my dad—he was kind of my hero. And I'm really dreading telling my mom what he did."

It was hard to spill her guts when Julia stood with her arms crossed, looking so formidable.

"But, Julia, I want you to know . . . you're the one bright spot in all of this—I just kind of forgot that for a minute."

Julia's mouth wobbled, and her eyes went glassy.

"You know . . . ," Daisy said. "I never told you this, but I always wanted a sister. I kind of envisioned a little sister who arrived a long time ago, but hey."

Julia huffed a laugh, her posture relaxing even

as her face softened. "I always wanted a sister too."

They flew into each other's arms as if drawn by a magnet, holding each other tightly. Emotions welled up, a hard knot forming in Daisy's throat. They were family. She knew next to nothing about this sister of hers, but she was going to remedy that. She didn't know how all this was going to work out, but she knew that much.

And it was enough for now.

SEVENTEEN

The woman in charge of Peachfest, Harper Reed, lived twenty minutes outside of town on a slice of acreage nestled against the Blue Ridge Mountains. She was a young widow and a renowned dog trainer. She'd been chairing the festival for a few years and had agreed to meet with Daisy when she'd called three days ago.

Of course, Daisy hadn't known then that she'd be operating on four hours of sleep and a dump-truck load of worry on the morning of their appointment. All night long she'd tossed and turned, trying to figure out how and when she was going to tell her mom what she had learned.

The sun had only just chased away the morning fog when she stepped from her car. Dogs barked from the kennels at the side of the old farmhouse, and a German shepherd stood with his nose pressed to the chain-link fence, his tail wagging like crazy.

The grass was damp, the morning air laden with pine and the fresh scent of morning dew.

"Hey, big guy." Daisy approached the kennel as Harper exited the barn.

The woman was tall and lean with a confident

but gentle way about her. Her brown hair was tied back in a low ponytail, her sideswept bangs exposing a pair of wide-set brown eyes.

"Morning." Harper set down a pail, then approached Daisy.

"Morning." Daisy reached out toward the shepherd. "Who's this?"

"You don't want to do that," Harper said with a light tone. "He bites on sight."

Daisy pulled her fingers back. "Oh. He looks so friendly."

"He's an enigma, that one. Having some behavior issues. Coffee?"

"That'd be great."

A few minutes later they were seated on Harper's porch with steaming mugs of java. After some small talk, Daisy homed in on the topic she'd come to discuss.

"So I mentioned on the phone that I wanted to talk with you about doing a fundraiser during Peachfest."

"Right. What did you have in mind?"

Daisy explained about the Hope House's needs. Harper knew about the storm damage, of course, and seemed eager to help any way she could.

"You know, Ava Morgan is our reigning Miss Georgia Peach," Harper said. "I'll bet she'd be willing to help."

"I'll have to talk with her. I see her almost every day since she's living in the apartment above the flower shop now." But Ava already had too much on her plate, and Daisy wasn't about to burden her with more.

"I didn't know that. Good for her. So were you thinking of setting up a food tent or something?"

"I'm afraid we're going to need something a little more profitable than that. There's already so much competition in that area. So I thought I'd ask you: Are there any 'holes' you see that we could fill?"

Harper gave a wry laugh. "Not unless you happen to know Brad Paisley or Jake Owen." She took a cautious sip of the hot coffee before giving Daisy a wan smile. "Our band canceled last minute."

"Oh no. That's terrible." Music was one of the festival's highlights, and they usually managed to book a regionally popular band that could draw a decent crowd.

Harper shrugged. "The lead singer was in a motorcycle accident. Nothing we can do about it. I've been busting my butt trying to get a replacement, but on such late notice . . ."

"What about Last Chance?"

"Rawley was my first phone call. They have a gig in Atlanta that weekend."

"That's too bad." Well, there was the hole. Too bad Daisy couldn't do anything to fill it. "I wish I could help."

"You and me both. Well, let me give it some

thought. I'm not usually given to brilliant flashes of genius. I'm more of a slow-brew kind of girl."

"I don't know . . . I've heard you're quite brilliant with animals."

Harper waved her off. "Dogs aren't that complicated. People, now . . . another matter entirely."

Daisy smiled. "We can definitely agree on that."

Her phone vibrated in her pocket, and Daisy checked the screen. Why would her mom be calling so early? The shop wasn't even open yet, and Karen wasn't scheduled to work today. Maybe she was sick.

"It's my mother, do you mind?"

"Not at all. Go right ahead."

Daisy touched the button. "Hey, Mama."

"Honey . . . I'm going to need you to pick me up."

The odd tension in her tone made Daisy's spine lengthen. "What's wrong?"

"I was just . . . cleaning out some things in the office closet . . . and I fell. I've hurt my arm." Her sentences were punctuated by gasping breaths.

Daisy looked at Harper. "I have to go," she whispered.

Harper nodded as Daisy left. "Mom, I'm twenty minutes away. Call an ambulance."

"I'll wait for you."

"You might've broken it. I'll call Mrs. Rose to come get you, and I'll meet you at the hospital. Sit tight."

She hung up without waiting for her mom to argue. Daisy made the call, and her mom's neighbor was happy to help. She called her grandma too and asked her to cover the shop, assuring her she'd call as soon as she had news.

But an hour and a half later the news was not good. Her mom had a forearm fracture that was going to require surgery once the swelling went down.

It wasn't until later that night at the house that Daisy realized she'd have to put her bad news on hold. She couldn't possibly disrupt her mom's life with that surgery on the horizon. And as terrible as she felt about the injury, she couldn't help feeling relieved about the reprieve.

Under her mother's watchful eye, Daisy made up a eucalyptus and peppermint essential oil blend and helped apply it to her bruised, swollen arm. Karen had refused the painkillers the doctor prescribed.

Once her mom was settled in bed for the night, Daisy went to the office and found the tipped chair and box of spilled things. She cleaned up the mess and returned to the living room. Maybe selling the house wasn't such a bad idea. The place was a lot to keep up, and her mom wasn't getting any younger. Besides, all those sweet memories of her dad had been sullied by the recent revelations. Her mom wasn't the only one who'd taken a hard fall from a lofty place.

But Daisy didn't want to think about that tonight.

She settled on the couch with her phone. The glow of the TV flickered in the dark room, but she wasn't interested in the drama playing out on the screen. She was very interested, however, in seeing if TJ had responded to her message. With everything that had happened in the past twenty-four hours, she hadn't had a chance to check the app.

She logged on to her profile, her heart fluttering a little at the sight of the waiting message. There were also two nudges from other men, but she ignored those and opened the note, pleased to see it was nice and long. She read it, absorbing his words, smiling at his obvious joy as he talked about his faith.

He seemed more sensitive than the average guy—and she meant that in a good way. He was plenty masculine, she could see that from his sporty pictures, but he also didn't shy away from talking about important things. She liked that. Liked it a lot. It was tempting to bring up the subject of meeting. But she had a lot going on now with a new sister, her mom's injury, and the fundraiser. Besides, she didn't want to rush the relationship.

Since it had been a full twenty-four hours since he'd written, she didn't hesitate to start a letter back.

Hey there!

I love your enthusiasm about your faith. It rings through pretty loudly in your words. To be honest, my life is a little complicated right now, and your letters are a real bright spot in my day.

Speaking of days . . . My mom broke her arm today, and we spent hours in the ER. Unfortunately, she's going to need surgery soon. I'll be staying with her for a while, despite her assurances that she'd be fine on her own. My mom has quite the stubborn streak, which, you'll be happy to know, I did not inherit. ☺

That's so funny about the "Bon Voyage" arrangement! I'll bet a lot of people wondered . . .

So, you asked about unusual things on the job.

Daisy stopped, her mind immediately going to Julia's first visit to the flower shop . . . to finding the flowers at the grave . . . to ultimately learning Julia was her sister. That was definitely one for the books, but it was also very personal. Too personal for such a new relationship. She spoke softly into the phone.

When I was in high school I had a terrible crush on an older boy—Tyler Stevens.

163

He was so smart and handsome and on the football team—an all-around good guy. I nursed that crush for over two years, but he didn't even know I was alive. He did, however, know Ella Montgomery was alive. Ella was smart and beautiful and, of course, a cheer-leader. And, as it turned out, Tyler was a very attentive and romantic boyfriend. He ordered flowers every week for Ella, and guess who got to deliver them after school?

I used to read all the sweet things he wrote on the cards and torture myself by fantasizing that the notes and flowers were really for me. The fantasies went *poof!* about the time Ella opened her front door and took them off my hands. Haha. The lovebirds ended up getting married after high school. He still sends her flowers—but I've since moved on. ☺

Okay, so that story was pretty pathetic. We have one customer who regularly sends "doghouse flowers" to his wife. Sometimes she doesn't accept them. We have another customer who orders a fresh arrangement each week just for the purpose of painting them—he has a crush on my mom, and I feel so sorry for him as he blushes and stammers and tries to get her attention. I actually think he'd be a good match for her if she could just let down her guard a bit.

Well, speaking of my mom, I should probably go check on her.

Chat soon!
Daisy

EIGHTEEN

Daisy helped her mother wash her hair, then insisted on drying it for her. Karen was scheduled for surgery the next day, and Daisy was trying to help her get ready. Over the past two days Daisy and her grandma had taken turns running the shop and keeping watch over their patient. But it was clear Karen Pendleton had had enough of being coddled.

She batted the hairbrush away, glaring at Daisy's reflection in the mirror. "That's enough! I can do it myself."

"Mama, you can't style your hair with one arm."

"Watch me."

Daisy tried to stare her down, but her mom always won that contest. The smells of eucalyptus and peppermint filled the bathroom along with a vague hint of some other essential oil that was supposed to help with bruising.

Maybe Daisy could slip a little something into the next blend for her mood. "Fine, Mama. Do it yourself. I'll go get supper started."

"No, you won't. I can do that myself. I don't need you and your grandma fussing over me

24/7—and you're going to sleep in your own bed tonight too."

"Mama, it's really no bother."

"No. I mean it. I've had enough help, and you need some fresh air. Go out with your friends or something."

Daisy considered her mother for a long moment as she brushed her hair. Her movements were clumsy, the injured arm being her dominant one.

"Go on now. I'm not going to tell you again."

Daisy sighed. "All right. But promise you'll call if you need anything."

"I promise. Now go. And tell your grandmother to stop checking on me. She sends a text every hour on the hour."

"I'm not getting in the middle of that."

Daisy collected her things and said good-bye to her mom. Once in the car she considered what she might do next. She didn't feel like going home to her empty refrigerator and reality TV. She didn't even feel much like reading.

On a whim she dialed Julia. She'd told Daisy she was going to stick around awhile. She was a college professor, and she had the summer off—nothing urgent to get back to, she'd said.

"Hi there," Julia answered.

"Hey yourself. I got a reprieve from mom-sitting. Any chance you're free for supper?"

"I was just leaving for the diner. Want to join me?"

Daisy smiled at Julia's welcoming tone. "I'd love to. See you there in a few."

Ten minutes later Daisy slid into the booth across from Julia, inhaling the yummy aroma of grilled burgers and onion rings. The diner was reminiscent of another time with its red vinyl booths and black-and-white checked floor. The silver barstools up at the counter were full tonight, and the servers bustled around in their white aprons filling orders.

"How's your mom doing?" Julia asked after she'd settled.

Daisy gave her a droll look. "She's grumpy and bossy and even more impossible than usual."

"Aw, you know you love her."

"I do. And she's in pain and frustrated and probably worried about her surgery. I get that. But she's driving me crazy."

"I used to say the same about my mom. Funny thing is, now I'd give anything to have her back, driving me crazy again."

Daisy's face fell as she grabbed a menu. "Oh sheesh. Now I feel like a jerk."

Julia laughed. "I wasn't trying to guilt you. Mothers and daughters . . . It's complicated."

"You've got that right." Daisy dropped the menu. "I don't know why I'm looking at this thing. I always get the chicken fried steak and mashed potatoes."

"Mmm, that sounds good. I haven't tried that yet."

Barbara came by and took their order, then they settled into conversation. Daisy let her eyes scroll over her sister's face as she talked. The shape of their eyes was the same, even if the color wasn't, and they both had full lips. While Daisy's hair was blond and Julia's was a rich mahogany color, they both had full, silky locks.

Julia was seeing someone casually, and Daisy told Julia she was single—she didn't admit to having joined a dating website or to the relationship she was building there.

"So, since you're not telling your mom about me just yet," Julia said after their food had been delivered, "who are you going to tell people I am?"

"If anyone asks, I thought I'd just say that you're visiting Copper Creek for a while and we hit it off. I did tell one person, though—my pastor. He's great, and very discreet."

"Daisy . . . are you sure it's okay that I stay? I don't want to impose on your life or cause more trouble."

Daisy forked off a piece of her steak. "I'm glad you're staying. I'd like to get to know you better."

"Me too. But I don't want to create any problems

for you." She gave Daisy a wry look. "Well . . . at least not more than I've already created."

"You didn't create the problem, Julia. Not really. My dad did that."

"And my mom, I'm sorry to say."

The other night when Daisy had gone back to the motel, Julia had confided that their dad had known about the pregnancy. He'd broken off the relationship with Julia's mom shortly after finding out about it, which only made Daisy more disappointed in her father. How could he have just deserted his own child like that?

Julia asked her a lot of questions about Paul Pendleton, and Daisy answered them all. She promised to dig up some pictures for Julia. Her sister didn't seem to carry a lot of animosity toward their dad, and Daisy wished she could say the same.

They were just finishing their meals when Julia's phone rang. The ringtone was a popular country tune.

Julia turned off the ringer. "Sorry. It's a friend from back home. I'll call her later."

"We even like the same music," Daisy said, gesturing toward her phone. "That was my favorite song last year."

"It's great, isn't it? I actually know the lead singer of the band. We went to high school together." She scooped a bite of mashed potatoes into her mouth.

Daisy's jaw dropped. "You know the lead singer of Grainger? Kade Patrick?"

"The one and only. He was friends with my brother—and very popular with the girls, I might add. I guess that's not much of a surprise now that he has women falling all over him."

"Hardly. Did *you* go out with him?"

Julia chuckled. "No. Sadly, I was just his friend's big sister. He never looked at me twice."

Suddenly Daisy remembered the fundraiser and the Peachfest's lack of a band. Surely Grainger wouldn't be available on such short notice. Besides, she'd only just met Julia. She couldn't go asking favors already.

Could she?

"What's that look on your face?" Julia asked, eyeing her sideways. "It's a little scary, but I don't know you well enough yet to read it."

Daisy winced. "How well do you know Kade Patrick?"

"I haven't talked to him in years. But my brother still keeps up with him, I think. Why?"

She shouldn't be imposing. She didn't want to ruin their relationship before it even got off the ground. "Never mind. How'd you like the chicken fried steak? It's pretty good, huh?"

Julia tilted her head. "You can't say 'never mind' after you brought it up like that. Just tell me. I won't get upset."

Daisy waffled. What could it hurt, really?

She wouldn't push Julia into this if she was uncomfortable with it. Daisy told her about the Hope House and about volunteering to organize a fundraiser. Then she filled Julia in on the Peachfest dilemma.

"The band canceled at the last minute, and if I could find a group to take their place, the chairperson told me we could keep the festival's share of profits from the concert."

"Wow, that's a great offer. When's Peachfest?"

Daisy grimaced. "In four weeks."

Julia's face fell. "Oh. Listen, Daisy, I'd be happy to have my brother call Kade for you. But the chances of Grainger's schedule being open are probably pretty slim. I know they were touring recently, and they book up well in advance."

At least she was willing to try. Daisy whipped out her phone. "Let's check their website. We can at least see if they have a concert scheduled. If they do, there's no point in asking."

"Good point."

Once Daisy found their website, she scrolled the tour dates. "Nothing for that weekend . . . which doesn't mean they're not busy, of course. They might be recording or whatever."

"True, or just taking time off. But I can have Josh make a call and find out."

Daisy leaned forward. "Are you sure you don't mind? The last thing I want to do is take advantage of our relationship."

Julia smiled. "We're sisters, Daisy. You can ask me anything. Let's try him right now."

The server came to take away their empty plates as Julia placed the call. But a few seconds later she shook her head and left a voicemail asking Josh to call her back.

"I'll let you know when I hear something," she said. "Josh is pretty good about returning calls."

Daisy would be holding her breath till then. She didn't know what kind of fundraiser would raise as much as a concert would, even after the band's cut. "You want to grab a movie or something?"

Julia frowned. "I wish I could. But I'm taking an online course, and I have an assignment due tonight. I'm afraid I've been procrastinating all week."

"Another time then. What kind of course is it?"

"It's called Historical Ecologies."

"Oh, that sounds . . ."

Julia laughed. "Utterly boring. But it's a required course for my doctorate."

A PhD? Her sister was probably as intelligent as their dad had been. Daisy was glad one of them had gotten those genes.

NINETEEN

Jack was toting a bag of groceries to his car when he spotted Daisy pushing a cart across the Piggly Wiggly parking lot.

His stubborn heart stuttered, but his legs didn't think twice. He skirted a puddle or two, his dress shoes grinding against the loose pebbles. Twilight stretched across the sky in purple hues, cooling the evening, but the smell of asphalt still emanated from the steaming pavement.

He caught up to Daisy just as she reached her car. "Daisy . . ."

She turned, that beautiful smile blooming on her face. "Pastor Jack. Fancy meeting you here."

"It was an emergency." He gave a sheepish look. "I was out of cheese."

She laughed. "My emergencies usually involve chocolate or tea." She gestured to her full cart. "Tonight they involve virtually every item the store carries. I'm afraid I was down to mustard and pickles."

"How's your mom doing? When's her surgery?"

"It's tomorrow. She's doing all right, I guess. I'll probably end up taking half this stuff over there."

"Can I stop by the hospital before her surgery and pray with her?"

"That's awfully nice, but it's at six in the morning. And just between you and me, she hasn't been in the mood for company, if you know what I mean. We'll take all the prayers you're willing to offer, though."

"You've got them." He could read every emotion on Daisy's open face. "It'll be over soon. I hope you're not wearing yourself out in the meantime."

"Mama tossed me out on my ear tonight. I just had supper with Julia at the diner— Oh! I have some exciting news. You have a minute?"

"Sure. I'll help you load up your groceries if you like."

"Thanks." She opened her trunk, and they loaded her groceries while she filled him in on her meeting with Harper Reed and Julia's relationship with Kade Patrick.

"Isn't that exciting?" she said. "We could raise so much money if Grainger agrees to a concert. I know it's a long shot, but it could actually happen."

"I'll certainly be praying toward that end. If this pans out, it'll be huge for the Hope House. Nice work, Daisy."

"Well, I haven't really done anything yet, Jack." She halted, holding the bag of fruit midair, her eyes widening. "Sorry. *Pastor* Jack, I mean." She set the bag in the trunk and reached for another, looking flustered.

Two steps forward, one step back. He tugged the package of water bottles from under the cart. "You know, Daisy, it's okay if you just call me Jack. Whatever you're comfortable with."

After he stowed the water she closed the trunk, turning with a smile that suddenly froze on her face. She was staring at him with dismay, a flicker of guilt in her eyes.

He cocked his head. "Uh-oh. What's wrong now?"

"I just . . . I just realized something that really embarrasses me."

Curiosity tweaked him as he grabbed the cart, ready to take it to the corral. "Dare I ask?"

She grabbed her purse from the cart, hitching it on her shoulder, not quite meeting his gaze. "We've talked so many times . . . have literally spent hours talking and . . . I've never once asked about you. I rattle on and on about me and my problems, and I hardly know a single thing about you—except that you have a fondness for cheese. I'm so sorry. I can't believe how—"

She stopped when he raised his hand, palm out. He hated to remind her, but . . . "You don't owe me an apology, Daisy. I'm your pastor. That's what I'm here for."

"But you were right, what you said the other

day. I do think of you as a friend. And I've been a terrible friend!"

He chuckled at the adorable chagrin on her face. "I'd just say there's been a natural progression from pastor to friend. No worries."

He moved the cart to the corral, right next to the parking space, and collected his own bag. But instead of saying good-bye and leaving, Daisy leaned against her car and folded her arms.

He stuck one hand in his pocket as he made his way around the corral. She'd tilted her head and was peering at him in a way that made his breath hitch.

"So . . . ," Daisy said. "Tell me something about your life outside of church, Jack."

He did like the way his name just rolled off her tongue. "I'm not sure I *have* a life outside of church."

"Oh, come on. You must have a hobby, a family, a love life—is that too personal?"

"Not at all. My parents live in Minnesota, as do my married sisters, so I don't see them as often as I like, but we're pretty close. As far as hobbies go, I'm a history buff, and I enjoy physical activities—maybe because I'm at my desk so much or always meeting people over coffee or supper. I have to work out or all that pie will go straight to my waistline."

"I tried jogging last year—not my thing."

His lips twitched as he remembered her limping

into the Rusty Nail that week. "You should try rock-climbing. It's a lot more fun."

She made a face. "I'm not sure heights are my thing either."

"You should go with me sometime. I think you'd change your mind." His boldness took him by surprise, but she seemed to be considering the offer.

"I might just take you up on that after my mom recuperates from her surgery."

"It's a deal." His chest barely contained his thumping heart. That was almost . . . sort of . . . a date.

Daisy glanced at her phone. "Speaking of my mom, I should drop some of these groceries at her place before she goes to bed."

He took a step backward and gave a nod. "Let me know how things pan out with your mom . . . and Grainger."

"Will do. See you."

"Bye, Daisy." He turned toward his car. The parking lot lights had flickered on and buzzed overhead. But he could hardly hear them over the buzzing of his blood through his veins.

"Hey, Jack!" Daisy called.

He turned, walking backward.

"You never answered my question about your love life."

His lips twitched as a flush of pleasure warmed the back of his neck. "Another time."

She quirked a brow. "I'll hold you to that."

He gave her a smile, then turned and resumed walking. He might've even been strutting—and that was something that had never before been said about Pastor Jack McReady.

TWENTY

The Rusty Nail was crowded Saturday night as Last Chance was playing, and Jack was sitting with his friends at the back of the restaurant. Conversation and laughter had flowed among the group, but now that the band was playing, it was too loud to talk.

The smell of grilled burgers dominated the room. The Braves game played on the muted TVs, giving Jack a convenient place to stare whenever his eyes felt inclined to stray toward Daisy.

She'd come in late, looking a little tired, and no wonder with the pace she'd kept this week.

Jack pushed back his empty plate, his belly comfortably full.

When the band's tempo kicked up, Cruz hauled Zoe onto the dance floor, taking little Gracie with them. He took turns spinning his girls around, then picked up Gracie, holding her in one arm while he attempted to two-step with Zoe.

Brady had also claimed his wife for a dance. He and Hope had gotten a sitter for baby Sam tonight. They looked as in love as they had when they'd gotten married the year before. Jack had thought he'd sensed something a little off during their premarital counseling, but clearly it was his spidey sense that had been on the blink. The lovebirds only had eyes for each other.

Down the table a bit, Daisy finished her salad. They'd spoken briefly before the band went on. He knew that the moment she finished eating, some guy would ask her to dance, and then he'd be watching from the sidelines again. He wasn't sure why he signed up for this torture every Saturday night.

He wished she were home instead, writing a letter that would be waiting for him when he got home.

Next to him, Noah leaned in close and all but yelled in Jack's ear, "Too bad you deleted that Flutter account, buddy."

Jack jerked his eyes away from Daisy and back to the ball game, his cheeks heating. So he'd never exactly admitted to Noah that he and Daisy were communicating via Flutter. It really wasn't his business.

"Wait a minute . . ." Noah leaned forward in his seat. "Did you not delete the account?"

Jack spared him a glance.

"You didn't, did you?" Noah nudged him. "You made a move on her."

Jack scowled at him.

Noah laughed. "Oh, man. You're working this out, you little Romeo, you."

"That's enough. We're just talking." When some of the other patrons clapped in response to the ball game, Jack joined them. He had no clue what the score was or even what inning they were in.

"Well, that's how it all starts, you know. Well done. Bravo."

Jack frowned. Nothing like being patronized by your best friend.

Last Chance moved into another song, a haunting melody that had the lovers coupling up on the dance floor. Daisy was the only woman left at their table, but Jack knew that wouldn't last long. His lips twisted, and he mentally prepared himself for the sight of her in another man's arms.

"Why don't you ask her to dance?"

Jack ignored Noah, his eyes glued to the game. Even if he got up the nerve to ask, even if Daisy said yes, he still had two left feet. He wasn't going to impress her on the dance floor, that was for sure.

"Did you hear me?" Noah asked.

Jack gave him a flinty look. "All of Copper Creek heard you."

"So do it before someone else beats you to it, man."

As if Noah had spoken the idea into action, Jack saw Bryce Carter zero in on Daisy from across the room. And then he was making a beeline for her table.

Noah gave him an *I told you so* look.

In about thirty seconds young Bryce would be holding Daisy in his arms, his palms resting on her slender hips. Her hands would be clasped around his neck, and Jack would be sitting here eating his heart out.

Before Jack could stop himself, he pushed to his feet and approached Daisy. His supper churned in his stomach as he called himself ten kinds of fool.

When her eyes met his, he held out his hand. "Would you like to dance?"

Her brows shot up, her lips parting.

His heart gave a heavy stutter at the thought of being shot down.

"Uh, sure."

He gave a deep sigh as she pushed back her chair.

Her hand was small in his as he guided her to the floor, and his palms were already damp with sweat. His thumping heart outdid the heavy bass coming from the speakers. What was he doing? He was going to make a fool of himself. But it was too late to chicken out.

Stupid Noah. Look what the guy had gotten him into now. He had to find better friends. He led her to the middle of the throng where he could hide and drew her into his arms.

When he failed to move, she looked up at him, arching a brow. "I thought we were going to dance."

"Listen, Daisy. I should've told you. I'm not a good dancer. My sense of rhythm is . . . somewhat lacking," he finished with a shrug.

She gave him a sweet smile. "I already know that, Jack."

He felt affronted, even though it was the truth. "Why? Is it because I'm a pastor? You know, just because I'm—"

She laughed. "No . . . It's because at church when the choir kicks it up a notch, you clap on the one and the three."

The one and the . . . "I don't even know what that means."

"Listen, you're overthinking this. We don't have to two-step. Slow dancing is very basic—just shift your weight from one foot to the other. Like this."

She swayed from side to side, and he went along with her, letting her lead. This wasn't so bad. It felt a little eighth-grade-dance—which was about the last time he'd done this—but he was managing. At least he thought he was.

"I look like a dork, don't I?"

Her eyes danced. "You're doing just fine."

He'd look like a dork all night long if she'd just keep smiling at him like that.

"Is that why you never ask anyone to dance? I've wondered. There are plenty of ladies who'd say yes, you know."

Fact was, he didn't want to dance with

anyone else. In answer he lifted his shoulders, conscious of the delicious weight of her hands. It felt like a colossal privilege, having her in his arms. He wondered if he could bribe Last Chance into playing slow songs the rest of the night.

"Well, I'm happy to be your guinea pig anytime," she said. "And look at you, moving like a pro. Let's start rotating a little."

His muscles locked up. "That sounds like an advanced move."

She laughed and started turning them in a circle. "You're so funny. There you go. You're doing it."

"I'm too stiff."

"So loosen up." She gave a little upper-body shimmy.

"You make it look so easy."

He gave it an honest effort, but it was hard to relax with Daisy only inches away, her breath warm on his collarbone. His hands twitched reflexively on her hips. He'd never held her this way before. Might never get this chance again. He tried to memorize the feel of her fingers pressing into his shoulders, the curve of her waist that seemed custom-made for his hands. Her scent wove around him like a spell.

He stepped on her foot and quickly corrected himself. "Sorry."

"No worries."

He had to stop daydreaming. "Are you okay? I didn't break a toe?"

"No *permanent* harm done," she teased.

He needed to make conversation. He'd already asked if she'd gotten news about Grainger. Julia's brother was now waiting for Kade to return his call. If that worked out, they were well on their way to a successful fundraiser.

"So . . . ," Daisy said. "I believe you promised to dish out all the dirt on your love life."

"I don't recall promising that exactly. Besides, there's no dirt to speak of. It's more like a rather unspoiled meadow."

She gave him a speculative look. "Intriguing."

"Deadly boring, more like."

She swatted his shoulder. "Oh, come on. I see all the single women at church making eyes at you. If you so much as sneeze you probably have a dozen casseroles in your freezer."

His cheeks burned. There was some truth in that, but he wasn't interested in those women. "I don't find forwardness an especially attractive quality. It actually embarrasses me a little."

She gave him a searching look. "I can see that. But I'm sure you'd like a wife and a family someday. So what are you looking for, Jack? Someone selfless and devoted? Someone gifted in hospitality? Someone who plays the organ?"

He saw with a glance she was teasing, but he thought he detected a serious question under there somewhere. "I don't even like the organ—don't tell anyone—and I'm not looking for a saint. I just want the same thing every man wants: a woman who loves me and a woman I can love and cherish in return."

She gave him a long, speculative look that made his breath catch in his chest. Was something flickering in her eyes? Wishful thinking on his part, no doubt.

"That sounds reasonable," she said.

"I'm a very reasonable man."

Daisy peered at Jack from beneath her eyelashes. It was kind of cute the way he shuffled awkwardly in circles. She was used to seeing him behind a pulpit, behind his desk, all calm and confident. Seeing him out of his element . . . It was kind of endearing.

She studied him, trying to view him as an ordinary man. Oh, she knew that's just what he was, but somehow that title of "pastor" made her forget sometimes.

Jack had nice facial features, the classic good looks of a forties movie star. With his black hair, dark brown eyes, and aristocratic nose, he kind of put her in mind of Cary Grant. Up close she noticed the long sweep of his lashes, the hint of stubble on his jawline.

He was looking at her, she realized with a jolt. She gave an awkward smile and jerked her eyes to a spot over his shoulder. The song's last notes played out and the next began, something faster.

She drew away from Jack with a smile, eager to part after being caught staring. Mercy knew he got enough of that at church.

She dipped in a curtsy. "Thank you for the dance, kind sir."

He gave a wry grin. "Thank you for the lesson. I'm going to grab something to drink. Can I get you anything?"

"I'm good, thanks."

She followed him off the floor, and they parted ways. Hope gestured her over to where she stood in the hall by the bathroom.

"It's about time you two got a clue," Hope said when Daisy reached her.

"What? Me and Jack? We're just friends. It was just a dance. There's nothing there, nothing at all."

Hope's brows spiked. "Defensive much?"

"Funny." Daisy crossed her arms. "That's my pastor you're talking about. He is so not my type."

"Really?" She gave Daisy a rueful look. "You don't like handsome men who are amazingly nice and genuinely caring?"

"No, I prefer them mean and selfish. Besides, what he needs is a pastor's wife. I'm hardly fit for the job."

Hope rolled her eyes as Jack's words played through Daisy's head.

I just want the same thing every man wants: a woman who loves me and a woman I can love and cherish in return.

She shook the words away. That sounded very simple, but the fact was, she was so not pastor's-wife material. Her with her high school diploma and reading disability. Besides which, she'd had quite enough of the fishbowl life when her dad had been mayor, thank you very much.

Not to mention she'd recently learned the hard way that people you knew—even people you knew well—weren't always who you thought they were. For all she knew, Jack was an entirely different person from the one everyone saw at church. It seemed hard to imagine, but then, she'd thought the same about her dad.

Daisy glanced at Hope, realizing belatedly that her own eyes had been plastered to Jack's retreating back.

"What?" Daisy snapped.

Hope gave her a *get real* look. "Did you not see the way he was looking at you when you were dancing?"

"He wasn't looking at me in any particular way. I was teaching him to dance. We're just friends. Besides . . . I'm kind of talking to someone else right now."

In fact, she'd been reluctant to even come

tonight, eager to get home and write TJ back. But she'd kind of forgotten about that the last little while, she realized.

Hope lit up. "Is that right? Did you meet him on that website?"

"Yes . . . and I'm taking it slow just like you suggested. He seems really great so far."

Hope nudged her. "That's awesome, Daisy." She was about to say something else, but Brady returned just then and claimed his wife for a dance.

Daisy watched them go, hand in hand, so in love, and once again Jack's words were ringing in her ears . . . *A woman who loves me and a woman I can love and cherish in return.*

TWENTY-ONE

The church vestibule was packed as Daisy made her way out of the sanctuary. Jack had brought another thoughtful sermon, and now the members gathered in small groups, catching up and making dinner plans. Daisy sometimes met her friends at the diner after church, but today she was picking up food for her grandma and her mom, who was still recovering.

Daisy glanced at Jack as she drew near. Monica Davis, a pretty thirtysomething single, was at his side, listening raptly to whatever he was saying. The woman laughed, touching his arm as she smiled sweetly up at him.

Daisy wanted to vomit.

And then Leah Sanders appeared at his other side, handing him a foil-wrapped dish. As he took it, a mottled flush climbed his neck. He tugged at his collar.

Part of Daisy wanted to rescue the poor guy. Another part of her wanted to encourage him. Either woman would make him a good wife. Leah was a local veterinarian and director of the children's program at church. Monica taught Sunday school for the preteen girls and was an RN at the Piney Acres nursing home. Both women were smart, hospitable, and well regarded in the community.

Daisy's eyes met Jack's as she passed, and his gaze sharpened on her.

She gave an impish smile and waggled her fingers. "Careful not to sneeze, Pastor Jack."

She watched the meaning register on his face, first as a twinkle in his eyes, then as a twitch of his lips.

"Have a good afternoon, Daisy," he said when he found his tongue.

She was smiling broadly as she exited the church, and her heart seemed twitchy in her chest. She shook the feeling away as she wove through the parking lot to her car. She was just getting in when a text buzzed in. Julia.

Call me when you have a minute.

She must have news from Kade Patrick. Daisy's fingers trembled as she dialed. *Please, let it be good news.*

Julia picked up on the third ring.

"Hey," Daisy said. "I just got out of church. Any news from your brother?"

"He called a few minutes ago. He and Kade have been playing phone tag for a few days. Grainger's in Nashville for a month, recording."

Nashville was only a few hours away, but it

sounded as if they were busy. "That doesn't sound good."

"Actually, Kade said he'd like to do the concert, Daisy. He has to discuss it with their manager and agent, but the band is on board."

"Really? That's wonderful!"

"And that's not all . . . They'd like to donate the band's share of the profits to the Hope House."

Daisy gasped. "What? Are you kidding me?"

"I'm hopeful it'll all work out. I'd forgotten something about Kade—he grew up in foster homes. He really wants to help the Hope House."

"Wow, this is just . . . I can't believe this is happening. This is the answer to our prayers."

"Well, it sure sounds promising. There's the contract and legal stuff to make it all nice and tidy, but if his manager and agent are in agreement, and he thought they would be, this thing is going to happen."

Daisy closed her eyes, her breath tumbling from her chest. "I don't know how to thank you, Julia. This is amazing. I can't wait to tell Jack."

"Who's Jack?"

"My pastor. We've kind of been working together on this."

"Oh, right. Well, Kade's supposed to get back with the final word tomorrow. If it pans out, there'll be a ton of details to work out. The good news is, if you don't mind my staying on awhile, I'll be on hand to help."

Daisy smiled. "I'd love that. But are you sure you can be away so long? I'm not keeping you from anything?"

"I've only got my online course to keep up with this summer, and that only requires a few hours a week."

"I'd love the help then. Thank you so much."

"My pleasure. I'll let you know when I hear back from my brother."

After getting off the phone, Daisy flipped over to her contacts. She'd only ever called Jack a few times, and she'd never texted him. But she couldn't wait to tell him the news, and she didn't want to interrupt his conversation with Monica or Leah or whoever had him cornered now.

She clicked on his name and started the message.

Good news! It looks like Grainger will probably be saying yes!

She added a prayer emoji, sent the text, then started her car. She should let Harper know too. She'd give the chairwoman a call when she reached her mom's house. Before she could put the car in drive, a text came in from Jack.

Terrific news! Well done, Daisy. Everyone at the Hope House will be so appreciative. (BTW, you could've rescued me in here!)

Daisy laughed and texted back.

Where's the fun in that? Keep the good news under your hat for now, okay?

He sent an emoji of a monkey with his hands over his mouth.

Daisy smiled. She liked Jack's sense of humor—she hadn't realized until lately that he even had one. She thought of what Hope had said on Saturday night and shook her head. Pastor Jack was so not interested in her.

Anyway, she had a perfectly nice man she was talking to, and she owed him a reply. She put her car in drive and went to pick up some dinner.

The call she'd been waiting for came the next evening.

"It's a go," Julia said. "Everyone's on board."

"Yes!"

Daisy could hardly contain her excitement. She couldn't believe things were working out so well. She and Julia talked over some details, and when they got off the phone she immediately texted Jack.

He replied, congratulating her. He was eager to let Lucille Murdock, the Hope House's CEO, know, but Daisy told him she'd have to check with Harper first, since a contract would have to be signed before it was official.

She called Harper and offered to take on some of the responsibilities of the concert. It was the least she could do since the festival committee was being so generous with the Hope House. Harper put her in charge of the performance contract, since Daisy's mom was a lawyer. She also said to keep the news quiet until the contract was signed.

She settled against her pillows with her phone. It was her first night back in her own bed, and she'd missed her soft mattress and favorite quilt. Her mom's arm was healing well, and she was tired of being hovered over. It was only a matter of time before Daisy would have to break the news to her about Julia. But she wasn't going to think about that tonight. She had a letter to write.

She reread TJ's last note, sent just this afternoon.

Daisy,
You have such a kind heart. It sounds as if you already have your hands full with your shop and your mom's recovery, and now this fundraiser. I hope Grainger comes through for you. I'd think it would be good publicity for the band as well. A win all the way around. Let me know what you find out.

You asked about my high school years—to tell you the truth, they weren't

198

the best. I was gangly, pimpled, and socially awkward. And that was before my mom made me get braces! Of course, eventually I filled out, the bad complexion cleared, and the braces did their thing. But those years took their toll. Some days I still feel like that dorky kid inside.

Write soon.
TJ

Daisy's heart gave a squeeze at his words. She started a note back.

TJ,
Thanks for your kind words. I can't help but want to give back to a community that's done so much for me and my family. Those girls at the home are so deserving of a real chance. And I got the good news tonight: Grainger is officially coming for our festival! I'm so relieved. There'll be a lot of work in the next few weeks, but it'll be worth it.

Thank you for sharing about your teenage years. You have no idea how easily I can relate.

Should she tell him about her dyslexia? She was still self-conscious about it, and she didn't want him to treat her differently.

She looked at TJ's message on the screen. Maybe it was better to lay it out from the beginning, before she cared so much. And the way he had opened up to her gave her the courage to be honest.

I also had some traumatic years at school. I was diagnosed with dyslexia when I was twelve. But by then I was already behind in school, had been held back a grade, and my self-confidence suffered a hard blow. The other kids called me names, and all these years later, those words still haunt me.

It affects not only my reading and writing but can affect my verbal skills as well, especially if I'm nervous. I actually threw up in the middle of a seventh-grade presentation on *Jane Eyre*. It was awful.

I learned how to cope with the dys-lexia, but unlike with you, there were no true fixes for my problem. Even now I sometimes write a customer's address or credit card number down wrong or dictate their message incorrectly. Paper-work is overwhelming. If it weren't for voice-to-text you would've caught on to my disability by now. So I do know what you mean about still feeling like that insecure kid.

I felt that way tonight when the festival chairperson assigned me the performance contract for Grainger's concert. Silly, since I'll only be passing it along to my mother to handle.

Thanks for sharing your heart with me. Chat soon—if I haven't scared you away yet!

Daisy

TWENTY-TWO

Jack hadn't seen Daisy since Sunday, and he was experiencing a bit of withdrawal. Sure, he'd gotten a few texts and that was gratifying. And he had her letters to TJ. But he couldn't resist seeing her up close and in person, so he decided to stop by her shop after lunch on Friday.

He'd taken heart in the way she'd confided in him about her dyslexia. He'd had no idea. He'd noticed errors in her messages sometimes, but that wasn't uncommon, especially when using voice-to-text, as she did.

The bell jingled as he entered the shop. Daisy straightened from watering the plants in the front window. "Jack! How nice to see you."

"I was just on my way back to the office and thought I'd stop in and see how your mom's doing."

"She's fine. In fact, she's in the office right now doing the books"—she raised her voice—"despite the fact that she's supposed to be home resting."

"I'm fine!" her mother called from the back.

Jack bit back a smile as Daisy rolled her

eyes. "She's impossible. She refuses to listen to anyone, even her own doctor."

"I'm sure she's just bored and lonely being at home."

"Do you always have to be so kind and compassionate?"

The bell jingled again, and Daisy turned to greet her customer. "Hello, Mr. Francis. How are you?"

"I'm faring well, Daisy, and you?"

"Oh, not too bad." Daisy introduced the two men.

Jack gave the middle-aged man a firm handshake.

"Your arrangement is all ready for you," Daisy told him. "My mom will be right out."

Jack startled when she grabbed his arm and began tugging him to the door. "Mama," she called over her shoulder, "I have to step out a minute."

"What?" her mother called.

"You'll have to cover the counter for me. Mr. Francis is here for his flowers. I'll be back in a few."

Her mom said something in return, but the jingle of the bell covered it. Jack followed her down the shaded sidewalk until they came to a bench facing Magnolia Lane.

"Sorry about that," she said sheepishly as they settled there.

"Is everything okay?"

"I'm fine. It's Mr. Francis. He has a crush on my mom."

The artist. Jack remembered her mentioning him and opened his mouth to say so. Then he remembered she hadn't told *him*. She'd told TJ.

"My mom always avoids him, and I just thought—you know, if I gave them a chance to interact . . ."

"Playing Cupid, Daisy?"

She breathed a laugh. "Oh, why not? He's a nice enough man, and it's so sweet the way he comes in every week all nervous and blushing."

"I'm not sure she'll appreciate your gesture."

"Oh, she definitely won't."

"So I'm basically your decoy right now."

She winced. "Sorry. You can leave if you have somewhere else to be. But I did want to ask if you'd pray for me. I'm going to have to tell my mom about my dad soon. Tonight, actually. I just can't put it off any longer. It's already been a week since her surgery."

"You definitely have my prayers. I'm sorry this is falling on you."

"Thanks. I'm really dreading it. This is going to tear her heart in two, I'm afraid."

He squeezed her hand. "Let me know if I can help in any way. I'm happy to counsel with your mom if she feels it would be beneficial."

Daisy gave him a long look that made him

want to clutch his achy chest. "I don't know what I'd do without you, Jack. Thanks for being my sounding board more times than I can count. You've always been there for me."

"Anytime, Daisy."

She looked down the sidewalk toward her shop. "Maybe I'm just being selfish—hoping Mr. Francis will soothe the pain of her heartbreak."

"Whatever is meant to be will be. Your mom's heart will mend, and you'll feel much better after you unburden yourself."

"You've got that right. The dread is sitting in the center of my chest like a cement block."

"These things can actually bring people closer together when they're handled the right way. That's what I'm praying happens for you and your mom."

"That would be great. But honestly, if it weren't for Julia, I think I'd just keep all this to myself and find a way to put it behind me."

"But there *is* Julia—awfully hard to pretend you don't have a new sister. Tell you what. Once it's done, let me take you rock-climbing—get your mind off it." His heart hammered at his sudden attack of nerves. His face warmed and he tugged at the collar of his shirt.

Her lips tipped upward. "I'll take you up on that, Jack. How about tomorrow? Gram and Mom are working, and that should give them time to talk about this."

"Won't your mom want the day off after getting such news? Time to process things?"

"Oh no. She'll want to stay busy. She worked like an industrious little ant for months after Dad passed. It's her way of coping."

He gave a nod, feeling as if his heart just might explode for joy at the thought of an outing with Daisy. "Sounds like a plan."

"What were you thinking?" Daisy's mom asked before the shop door had even swung shut.

"Why, whatever do you mean?" Daisy blinked innocently.

Karen rested her uncasted fist on her hip. "You know very well what I mean."

"I had to speak with Pastor Jack for a moment."

"You left me alone with that man on purpose. And he asked me out for coffee!"

Daisy's hand flew to her chest. "Oh no! I hope you told him that was highly inappropriate."

"Don't be smart with me, young lady."

Daisy tilted her head, reaching for patience. "Mama. He's a very nice man. And kind of cute, don't you think? I hope you said yes; it probably took him all week to work up the courage."

"Of course I didn't say yes." Her mom made a beeline toward the office.

Daisy followed. "Well, why in the world not?"

"You need to stop meddling!"

Daisy laughed outright. How many times had

her mother set her up on blind dates and otherwise interfered in Daisy's love life?

"This is not funny," her mom said. "It was so awkward."

"It would've been less awkward if you'd only said yes."

The last thing Daisy heard from her mom was a soft *humph* before the office door clicked shut behind her.

TWENTY-THREE

Daisy thought she looked the part of rock-climber the next morning in her yoga pants, T-shirt, and ponytail. Jack had promised to bring the rest of the gear. While she waited for him to pick her up, she found a new message from TJ waiting on the dating site. His response to the news of her dyslexia. She perched on the sofa and opened it on her phone.

Hi Daisy,
Thanks for sharing so openly about your dyslexia. I'm sorry it left some childhood scars. I can tell just from your letters that you're a smart, capable woman, and it breaks my heart that you might believe otherwise. However, I know how hard it is to shake those old perceptions. I pray God will show you your true value and continually remind you how special you are. I have a busy day ahead, but I just wanted to check in with you and let you know that. Have a wonderful day.

Daisy's heart gave a sigh. She reread the message, savoring his kind words. What a nice guy. She wondered how he could still be single. They hadn't talked much about previous relationships, but maybe it was time to go there. For all she knew he could be twice divorced with six children—although surely he would've mentioned that by now.

Then again, she had her own upheaval going on—a new half sister and a philandering father—and she hadn't mentioned that.

Gravel popped outside her screen door, alerting her to Jack's arrival. She grabbed her purse and joined him in the drive just as his car came to a stop.

"Ready for this?" he asked as she got in. He looked very un-pastorlike in his rugged pants, athletic top, and tennis shoes.

She gave him a wry grin. "Trying not to think about it too much."

Jack put the car in reverse and set his hand on her seat back as he backed from the drive. His fingers brushed her shoulder, and a fluttery feeling stirred in her stomach.

"So," he said as they set out toward the mountains, "I thought I might get a call or text last night. It must've gone well with your mom?"

She winced, remembering the night before. "It didn't go at all—I didn't tell her."

Jack glanced at her. "What happened?"

The whole thing had been a disaster. "She put me to work packing up things in the attic. I couldn't decide whether to bring up my dad's infidelity before the wedding album or after the box of love letters he sent her when they were dating."

"Ouch." Jack shared a commiserating look. "Bad timing."

"Horrible. I thought I was just coming over for supper—and, of course, that heavy conversation—but she was on a mission to get the house packed up. She put me to work before I could swallow my last bite of salad. And her arm was hurting, so she wasn't in the best of moods either." Understatement of the year. "Not enough frankincense in the whole world."

"Did you say frankincense?"

"Essential oils—never mind. I just couldn't tell her."

"I'm sorry. I know you were eager to get it over with."

"I'll have to do it tomorrow after church. Julia must be weary of hanging out with me at the motel, but I'm afraid my mother will see us out and about, and then I'll be forced to lie or come clean. Julia probably feels like my dirty little secret."

"I'm sure she understands this is a delicate situation."

"Thing is, even after all this blows over, I'm

afraid my mom's going to feel betrayed that I want a relationship with Julia at all."

"I don't think you're giving her enough credit. It might take some time, but I'm sure she'll understand eventually—you can't ignore the fact that you have a sister."

"I hope you're right." Daisy rubbed her face. "But in the meantime, can we just forget about all this today? I want to put it aside and enjoy the lovely weather and good company."

Jack tossed her a smile. "You've got it."

Thirty minutes later Daisy stared up the face of a jagged cliff, her stomach churning. "I'm sorry, did you say we're starting here? 'We' as in 'you and me'?"

The wall went up at least thirty vertical feet and looked impossible to scale. Her legs felt unstable, and they hadn't even left the ground yet.

"It's a great beginner's crag." Jack dropped the dusty duffel bag and began pulling out hardware.

The sun glinted off the top of the cliff, and Daisy got dizzy from tilting her head back. "You know, I think maybe I'll just observe today."

"Oh no you don't. It's perfectly safe, and you're going to love it. Trust me."

"I'm kind of fond of solid ground, and I'm currently on good terms with gravity—I'd like to keep it that way."

He handed her some climbing shoes. "Try these on. I borrowed them from a friend."

She gave him a look but took the shoes. "Did I mention I'm afraid of heights?"

"Just try it once. If you don't like it, we'll pack up and I'll take you home."

"But I might die."

His chuckle was deep and rich. "I've done this a hundred times, Daisy. I won't let you fall."

Her heart stuttered—at the thought of defying gravity, not at his very pleasant-sounding laugh. "Although death would get me out of that conversation with my mom."

He gave her a mock scowl. "Don't even say such a thing."

She looked up the face of the cliff, then back at Jack. He was studying her with those patient brown eyes, waiting for her to acquiesce. She knew he wouldn't push her into something she didn't feel comfortable with.

And there was no one she trusted more. "Promise you won't let me fall?"

His lips curled upward. "I promise."

Jack could see Daisy's hands shaking as she stepped through the leg loops and pulled the harness to her waist.

"Okay, let's adjust this," he said. "You'll want it nice and snug."

He started tightening the waist belt of her

harness and caught a whiff of her floral shampoo. She was in the flat climbing shoes, causing him to tower over her. He tried not to think about the way the backsides of his fingers brushed her stomach as he checked for fit.

"How's that feel?"

"Like I can't breathe."

"Too tight?"

"No, I just forgot how."

She was cute when she was nervous. "Well, we definitely don't want it too loose."

She fixed her wide eyes on him. "Why not? Will I fall out?"

"Not unless you turn upside down."

Her lips slackened.

"Kidding. It'll just ride up and be uncomfortable." He slipped two fingers between her body and the waist strap. Next he gave the harness a hard tug downward to make sure it stayed put.

"That should do it." He squatted beside her and got up close and personal with the leg loops. His face heated at their proximity as he began adjusting the straps. "We want these slightly loose or they'll inhibit your leg motion."

"My legs aren't feeling inclined to move anyway."

He finished the second strap and checked for fit before standing again. "All right. That should do it."

"It feels like I should have more protection,

like a padded vest or bubble wrap or something."

"Well, we can't forget about your noggin." He set a red helmet squarely on her head and reached for the knob at the back. It clicked as he turned it, tightening the fit.

"Shake your head around a little."

The chin straps waggled as she followed his instructions.

"Look up. Make sure it's not moving around."

"It's not."

He clipped the straps together under her chin and checked for fit at the sides, making sure they formed a comfortable Y around each ear. He couldn't help but notice how warm and soft her skin was. His heart leaped in his chest when she turned her vulnerable eyes up to him. Her breath hit his forearm, teasing the hairs, making him lose all thought for a long beat.

Rock-climbing. Safety. Helmet.

He cleared his throat. "How's that feel?"

"Okay, I guess?"

He hoped his smile looked steadier than it felt. "You're going to be fine, Daisy. I won't let you fall. Even if you let go altogether, you'll just hang there. Nothing bad will happen."

He gave her some last-minute instructions as he attached the rope to the belay loop of her harness. "Okay, we're anchored in up top, and you'll be hanging from that rope. I'll keep my eyes on you every second and help you find handholds and footholds as you climb. If you have to let go altogether, go ahead. I've got you."

"You've got me," she whispered.

He cupped her shoulder. "You can do this, Daisy. Ready?"

Her gaze drifted up the jagged face of the cliff. "As I'll ever be."

She couldn't feel her legs. Or her arms, for that matter. But her heart—oh, her heart was making itself known. It threatened to burst from her rib cage and explode against the rock face she was pressed against.

"Right hand, Daisy," Jack called from below. Way, way below.

She reached out with her hand, her face so close to the rock her vision was blurry. She was almost to the top. At least she thought she was. She was too afraid to look up, and she'd already looked down once. Big mistake.

"A little higher and to the left," he called. "You've got this."

She groped for the hold, her cheek pressed to the cool rock face. Her feet were turned outward, clinging to the almost nonexistent ledge. Her legs quaked beneath her. Surely Jack could see her shaking from the safety of the ground.

Ground. She'd never realized what a lovely, solid word that was.

"There you go!" he called just as her fingers

found a minor bump in the surface. She curled her hand around it and pulled up, pushing her legs straight.

"You're there, Daisy! Reach up and touch the top."

She felt blindly with her left hand and felt grass. "Is this it? I'm at the top?" She sounded as breathless as she felt. The rush of adrenaline made her blood hum through her veins.

"You did it! Now . . . as loud as you can, shout, 'I'm on top of the world!' "

"Why?"

"Just do it!"

Daisy drew a deep breath and bellowed, "I'm on top of the world!" She felt a little silly, but good. No, she felt great! She'd done it! She laughed even though she was very aware she was still clinging for dear life to the top of a cliff.

"Is—is that some kind of rock-climbing tradition?" she called.

"No, I just wanted to hear you say it."

She could hear the humor in his tone.

"Funny. Now how do I get down from here? You neglected to cover this part, and it suddenly seems very important."

"Now it's time you learn to rappel. You've seen this before. First you have to sit back in the harness until your legs are straight out in front of you."

"I'm sorry—did you just say, 'Sit back in the harness'?"

"I've got you, Daisy. Just trust me."

"Just trust him," she muttered. "No problem, just ease back from this cliff I've been clinging to for twenty minutes and sit back into thin air. Don't mind the fall. You won't feel a thing."

"Did you say something?"

"Never mind!"

As much as she hated the thought of sitting back, her fingers and toes ached something fierce. And it wasn't as if she could climb down the way she'd climbed up.

"Daisy? Are you ready?"

"The question is, are *you* ready?"

"I'm good to go."

She heard the smile in his voice.

"Just sit back, I've got you."

She slowly loosened the grip of her fingers and tested her weight on the harness.

"That's it. Feel the rope holding you? You're not going anywhere."

She let loose from the rock entirely, her heart a bass drum in her chest, pounding out a punishing rhythm. She clung to the rope for dear life—as if that would help—until finally her legs were at a ninety-degree angle from the wall.

"When you're ready, push off, and keep your feet in front of you. I'll lower you a bit, and you'll come back to the wall."

"Here goes nothing." She gave a little push and found herself going down, down, down before her feet touched the wall again.

"Hey, look at that! You're a natural, Daisy."

"You're full of baloney, Jack McReady!"

"Do it again," he said, chuckling.

She pushed off again and returned to the wall a bit lower with no problems. She did it again. And again. She was starting to get the hang of this. She even laughed at her pun. And best yet, she was getting nearer to the ground. She might just kiss it when she got there.

The descent went quickly, and before she knew it, her feet were again on terra firma and Jack was high-fiving her.

"Way to go, Daisy!" He wore a huge grin, and his eyes gleamed with pride. "That was amazing."

He was proud of her, and that felt so good. Almost as good as the adrenaline flooding through her system.

She threw her arms around him. "I can't believe I did that! I was so scared!"

His arms came around her, and he hugged her tight. "You did great. You really are a natural."

"My legs are shaking. I'm shaking all over!"

His chuckle stirred the hairs near her ear. "That's bound to happen. You're using new muscles."

"I was clinging for dear life." She let loose and

backed away, still breathing hard, her hands still gripping Jack's biceps. They were as solid as the rock face she'd just been clinging to. She'd never noticed that before.

And so was his chest, she realized belatedly. She blinked, gave her head a shake, and stepped back. "That was such a rush."

Jack beamed at her. "I told you. Have you had enough for today? Want to call it quits?"

"Oh, heck no. I want to go again. You know, if you'd asked me five minutes ago, I would've said no way. I think I may be an adrenaline junkie."

His smile broadened, that look of pride coming over his face again. "There are worse things. All right then, let's do it again."

And Daisy thought she just might be able to get used to that look on Jack's face.

TWENTY-FOUR

The euphoria from Daisy's successful climbs yesterday was gone.

Long gone.

She glanced at her mom from beneath her lashes, a heavy dread weighting her middle like a lead brick. Today was the day. She couldn't put it off any longer.

After church she'd followed her mom home, and they'd eaten chicken Caesar salad. Daisy had hardly tasted it. Her mind was playing with words, trying to find just the right way to break the news.

Karen's chair scraped back as she stood and took her salad bowl to the sink.

"I'll get that, Mama." Daisy rinsed the bowls and utensils and put them in the dishwasher.

When she was finished, she found her mom with her arms crossed as effectively as she could with one of them casted. She was tilting a knowing look at her daughter.

"What?" Daisy asked.

"You've been brooding all weekend. Are you going to tell me what's on your mind?"

Daisy faltered, dish towel in hand. She was never going to get a better opener.

"Is it the house?" her mom continued. "Because it's time, Daisy. I need to do this, and I'd really appreciate it if—"

"No, Mama, it's not the house." She didn't even care about that anymore.

There was a long pause as her mom studied her. "Well, what is it then?"

"Can we sit down?"

After a short pause, she followed her mom to the living room where they'd gathered so many times as a family. Watching the Braves, playing board games, enjoying late-night chats and movie nights. And now Daisy was about to cast a horrible black cloud over all those memories.

"Out with it now. You're scaring me." Karen's back was ramrod straight against the sofa back. "Are you all right? Did something happen?"

Daisy had the ridiculous urge to add lavender to the glowing diffuser that was pumping out vapor on the hearth. There wouldn't be enough lavender in the world to calm her mom after this.

"I'm fine. I just . . ." Daisy leaned forward in the chair catty-corner to her. "Mama . . . I don't know how to say this . . . It's about Daddy."

Karen shook her head. "Your father? What about him?"

"I found out something, and I have to tell you what it is. I don't want to hurt you—but you need to know."

"Daisy, I hardly think there's anything you

could tell me about your father that I don't already know."

"Oh, Mama . . . Daddy wasn't—he wasn't always faithful to you." She paused, her throat closing up around her words.

Her mom had gone still, unblinking.

Daisy took her hand. "It was years ago, before I was even born."

Her mom slowly shook her head. "Oh, Daisy . . ."

"I know it's hard to believe, Mama, but it's true. I have proof. I wouldn't be telling you this at all, but . . . I know how difficult this is to hear. Believe me, it wasn't easy even for me, but—"

"How did you find out?"

Daisy jerked back. That sounded like . . . She blinked.

Her mom was staring at her, not with horror, but with something akin to sympathy. Her eyes had gone a little glassy, and her head tilted to the side.

Her grip on Daisy's hand tightened. "I never wanted you to find out."

"You already knew." Saying it out loud didn't make it any easier to believe.

Her mom sank into the couch, wordless. "Yes, I did."

Daisy could hardly wrap her head around it. Her mom was stubborn, fearless. She didn't put up with anything. "And you stayed with him?"

"It was a difficult time for both of us. Our marriage didn't start off on the best foot. My parents didn't approve of him, and we had financial difficulties for a while. It wasn't good."

Daisy shook her head. "You've never said anything like that before."

"Honey, you're our child. We protected you from many things."

"Protected me! More like let me believe a lie. Mama, I thought you had the perfect marriage—"

"Oh, honey. There's no such thing."

"And I had Daddy on a pedestal! I thought he hung the moon, and you let me believe it." Daisy gave her head a hard shake. Had the world just turned on end? In what universe did her mother put up with a philandering husband?

"It wasn't a lie. Your daddy was a good man. A good husband and a good father. You meant the world to him."

"How can you say that? He cheated on you! He had a chi—" Daisy stopped just in time.

Just because her mom knew about the affair didn't mean she knew about Julia. She gulped a few deep breaths, forcing herself to calm down. She realized she had her mom's hand in a death grip and released it. Wiped her sweaty palm down her leg.

A resignation had settled over Karen's face. It was clear in the tense corners of her eyes, in the tilt of her chin. "A child? Is that what you were going to say?"

Daisy's mouth slackened. She could only stare as her mom slowly stood and walked across the room.

"Yes, Daisy, I know about that too." Her mom straightened the afghan on the recliner with her one good hand.

It had never even dawned on her that her mom could know about Julia. If her mom had known, then there was no good reason for her dad to have abandoned Julia.

"I don't understand," Daisy whispered. Or maybe she just didn't want to.

Her mom made a final adjustment to the afghan and turned. "It's not really yours to understand, Daisy. It was between your father and me, and we handled it as best we could at the time."

"Not mine to understand? You didn't think it was my business that I have a sister I didn't even know about?"

Her mom lifted her chin. "That was an unfortunate consequence of your father's decision. It was a very complicated situation. Things aren't always so black and white, you know."

"He abandoned a child, and you let him! That's not fair, and it seems pretty black and white to me."

"Don't you judge me." Karen's voice wobbled. "You want to talk about unfair? You have no idea what I went through back then. I was devastated about the affair, not to mention the fact that my husband's lover was pregnant with his child!"

Daisy came to her feet, her mind awhirl. There were so many things to say, so many thoughts buzzing through her brain, so many things wrong with the way her parents had handled this . . .

She shook her head, not even knowing where to start.

"We made a mutual decision based on what we knew at the time," her mom said. "We had a marriage to put back together—we both wanted that. You haven't walked in my shoes, Daisy. Do you know how hard it was to forgive him for what he had done? How was I supposed to let his love child into our family? A constant reminder of his unfaithfulness? It would've completely changed our lives—changed your life. Can you imagine the talk in town? Do you think he would have become mayor? His political aspirations would've been over before his career had even begun."

Daisy looked at her mom as if she'd just sprouted a second head. "Talk in town? Political aspirations, Mama?"

"We did what we thought best, Daisy. We don't always have the benefit of hindsight."

Something occurred to her. "Does Grandma know too?"

The pause was so long Daisy wondered if she

was going to answer. Then finally she made an effort to cross her arms. "She knows."

Was Daisy the only one who hadn't? "And she just went along with this?" Daisy couldn't believe it of her grandma. She just couldn't.

"It wasn't her decision to make. She didn't approve of it, if that makes you feel any better. And just how did you find out about this anyway? Did you find something in the attic? Did you go snooping through our things?"

"No, I didn't go snooping through your things." She told her mom about the first time Julia had come into the flower shop.

Karen's eyes flashed. "She was here in town?"

Daisy ignored her and went on to tell her about finding the flowers at her dad's grave. About chasing down Julia and demanding answers the next week.

"Oh, Daisy." Her mom shook her head. "You couldn't have just left well enough alone?"

Daisy gaped at her. "So this is *my* fault?"

"Of course not. That *girl* never should've come here to begin with. And she surely had no business in our shop."

Daisy thought of Julia, of the vulnerability she'd seen in her eyes when they'd gotten the test results. Of the gentle, careful way she had with Daisy, trying so hard not to overstep invisible boundaries.

Daisy's shoulders went back. She had to leave

before she said something she would regret. "I should go now, Mama. We can talk about this later."

She collected her purse and headed toward the door. But before she did, there was one more thing that had to be said.

She turned, one hand on the doorknob, her heart stuttering in her chest. "Just remember, Mama . . . That *girl* is my sister. And regardless of what Daddy did, she's as innocent in this as I am."

Daisy sat in her car in front of Jack's house and drew a deep breath. She'd already knocked on his door even though his car wasn't out front. The neighbor lady was outside again, at the side of the house, and she'd drilled a hole in Daisy's back until Daisy retreated to her car, out of sight.

She wondered where Jack was. Was it still Sunday? It seemed like a week had passed since she'd left church. One of the members was probably hosting Jack for dinner. It happened almost every Sunday, him being a bachelor and all.

The afternoon sun heated the inside of her car, and she started it up. Cool air blasted through the small interior space, making the colorful lei hanging from her rearview mirror sway.

She had no idea where she was going or what

she was going to do. She wasn't ready to face Julia yet. Not only had Daisy's dad abandoned Julia, but her mom had had a part in it. Daisy felt guilty by association.

But she couldn't sit here any longer. She put her hand on the gearshift just as Jack pulled into the drive, coming up along her right side.

He gave her a cautious smile as he got out of his car, no doubt sensing what this visit was all about. He'd known today was the day.

He gestured toward the porch, but Daisy thought of the nosy neighbor and reached over to open the passenger door.

"Can we talk in here instead?"

"Sure." Jack folded himself into her car, then put the seat back as far as it would go. Only then could he get the door shut.

"Are you all right?" he asked. "Do you want to go somewhere and talk?"

"Not really." She angled a glance his way. "I just told my mom."

"I figured. It didn't go well?"

Her eyes glazed over, the dashboard going blurry. She turned to Jack. "She already knew, Jack. She already knew about Daddy's affair."

He studied her for a long, thoughtful minute. "All right . . . But that's good news, isn't it? You didn't have to hurt her with your dad's infidelity."

"There's that." Daisy swallowed hard, choking back the tears. "But she also knew about Julia.

She knew my dad fathered a child, and she supported his abandonment of her. She kept my sister from me. They both did."

"Oh." His head tipped back. "I see."

Her chest constricted until breathing became difficult. Until the ache spread outward from the epicenter, consuming her.

"Neither of them were who I thought they were, Jack. The dad I knew never would have broken his marriage vows, much less abandoned his child, and the mother I knew never would have condoned it."

"I'm so sorry, Daisy." The compassion in his eyes was her final undoing.

The warmth of tears trickled down her face, and she covered her face with her hands.

"Hey . . . it's going to be okay." His low voice scraped across her heart.

She felt the weight of his hand on her shoulder, and it was all the encouragement she needed. She turned into his touch and found her face buried in his chest. His arms reached around her, solid and comforting.

He reached into the glove compartment, withdrew a fast-food napkin, and pressed it into her hand.

"I feel like my world's turned on end."

"You've had a series of shocks. It's a lot to digest."

"I don't know how I can face Julia after this."

"What do you mean? You didn't do anything wrong."

"Well, I feel guilty anyway. I got a father, and she just got ripped off."

"Hey . . ." He leaned back, taking her chin. "Now, I know you've got a raging guilt complex—you told me about the banana bunch you left in aisle six of the Piggly Wiggly last year . . ."

She huffed a laugh.

"But this is not your fault. Your parents are responsible for their own choices, Daisy, not you. Even if you ended up being the one to benefit from them."

"But that's just it. Not only did Julia miss out on having a dad, I missed out on having a sister. It didn't have to be that way, if they'd just done the right thing."

"Do you think it would've been all you dreamed of, given the situation?"

She stared at the wet spot she'd made on his blue dress shirt. "No, I guess not. And I can only imagine how hurt Mom must've been when she found out. Accepting Julia would've been a challenge for any woman. But I just thought . . ."

He let the pause draw out. "They were better than that?"

Their eyes connected, and Daisy melted at the understanding there. "Yes. And if my dad completely abandoned one child . . . how much could he have loved me?"

"Daisy . . . your dad loved you. Don't doubt that. He sinned, and he suffered the consequences, as did other people—your mom, Julia and her mom, and now you. I'm afraid people are hopelessly fallible. There's only one who'll never let you down, Daisy. Only one who'll never disappoint. Sometimes we have to remind ourselves of that."

He was right. Part of her disappointment was her own fault. One last tear leaked out. "I never should've had Daddy on that pedestal."

He gave her chin a little pinch. "You're a strong woman, Daisy. You'll get through this."

Their gaze held for a long moment. A flicker of something passed over Jack's face, and Daisy's pulse fluttered. What was that look? It was almost as if . . .

But then it was gone.

Jack settled back in his seat, running a hand over the back of his neck.

She drew a deep breath, remembering what Hope had said about Jack at the Rusty Nail. Did he really look at her a certain way? Was that what she'd just seen, or was she really losing it? It was hard to trust her instincts when she'd been so off base about the people she loved most.

Besides, if Jack really was interested in her, she needed to nip that in the bud. She was the last person he should be considering. She remembered what he'd said about finding someone to love and be loved by. He deserved that. He was always thinking of others, and he'd been so good to her. Maybe she could return the favor by finding him a worthy woman to love.

Her stomach gave a little twist.

"You feeling better now?" he asked.

"I am. I guess I need to talk to Julia next. She's already texted twice asking how it went." She squeezed his hand. "Thanks for listening, Jack."

He gave her a sympathetic smile as he reached for the handle. "Anytime, Daisy."

"And don't think I've forgotten that conversation we still haven't had," she called before he could exit the car.

He gave her a questioning look.

"Your love life, remember?"

He chuckled, and the sound of it reached someplace deep inside her. "I'm afraid that'll be a short conversation, Daisy." He gave her a final wave as he rounded the front of her car.

TWENTY-FIVE

Daisy took a sip of her iced tea and sat back in the porch chair. In the swing catty-corner to her, Julia gave a little push, and the metal links squawked quietly in the stillness of the evening. The front porch was one of the primary reasons Daisy had bought the house. That and the huge oak tree that shaded her entire front yard.

It had not been a restful afternoon. She kept thinking of her conversation with her mom. To keep busy, she'd printed off the Grainger contract she'd received Friday. She wished she'd given it to her mother the moment she'd received it. Now it would be awkward, asking for her help. And Daisy sure couldn't handle this part without her. She couldn't get past the first paragraph.

When she got home from Jack's, she let Julia know that everything was—more or less—all right. She'd asked her over, but Julia was in the middle of a paper for her online class, and they'd put off the discussion until tonight.

So for the first time in her life, Daisy had her sister over for supper. She had a sister. It was still a lot to digest. And although Julia was the elder, she wasn't in any way bossy. In fact, they seemed to be finding equal footing. It gave Daisy a bit of hope, and she was desperately in need of hope.

Now, with the meal and the official recap behind them, they relaxed as the evening shadows stretched across the porch.

Julia was dressed casually in jeans and a cute white blouse. With her mahogany hair swept back in a ponytail, her prominent blue eyes were striking, reminding Daisy so much of their father's.

"I'm glad you didn't have to break your mom's heart at least," Julia said, interrupting the silence. "I know you were worried about that."

"Me too. I just wish I didn't feel as if they'd lied to me all these years. I mean . . . if they lied about this, what else did they lie about, you know? How can I ever trust her again?"

Julia winced. "That's the problem with secrets, I guess."

"One of many, I'm sure." She thought of Jack then, and his words of wisdom. In some ways she'd set herself up for this. Where had she gotten off thinking her dad was so perfect? She'd never put someone else on a pedestal again.

"It's kind of surprising when you think about it," Julia said. "That this never came out before. I mean, your dad—*our* dad—ran for mayor. This is just the sort of scandal that usually finds its way into print before election day."

"This is Copper Creek we're talking about. Politics isn't as brutal here as it might be in a bigger city. My dad was golf buddies with the former mayor he ran against. Besides, my mom and grandma were the only ones who knew about the affair, and they sure weren't talking."

It hurt a little, too, that her grandma knew. After all, keeping her parents' secret had meant keeping it from Daisy too.

The swing stopped. "I'm sorry this is hurting you, Daisy. I never intended to cause you any pain when I came here. I hope you know that."

Daisy saw the same guilt in Julia's eyes that she saw in the mirror all too often. "I see we share the same guilty conscience. I've been feeling horrible about what my parents did to you. Guilty that he was a dad to me and not to you."

"I had a good upbringing, Daisy. My mom was the best, and I have a loving stepfather and a terrific brother. We got by just fine. Let's just agree to let each other off the hook and start fresh, all right?"

Daisy offered her a smile, grateful Julia was so reasonable about it all. "All right."

Julia held up her glass of tea. "To finding a sister."

"The silver lining in all this. Hear, hear." Daisy tapped her glass, the *ting* ringing out just as a car pulled into her drive.

Her mom's blue sedan rolled to a stop as dread

charged up Daisy's spine. Her fingers clenched the sweaty glass in her hand. She felt like a child caught with her hand in the cookie jar.

"Oh boy," she muttered.

"Who's that?" she heard Julia ask as if from a distance.

Her eyes were laser-focused on her mom, who still hadn't seen them sitting in the shadows of the porch.

"Daisy?" Julia said.

Her mom turned off the ignition and stepped from the car. This was not good. And completely unavoidable. Daisy set down her iced tea and stood as if facing a firing squad.

Her mom's confident stride faltered as she made eye contact with Daisy. Her eyes toggled to Julia and back. Daisy read the questions on her face a split second before Karen's shoulders went back.

"Mom . . . I wasn't expecting you."

"I thought we should talk. I didn't know you were having company."

That was her cue. It couldn't be avoided no matter how uncomfortable it would make them all. She sensed Julia tensing beside her.

"Mom . . ." Daisy swallowed hard and forced herself to go on. "This is Julia. Julia, this is my mom, Karen Pendleton."

The corners of her mom's eyes tightened, one of them twitching as her glance darted to Julia, then back to Daisy. Her lips drew tight, and her nostrils flared.

"Nice to meet you, Mrs. Pendleton," Julia said.

Her mom drilled Daisy with a look. "I can see I've come at a bad time. We'll talk tomorrow." And without so much as a word to Julia, Karen marched to her car, got in, and drove away.

"I don't know what to say," Julia said a long moment after Karen's engine had faded into the distance. "I'm feeling guilty again, so maybe 'sorry' is in order?"

"It's my fault. I never got around to telling her you were still in town."

Julia set down her glass. "I shouldn't be. I should've left days ago. This is all my fault."

"No." Maybe this was awkward, and her mom was obviously fit to be tied, but Daisy was only just getting to know her sister. "This isn't your fault. And I don't want you to go. I'm sorry she was so rude to you."

"Maybe we should just let this settle in with your mom. I don't want to cause problems between you two—though clearly I already have."

"The problems were already there—I just didn't know about them. And clearly you didn't put them there. My mom'll have to come to terms with all this sooner or later. It is what it is." Daisy set her hand over Julia's. "Please. I want you to stay."

Julia's eyes warmed as their gaze lengthened. "Are you sure?"

"I'll talk to my mom tomorrow and try to smooth all this over. Now, let's go watch a movie or something. This day has been way too heavy, and I need something to take my mind off it."

Jack didn't expect to hear from Daisy tonight, what with everything that was going on, but that didn't stop him from obsessively checking his Flutter app. It had been less distracting before he'd known about phone access.

He tossed his phone onto the sofa and went to make a late-night snack. Pizza rolls? Chicken strips? He had the cooking skills of a fifteen-year-old boy. Good thing he was a pastor. He opened his fridge and pulled out a foil-wrapped pie plate containing peach crisp.

He cut out a serving, set the slice on a plate, and heated it in the microwave. He felt mildly guilty for eating a dish from a woman he had no intention of ever dating. But Leah Sanders was a good cook, and surely she wouldn't want it going to waste.

At least that's what he told himself a few minutes later as he dished out a scoop of vanilla ice cream onto the steaming dessert. He thought of what Daisy had said last week about sneezing, and it made him smile as he carried the dish into his quiet living room. He flipped on the TV to a recap of the Braves game and settled into his favorite corner of the sofa. Even with the tempting dessert and game coverage, his phone taunted him from the sofa cushion beside him.

Just one more time. Then I'm not checking it the rest of the night.

He opened the app, and his heart gave a flutter as he saw a new message. He guessed it wasn't called Flutter for nothing. He set the dish on the coffee table and opened the note as happy feelings hummed through his veins.

Hey TJ,

What a weekend. Sorry I've dropped the conversational ball, but there's been a lot going on with my family. Talking to you is a nice reprieve from it all.

I went rock-climbing yesterday! It was a blast—and I didn't kill myself, so that's a plus. ☺ I'm definitely going again soon. Hard to think about life's little worries when you're hanging from a thirty-foot ledge. Haha.

I spent this afternoon trying to read through Grainger's performance contract for our festival chairperson. My dyslexia makes tasks like this very difficult. I'll get through it somehow.

How was church today? Learn anything new?

Daisy

Smiling, Jack tapped on the screen, opening up
a new text box.

Hey Daisy,
Church was good. I learned to check my
socks in better lighting before leaving
the house—among other things.

I'm sorry there's a lot going on with
your family. Is your mom's arm doing all
right?

I'd be happy to look over the contract if
you'd like an extra set of eyes. I've read
a lot of contracts as part of my job and
have a good eye for spotting problems.
On second thought, I also know an
attorney who'd probably take a look at it
as a favor to me if you wouldn't mind me
sharing it with him. I'd be glad to ask.

Just thought I'd get that out there
before you lose any sleep over it.

Jack sent the message and leaned back against
the sofa. He reread her message. She hadn't gone
into detail with him—TJ—about the family crisis
she was having. But that was understandable.
They'd only been writing a few weeks.

A new message came in.

242

That is so kind of you. Are you sure you wouldn't mind asking your friend? I was going to have my mom look it over, but we're kind of on the outs right now due to the aforementioned family issues.

Daisy was on the app right now, live. The thought of it made his pulse race for some reason. Made the back of his neck dampen with perspiration. It felt more . . . real somehow. But real was good, right?

He opened a new message box, his heart thumping.

Not at all. Send it over anytime.

He tapped his fingers on the back of his phone, staring at it as if he could make another message appear simply by force of will. And maybe it worked, because a minute later another message popped up. This time with an attachment.

He wrote back,

You don't waste any time.

Two beats later:

Oh, you have no idea how relieved I am to have this off my plate! And to avoid begging a favor from my mom right now.

Jack smiled. Tomorrow he'd ask Joe Connelly for help with the document. He was an elder in his church and always happy to lend his professional help.

Another message popped up.

Daisy: So . . . I guess we're talking live now.

TJ: Are you comfortable with that?

Daisy: I think I am. You?

TJ: Well, you don't seem to be a stalker.

Daisy: That's just because you haven't gotten to know me better.

TJ: The Flower Shop Stalker. I think I've seen that movie.

Daisy: It doesn't end well.

TJ: It never does. It's a thorny business.

Daisy: Groan.

TJ: Trouble blooming everywhere.

TJ: Victims wither and die.

TJ: And they don't get caught because florists can plant their own clues.

Daisy: Stop! LOL I had no idea you were so corny.

TJ: You could say I rose to the occasion.

Daisy: If you don't stop I'm going to poppy you over the head!

TJ: I knew you had a violet streak.

Daisy: Groan!

TJ: Okay, okay, I'll stop. (Though I've an
     endless supply of bad puns.)
Daisy: I don't doubt that!

Jack became aware of the huge smile on his face. This in-person chatting was the most fun he'd had since . . . Well, since he'd gone rock-climbing with Daisy Saturday. Hmm . . .

TJ: So, rock-climbing, huh? That sounds
     fun.
Daisy: It was such a rush. I was scared to
     death, but it's addicting.
TJ: I hope you were safe. Did you have a
     good partner?
Daisy: My pastor, actually. He's got a lot
     of climbing experience.
TJ: A rock-climbing pastor, huh? Sounds
     interesting.
Daisy: He's great.

Jack paused, feeling a prickle of guilt. He shouldn't have gone there. It wasn't fair. He should change the subject. Before he could write anything, another message popped up.

Daisy: So, we've never really talked about
     past relationships . . .
TJ: Uh-oh. Is this where you tell me
     you've been divorced five times?

Daisy: Or that you have ten kids by seven different women and a bad habit of leaving women at the altar?

TJ: A mere five kids—that I know of. I've only left two brides at the altar, and the second one was my cousin so she doesn't count.

Daisy: ACK!

TJ: Kidding! Never divorced, never engaged, no kids. You're too easy, Daisy.

Daisy: Whew! Had me scared. Ditto all of the above. Lots of first dates. Some disappointments. A bit of heartbreak.

TJ: I hear you.

Daisy: Sigh. Where are all the good ones?

TJ: Um, hello. Right here.

Daisy: We'll see about that. ☺

A short pause ensued. It was his turn, but he didn't know what to say.

Daisy: Well, it's getting late, and I've got a long day tomorrow.

TJ: I'll let you get your beauty sleep—not that you need it.

There was a short pause, wherein Jack second-guessed his last comment. He didn't want to come across as cheesy. Or like some kind of player. What if she— Another message appeared.

This was fun. Would you want to chat live again tomorrow night?

A smile spread across his face. She hadn't been judging his comment. She'd been getting up the nerve to ask that question. He pictured her biting her lip, waiting for his response.

Without hesitation he responded.

Jack: I'd love to.
Daisy: 8:00?
Jack: I'll be here.
Daisy: I had a difficult day, and you made me feel so much better. Thank you.
Jack: Glad I could help. I had a good time too.
Daisy: Good night, TJ.
Jack: Good night, Daisy.

He was still smiling as he closed out the app. His new favorite activity was talking to Daisy live. Of course, he talked to her live all the time, but this was different. Over the app he felt freer to flirt and be himself.

He was glad she'd mentioned the contract to him. It felt good to help her out in some small way. He wondered why she'd told TJ about her dyslexia even though she'd never mentioned it to Jack in all their conversations. But she must trust Jack too or she wouldn't confide in him about her family situation. Why did she trust TJ with the dyslexia and not him?

Oh, good gravy. He was jealous of himself.

Shaking his head, he checked the time on his phone, surprised to see it was after midnight. And on the coffee table, the dessert he'd been anticipating sat in a melted puddle, cold and forgotten.

TWENTY-SIX

Her mom exited the shop, and as the door closed behind her, Daisy let out a breath. Karen had been giving Daisy the cold shoulder all week, and the tension in the store had risen to an unbearable level.

Daisy felt a familiar hand on her shoulder.

"Come help me with the Connelly wedding," her grandma said, her brown eyes warm and kind.

Daisy closed the cash register and followed her to the back. The workspace was covered in roses, sweet peas, and hyacinth in muted pastel shades.

"You can do the bouquet," Grandma said, pushing back her short ash-blond hair. "You're so much better at it than I am."

Daisy set to work, gathering the flowers she'd need. She'd spoken at length with Tawny and felt confident she knew what the bride wanted. She loved this part of her job: meeting people during the most meaningful times of their lives and bringing a touch of beauty to those special moments.

Grandma snipped a pale pink rose and made

an ivy bed for it, her expert hands making quick work of the boutonniere. "I ran into Ava this morning as they were leaving for school. She said they were doing some evaluations for Millie, thanks to you."

"I feel for the girl. But if she does have dyslexia, there's so much they can do for her. I've been helping her with her homework when I can. She does quite well when I use some of the tools I've been taught. I don't want Ava to feel she's all alone in this."

"That's awfully kind, but you be careful not to overextend yourself."

"I will." Daisy selected a stem of ice-pink hyacinth. She loved the pale colors Tawny had chosen for her wedding. It was going to be so beautiful.

"So, this feud between you and your mom . . ."

"I thought you were going to stay out of it."

"Well, that was on Monday. Now it's Friday, and I've had about all the tension I can take."

"I'm right there with you, Grandma, but you know Mama. She's stubborn as a mule. I've tried to talk to her."

Grandma gave her a look over the straight line of her black-framed readers.

"I have! She refuses to even talk to me about this."

"Well, seeing that girl was quite a jolt. Can you blame her?"

"So you blame *me?* I want to get to know my sister—that's not exactly a crime."

Grandma began spiral wrapping the stems with floral tape. "Of course not. But she didn't even know the girl was still in town. You might have mentioned it at least."

"Julia. Her name is Julia."

"Fine. She was caught completely off guard to find *Julia* sipping tea on her daughter's front porch."

"I was going to tell Mama she was still in town, but I never got the chance. If she and Daddy had handled all this the right way in the first place, none of this would be happening." Daisy selected two more ivory roses and began stripping the stems of leaves and thorns.

"Honey, I know all of this has been a blow to you, and believe me, I understand how you feel. I never agreed with their decision to cut the child from their lives like they did, but it was their decision to make. Not mine and not yours."

Daisy heaved a sigh. She knew her grandma was right. It was just hard to accept that her parents had done something so selfish. Had hurt so many people.

"Your mom was heartbroken by your dad's betrayal, and I think he felt so guilty he was willing to do whatever was easiest for her. That doesn't make it right, but things can get very complicated in love, Daisy. When you're square

251

in the middle of the battle, things don't always seem so cut-and-dried."

Daisy could relate just a little. She thought of TJ and their conversations this week. They really did feel like conversations when they chatted live. She was growing awfully fond of the guy. He was funny and sweet and patient—he even pretended not to notice all her voice-to-text errors. There wasn't much time to check for perfection when messages were flying back and forth. And yet he treated her no differently.

And then there was Jack. Even though she knew she had no business thinking of her pastor that way, she found herself doing just that. He was so kind and wise and fun. Not to mention those deep brown eyes and rock-hard biceps. She kept remembering the feel of his arms around her in the car when he'd comforted her. She'd never felt so safe.

She gave her head a shake. All the more reason to follow through with her plan to set him up with one of her friends. She had to forget about Jack. He deserved better. He was so smart. When he preached on Sundays, she marveled at his insights and observations. He probably had more deep thoughts in one week than she had in an entire year. She was nowhere near his intelligence level, and he'd surely grow bored with her once he realized that.

The thought of it made her stomach twist hard.

It was one thing to have your fellow classmates know it. Quite another to have a man like Jack realize it.

Daisy winced as a thorn caught on her thumb. That's what she got for thinking about Jack at work.

"I met someone online, Grandma."

The woman gave her a double take. "You're giving me whiplash, child. We were talking about your parents."

She realized Gram had been talking the last couple minutes, and Daisy hadn't heard a word. She didn't want to talk about her parents anymore.

"He's really nice," Daisy said. "And funny. I might set up a date with him once this fundraiser is behind me."

"All this online dating . . . In my day we met people face-to-face and sized each other up in person."

"Well, life is busier now. It's harder."

"Oh, phooey. Young people today give too much thought to the wedding and not enough to the divorce. I knew your grandpa for all of four months before he proposed, and no one thought a thing of it when I was marching down the aisle two months later, no professional photographer, no live music, and no four-course meal."

"Well, you and Grandpa were a match made in heaven."

"Oh, don't romanticize it. He was a workaholic

and his feet stank to high heaven. But he was my best friend, and he loved the Lord. We made a life together and were determined to stick together come hell or high water. You don't need much more than that."

Daisy thought of her parents' marriage. "Didn't you ever, you know, hurt each other or go through awful times?"

"Of course we did. So we got really good at forgiving each other."

Daisy began gathering up the stripped flower stems into a bundle. "I guess Mama had to get good at that too."

"Every married couple does if they want it to work out. Granted, in a kinder world you'd be dealing with communication issues and financial problems, not the likes of an affair or a child conceived out of it. It wasn't easy on your mom back then—but it wasn't easy on your dad either, honey. He knew how badly he'd failed her, and he did love your mom, despite evidence to the contrary. He suffered terrible guilt for a long time. It took him even longer to forgive himself than it took your mom to forgive him, I'll tell you that."

The bell jingled in the front of the shop as a customer entered.

"I'll get that." Grandma set down her finished boutonniere and patted Daisy's arm. "You've got quite the beautiful bouquet going there."

Daisy watched her go, weighing the words she'd offered. Maybe she'd been too hard on her parents. Maybe she should be a little more patient with her mom and stop expecting so much of everyone. Including herself.

TWENTY-SEVEN

Jack was nervous as he entered the Rusty Nail on Saturday night. After chatting live with Daisy as TJ all week, things felt a little different. A little more real. And this was the first time he'd been with her since they'd talked in her car Sunday.

The restaurant buzzed with energy, and the smell of smoked ribs made his stomach growl. "All My Friends Say" was blaring through the speakers, and Last Chance was up front getting ready to go on.

His eyes landed on Rawley's tall, lean frame as the lead singer strapped on his guitar while flirting with two women who'd approached him side stage. Jack felt a moment's envy at the easy way Rawley had with the ladies. On the other hand, it wasn't Daisy the singer was flirting with this time, so maybe Jack should just count his blessings.

He worked his way through the crowd, saying hello to those he knew as he went. He found his regular group in the back corner, the round tables pulled together to form a caterpillar chain. There were a few empty chairs, including one across from Daisy.

"Jack!" Daisy called. "Over here!"

His heart gave a heavy thump at the way her face lit up at the sight of him. Her blond hair was pulled back at the sides tonight, calling attention to those moss-green eyes.

He greeted her with a smile as she pushed out his chair with her foot. Next he greeted Noah and Josephine, Cruz and Zoe, and Brady. He spotted Hope buzzing around in her apron, a washcloth in one hand and a bus tray in the other.

"Your wife looks busy tonight," Jack said to Brady.

Brady set his toddler, Sam, into the high chair next to him. "Two of her staff called in sick. It's going to be nuts tonight."

Jack caught up with the group, the topic swinging from work to town gossip to politics as quick as lightning. When the subject turned to cars—Brady and Cruz's topic of interest—the group began dividing up into more private conversations.

Feeling heady that Daisy had motioned him over when he arrived, Jack took the opportunity to engage her in conversation. "How'd the wedding go this morning? Any complications?"

She leaned forward on her elbows. "No major glitches, and the bride seemed pleased with the flowers."

The wedding had taken place at a sister church in Ellijay.

"I'm not surprised. You're very gifted, Daisy."

The color that rose to her cheeks was charming. "Oh, I don't know about that."

He gave her a long, pointed look.

Her eyes danced as she caught on. "I mean, thank you very much, Jack. That's awfully kind of you to say."

He gave her a nod of approval.

"But in all honesty, I just listen to what the bride wants and try to please her. It helps when they show me pictures of what they like."

"Pictures or no, I couldn't arrange a bouquet if my life depended on it."

She laughed, her eyes lighting up. "Thankfully, it doesn't."

"Maybe not, but our occupations really aren't so different, you know."

She raised a skeptical brow. "How so?"

He lifted a shoulder. "We both minister to people. We step into their lives when times are especially hard or particularly joyful. We attempt to bring hope and beauty during times of hardship and celebration."

She blinked at him. "That's so insightful. That happens to be one of the things I like best about my job, but I never thought about having that in common with you."

"We both care about people and count it a privilege to come alongside them during these moments."

"I guess we have something in common then."

"I guess we do." Their eyes caught and held for a long, poignant moment.

The server stepped up to the table to get drink orders, and by the time she left the moment had passed.

Jack leaned in closer to Daisy, being careful that no one else could overhear. "So how are the concert plans progressing?"

"The contract is in the works now, and as soon as the ink's dry there'll be a big announcement. Harper will get the media lined up, and hopefully the tickets will go fast."

He was impressed. "You're a godsend, Daisy."

"Thanks, Jack. That's sweet of you to say. I sure couldn't do it without Grainger and the festival committee, not to mention you and Julia."

"Don't be so modest. I really didn't know how we were going to raise that much money."

"Neither did I! But God heard our prayers. What a blessing that Julia knew Kade Patrick, huh?" Her eyes lifted to something over his head, and her mouth widened in a big smile as she waved. "Mary Beth! Over here."

Jack turned to see a pretty brunette wending her way through the tables. He'd seen her around town but had never actually met her. She was dressed casually in jeans and a blouse that hung a little loose on her lean frame.

The women hugged, and Mary Beth took the chair beside Daisy.

Last Chance greeted the audience and began their first tune, an upbeat Keith Urban song that had people scrambling for the dance floor.

Daisy had to almost yell to be heard over the music. "Mary Beth, this is Jack McReady. Jack, my good friend and customer, Mary Beth Maynor."

He shook the woman's hand, feeling a little put-upon at having his private conversation interrupted. He chided himself for being so selfish and dredged up a smile.

"Nice to meet you. Your father runs an orchard up in the hills, doesn't he?"

"Maynor Orchards." An easy smile complemented Mary Beth's girl-next-door looks as she shrugged modestly. "He wanted me to take an interest, but I'm a horse girl through and through. I'm an instructor at Sweetbriar Ranch."

"Ah, Noah's old place. He's mentioned you." He remembered now—it was Mary Beth who had rescued Noah and Josephine when they'd become stranded in the mountains a while back.

"Don't let her fool you," Daisy said. "She has a master's degree from one of the best equine programs in the country."

"Colorado State," Mary Beth said, punching a fist. "Go Rams."

"That's . . . that's great." Jack wondered why this was suddenly feeling like a sales pitch. "You must be very passionate about horses."

Mary Beth opened her mouth to respond, but Daisy beat her to the punch.

"Oh, she is. Just ask Noah. And she's so good with the kids. She loves kids, don't you, Mary Beth?"

The look the woman gave Daisy was a little uneasy. "Um . . . sure. What's not to like?"

Jack gave a polite smile and straightened his silverware. It was becoming obvious what was going on here. Mary Beth looked as awkward as he felt, and he wondered if she'd known she was being set up before she arrived.

He sure hadn't. So much for that heady feeling he'd had at Daisy's initial enthusiasm. She'd only waved him over so she could introduce him to Mary Beth when she arrived. He was such an idiot. When was he going to learn?

"She likes to rock-climb too," Daisy said.

"Is that a fact?" Jack squirmed in his chair, irritation pricking hard. *Way to go, Jack. The love of your life is trying to set you up with someone else. This must be some kind of new low.*

"Well, I haven't gone in years," Mary Beth said. "But I used to love it."

"Jack's a very experienced climber," Daisy interjected. "He introduced me to it, but I'm sure he was bored to death on my bunny cliff. Haha. Bunny cliff, like bunny hill . . . in skiing . . . ?"

He gave Daisy a direct look. "I wasn't bored."

"Um, I think I'll go grab a drink from the bar,"

Mary Beth said as she pushed away from the table. "Service is kind of slow tonight. You guys want anything?"

They declined, and Jack half expected Daisy to suggest Jack accompany Mary Beth. Maybe pay for her drink and invite her onto the dance floor.

This night had sure deteriorated in a hurry. Not only was the woman he loved trying to foist him off on someone else, but he had Mary Beth to consider. She seemed like a very nice woman, and he didn't want to hurt her feelings, but his heart was already spoken for.

The whole thing made him want to grind his teeth—something his dentist had broken him of. The fast song came to an end, and as the audience clapped, the band started a slower, quieter ballad. Couples swarmed the dance floor, most of their table included. Jack had to address this with Daisy before Mary Beth returned.

He leaned forward, catching Daisy's eyes and holding them for a full three seconds before he'd collected himself. "I don't need you setting me up, Daisy."

Her face went slack, a shadow coming over her eyes. "You're upset with me."

He took a few deep breaths, trying to hide his frustration. But it really rankled that she thought he was so pathetic that he needed her help finding a woman. He didn't need her help. He had women at church tripping over themselves to be his wife.

Just not the one he wanted. No, the woman he wanted was too busy pushing him off on someone else. And chatting online with another man.

Except . . . not exactly another man.

She set her hand over his. "Jack, I'm sorry. I didn't mean to—"

"Forget it." His tone was sharper than he would've liked.

He pulled his hand away before his heart could mistake her gesture for something more. He'd already done a lot of that, apparently. Starting with that little flicker in her eyes that he'd mistaken for interest. And the way she'd flung her arms around him when they were rock-climbing. And the way she'd come so easily into his embrace when he'd comforted her on Sunday.

At least she still liked TJ.

He shook his head. He was a joke. A big fat joke.

He pushed back from the table. "I shouldn't have come tonight. I have more work to do on tomorrow's sermon, and I have to be up early."

"Jack . . . ," Daisy began as he stood.

Her head was tilted in that apologetic way of hers, and her guilty eyes sucked him right in. Made him feel like a heel. But he wasn't fit for company anymore, and he sure didn't want to stick around for Mary Beth's return.

"It's fine, Daisy." He tried for a genuine smile, though he couldn't seem to maintain eye contact. "I know you meant well. Please make my excuses to Mary Beth, and I'll just see you tomorrow, all right?"

Daisy watched Jack go, a boulder sitting square in the middle of her chest. Jack was a virtual paragon of patience, and he'd never gotten upset with her before. She did not like it. At all.

When Mary Beth returned to the table, Daisy explained Jack's sudden departure. Mary Beth took it well, giving Daisy a little good-natured grief about her lame setup attempt.

They listened to the band, and Daisy made small talk with the group, but her heart ached just remembering the look on Jack's face. The unfamiliar tightness around his eyes and the grim set of his mouth.

The night dragged on. Daisy wasn't in the mood to dance, so she looked after baby Sam when Hope went on break and Brady claimed his wife for a dance. Daisy watched Nicolas and Gracie too. She'd become the babysitter of the evening, but that was okay. She liked being an honorary auntie to her friends' kids.

She wished Julia were here. She'd wanted to invite her tonight, introduce her around, but she figured she'd best wait for her mom to cool off. Everyone would want to know the story—Hope was the only one she'd confided in—and her mom might feel humiliated if the news spread around town.

By ten o'clock Daisy found herself looking for an excuse to leave. Once home she could see if TJ was available to chat, and then the night wouldn't be a total waste. And maybe she'd be able to get Jack off her mind. Speaking of which . . . This guilt was killing her.

She pulled out her phone, opened her last text to him. It was too loud for voice-to-text so she started typing, careful of her spelling.

I'm sorry about tonight. I didn't mean to make you uncomfortable.

She read it through, checking for errors, then sent the text.

"Whatcha doing?" Daisy jumped as Hope slid into the chair next to her.

Sam was sleeping soundly on her friend's shoulder, a pacifier dangling from his mouth.

Daisy pocketed her phone. "I was just texting Jack."

Hope waggled her eyebrows. "Hmm. Sounds promising. I thought he was here earlier." She looked around the restaurant.

"He was. I chased him off."

Hope set a hand on Sam's back and began rubbing. "Why'd you do that?"

266

"It wasn't on purpose. I was just being nice— trying to set him up with Mary Beth Maynor, and he got all cross with me and made some excuse about having to go."

Hope chuckled, looking at Daisy like she was crazy. "Are you dense, woman?"

Daisy bristled at the words. She knew Hope didn't mean it in an unkind way, but that kind of wording struck at her deepest wound. "No, I am not."

"He likes *you,* Daisy—"

"Oh, he does not."

"And you're trying to set him up with someone else. No wonder he scooted out of here so fast."

"I have no reason to believe that."

Even as her mouth formed the words, her heart tapped out an objection. Her mind suddenly provided vivid imagery. A picture of Jack beaming at her after she'd climbed that first cliff. A picture of his wide smile, blooming across his face when he'd seen her tonight. A picture of the compassion in his eyes right before he'd pulled her into his arms last Sunday.

The images were accompanied with sensory detail. The familiar waft of his woodsy cologne, the delicious depth of his chuckle, the gentleness of his fingers on her chin.

"I don't know how to tell you this, girl," Hope said, "but you're in some serious denial."

Daisy blinked at her friend. Was she right? It

was true, there'd been moments she'd thought she had seen interest in those brown eyes. But it was always gone so quickly she felt as if she'd only imagined it.

"If he were interested, he's had plenty of time to let me know."

"Haven't you noticed how shy he is?"

Daisy gaped. "Shy? He gets up in front of a whole church every Sunday and delivers a sermon. I could never do that. In fact, I've never met a more competent man."

Hope gave her a look. "I mean with women. He seems a little insecure about his masculine appeal, don't you think?"

Daisy gave a sharp laugh. "Have you seen Jack? He's like an Armani model. Only more approachable and humble."

"I know, right? And yet sometimes our perception of ourselves can be far from accurate."

The notion hit a bull's-eye square in the center of her heart. Wasn't that exactly what TJ had tried to tell her about her intelligence? She should've known better than to get into this with a woman who was pursuing a psychology degree.

Hope nudged her arm. "Why do you think he was so upset with you tonight, hmm? Could it be he didn't like you trying to pass him off to someone else?"

Daisy winced. That sounded terrible. And she wasn't passing him off. She was trying to set

268

him up with someone worthy of him. Deep down she knew her own feelings toward Jack were changing, and she just couldn't let that happen. She was all wrong for him.

Maybe she'd done this partly to soothe her own guilty conscience. There was no maybe about it. Oh, she was so selfish.

She didn't want to think about this anymore. She gave Hope a cheery smile. "So . . . you know that guy I'm talking to on Flutter? Things are progressing well with him. We've been chatting live all week, in fact, and I really like him."

Hope gave her a curious look at the change in topic. "Well, that's good, I guess."

Daisy's phone buzzed, and she pulled it out and checked the screen.

It's okay, Daisy. I'm sorry about my atti- tude. I was just in a mood I guess.

"Aha," Daisy said, turning the phone so Hope could read the message. "He was just in a mood."

Hope rolled her eyes. "Well, what did you think he was going to say? 'Sorry I got annoyed when you pushed me off on your friend and broke my heart'?"

Daisy snatched her phone back and gave Hope a withering look.

Hope held up a hand. "Hey, don't listen to me. I'm just the objective observer here."

Daisy was relieved a moment later when a kitchen emergency called Hope away from the table. She took the sleeping toddler and, as soon as Brady returned to the table, she handed over Sammy and made her excuses to the group. She was going home where she could put the whole evening out of her mind.

TWENTY-EIGHT

The next week was flying by. Daisy was so busy with work, concert preparations, and live chats with TJ, she dropped into bed exhausted each night.

TJ had returned the contract to her earlier in the week. The attorney he'd consulted with had suggested an important tweak in one of the clauses. She'd gotten Grainger to sign off on the change, and the news about the band's performance at Peachfest went live yesterday, on Wednesday. As anticipated, tickets were going fast.

Lucille Murdock from the Hope House had stopped into the shop that morning, tears in her eyes, to thank Daisy. She said the girls were so excited to know they'd all be back home soon.

Except for one of the girls—Laura Felger, who was staying with the Porters from church. Lucille seemed overjoyed to report that the couple wanted to adopt the twelve-year-old girl. The news made Daisy's heart sing. She'd whispered a prayer of gratitude as she watched Lucille leave the shop. She loved it when God used something bad to bring about something wonderful.

Once the news about Grainger was out, Daisy had put Julia in touch with Harper so she could help with marketing efforts. Harper had put Daisy in charge of the concert's setup and teardown, and with VBS behind them, Jack had offered to recruit help for the big event.

He'd seemed back to normal when she saw him Sunday and in a few subsequent texts. Daisy was happy to pretend her lame setup attempt had never happened. Even if she did still find herself admiring the broad set of Jack's shoulders, those crystal brown eyes, and that low chuckle she felt deep inside her chest.

May was rushing out with a heat wave that took Daisy's breath away every time she stepped outside. Her mom had graduated from a cast to a brace and started physical therapy on her arm. Their relationship was more or less back to normal, although the topic of her dad's affair and Julia was clearly off-limits. It had become the elephant in the room.

When the phone rang at work Thursday, Daisy took an order for a bouquet of roses to be delivered on Saturday, then went back to the concert plans. A moment later the bell over the door jingled, and Lydia Smith slipped into the shop. She was in her sixties, but with her sleek blond bob and carefully made-up face, she passed for much younger. She and her husband owned the gift shop/gallery on the corner of Main and Bluebell.

Daisy gave her a bright smile. "Hi, Mrs. Smith. How are you today?"

"Hello, dear. Your shop always smells so delightful. I love the scent of eucalyptus."

"Well, you've come to the right place then."

Daisy's mom came to the front and chatted with her old friend while Daisy went back to her concert plans. A few minutes later the mention of a familiar name dropped into the conversation drew her attention.

". . . Dan Francis?" her mother was asking.

"Yes, of course, Daniel Francis," Mrs. Smith said. "You'll have to pop in and see them. They're quite spectacular."

"Wait." Daisy straightened behind the counter. "What about Mr. Francis?"

Her mom's cheeks had gone to rosy pink, and she was straightening blooms in the artificial arrangement in the bicycle basket.

"We're showing his work now," Mrs. Smith said. "You should come by and see his landscapes. He's Copper Creek's best-kept secret, I tell you."

Daisy shot her mom a look. "No kidding."

"He has such a way of capturing light. I've known him for years and didn't even know he painted until one of my customers mentioned it to me."

"We knew it, didn't we, Mama?" Daisy's gaze toggled to her mom and back to Mrs. Smith. "We've never seen his work before, but he gets all his still life subjects from our shop, you know."

"Still life? Oh no, he only does landscapes, dear."

Daisy shared a puzzled look with her mom.

"I was in his little painting shed," Mrs. Smith said. "He showed me all his work. Landscapes, every last one."

A little grin sneaked onto Daisy's lips. "Is that a fact?"

"You really must come by the gallery. He's all the talk since we've displayed his work. We've already sold four pieces."

Her mom finally found her voice. "We'll have to do that. Now, is there something we can help you with, Lydia?"

"My niece mangled her ankle getting off the school bus, and she's a little down. I think some pretty flowers will perk her right up."

Ten minutes later Mrs. Smith left the shop clutching a bouquet of gerbera daisies from the floral case.

Daisy watched her go, then turned a look on her mom. "Well. What do you make of that, Mama?"

"I think she should've chosen the blue delphiniums with the yellow zinnias. Much more cheerful."

Daisy gave her a wry grin. "Very funny. I'm talking about Mr. Francis, as you well know."

Her mom began cleaning the already clean countertop. "I think it's wonderful his work is being displayed at the gallery."

"Mama . . . he doesn't even paint the flowers he's been in here buying every week for months."

"Then he's being very wasteful."

"It seems to me perhaps he's been coming in here for another reason entirely."

Karen picked up the broom and began sweeping. "I can't think what that would be."

"Really?" Daisy said, chuckling. "I can."

"Oh, stop it. He probably has a whole room full of still lifes Lydia knows nothing about."

"Or he's totally infatuated with you and needs an excuse to see you."

The phone rang, but before Daisy could move, her mom snatched it up.

"Saved by the bell," Daisy whispered.

"Oopsy Daisy," her mom said into the phone. "May I help you?"

Daisy shook her head, sighing. It was very sweet, really. The man was persistent, she'd give him that. If only her mom would give him half a chance.

Daisy grabbed the broom, sweeping up the fallen leaves and stems in the back room as her mom took an order over the phone.

A moment later the bell jingled again, and Daisy was surprised to see Jack coming in. Her heart gave a vigorous thump at the sight of him in his creased white dress shirt and fitted khakis. A thatch of his dark hair fell across his forehead, giving him a rogue-like appearance. Her fingers itched to brush it back into place.

"Hi, Jack." She put down the broom and met him up front with a smile. "What are you doing in town today?"

"I was over at the diner for lunch and thought I'd stop in and see if you wanted to go rock-climbing Saturday—if you're not working, that is."

The mention of rock-climbing reminded her of her snafu on Saturday with Mary Beth, and guilt pricked at her.

"Well . . . there's a lot to do with Peachfest only a week away."

He shifted awkwardly, and Daisy couldn't help but remember what Hope had said about his lack of confidence where women were concerned. And where she was concerned in particular.

"We can go over details on the way over and back. Besides, I have a feeling you're working yourself to the bone over this. You could probably use some time off."

He was right about that, but spending time alone with Jack wasn't a good idea. She didn't want to encourage him, and she especially didn't want to find herself falling for him. She'd already started down that slope, she was afraid.

But they were just finding their footing again

after her misstep Saturday with Mary Beth, and she didn't want to cause another rift between them.

"I have the day off, in fact. And I would like to rock-climb again."

Jack beamed, suddenly looking more relaxed. "Terrific."

"I do hope it'll cool off a little between now and then, though. It's supposed to hit one hundred today."

"If we get an early start, we should be able to beat the afternoon heat."

"Early would be good. I have a meeting at Harper's house at one o'clock to go over last-minute details."

He made arrangements to pick her up at six thirty, and Daisy went back to her sweeping.

"Looks like I'm not the only one with an admirer," her mom said from the front, eyes sharpened on Daisy.

Daisy spared her a glance. "So you admit Mr. Francis admires you."

"Don't switch the subject on me. We're talking about you. Our pastor's got himself a crush on my daughter—I can't imagine how that escaped my notice."

"We're just friends, Mama." Even Daisy was starting to disbelieve that tired old line. "He's teaching me to rock-climb."

"Well. I can think of safer activities," Karen

said as she headed to the office, probably to punch some numbers.

But it seemed to Daisy that no matter how her time with Jack was spent, it wasn't safe at all— not for her vulnerable heart.

TWENTY-NINE

Keeping his brake hand on the rope, Jack watched as Daisy tried to navigate the outcropping just ten feet off the ground. She'd vastly improved since that first beginner's crag. Today's cliff was a popular climbing site, just off the Appalachian Trail, but they had it all to themselves so far. This was her third time up this morning, but this climb was by far the most challenging.

Today she wore black yoga pants and a green T-shirt that set off her eyes. Her low ponytail hung down her back, the blond a sharp contrast against the green.

The sky was clear blue, and the air was heavy with the clean fragrance of pine and the loamy scent of earth. A light breeze ruffled the leaves overhead, and a dove cooed mournfully from a nearby tree.

"There's a handhold up a little to your— There you go. You found it." He took up the slack as she climbed, bringing the rope in his brake hand down to lock it in place when she settled into position.

"Are you sure I can handle this one? It seems like a challenging route."

"You've got this, Daisy. Trust me." But what he really wanted her to do was trust herself. Rock-climbing was good for self-confidence.

In the next twenty minutes she climbed steadily while he held his position, right foot forward, knees slightly bent, eyes trained on her. He coached her when necessary, but it wasn't often, and she practiced the commands he was teaching her so she could effectively communicate with him.

In a time that surprised even Jack, she reached the top.

"Great job, Daisy!" he called. "Couldn't have done it better myself."

Her laughter echoed off the surrounding rocks. "I find that very hard to believe, Jack McReady. My legs are trembling like an aftershock. That took forever."

"I've seen climbers take twice that long. You're ready for an intermediate climb, I think."

"I don't think my legs can handle any more today. I'm ready for terra firma. Get me down from here."

"You're awfully sassy for a girl dangling from a rope. What's the command?"

"Tension. Pretty please," she added with sugary sweetness.

"That's more like it." He tightened the slack, pulled his brake hand down, and leaned back. "Gotcha."

He was pleased with how comfortable she looked easing her weight back in the harness. She was trusting him. Trusting herself. It was nice to see.

"Lower me!" she called.

He brought his guide hand under his brake hand. "Lowering!"

She began rappelling, and he let the rope feed through the belaying device as she descended. She'd gotten good at this as well, maintaining a steady pace all the way down. He slowed the rope as she neared the ground, allowing her to touch down safely.

"Off belay," she said when both feet were steady on the ground.

He paid out the slack, momentarily blinded by her beaming smile. "Belay off."

He approached, giving her a hearty high five.

"That was awesome!" Those green eyes twinkled at him. "I think I'm addicted."

"Well, if you have to be addicted to something . . ."

"I'm getting all the fun. You're going to have to teach me how to belay so you can climb." She gave him a speculative look, reaching for her chin strap. "If you trust me, that is."

"I'll gladly put my life in your capable hands."

She chuckled self-consciously as she fumbled with the latch of her chin strap. "My capable hands are shaking like crazy at the moment."

"Here, let me." He brushed her hands aside, undid the clasp, then removed the helmet. The strap caught in her pulled-back hair.

"Ouch."

"Whoops, sorry about that." Jack used his fingers to untangle the strands. By the time he'd released the helmet, her ponytail holder was halfway down her back.

She pulled it out the rest of the way, releasing her hair in a cascade around her shoulders.

And that's when he realized how close together they were standing. Then he noticed the faint smattering of freckles on her nose and the amber flecks in her eyes—which were fixed directly on him.

His heart gave a heavy thump, and he froze. The moment hung between them, humming with tension, breathless and lengthening. The world closed in until there was only the two of them.

She hadn't stepped back, and he couldn't have moved if he'd tried. He was too mesmerized by the flicker of interest in her eyes. His gaze dropped to her lips of their own accord. They were slightly parted, the lower one plump and inviting. He could feel the warmth of her breath against his neck and knew an urge so sudden and desperate he wasn't sure there was a force on earth that could keep him from closing the gap between them.

• • •

Daisy couldn't take her eyes from Jack's. They had caught her like a riptide, pulling, tugging, until she was helpless against the current. Her body flooded with warmth, and her fingers itched to touch the smooth curve of his jaw.

They were pulled together, seemingly by a magnetic force. Their breaths mingled for a long, torturous moment, and she could think of nothing but tasting his lips.

A clatter came from somewhere outside their bubble, followed by voices.

Jack jerked back, blinking.

By the time Daisy returned to reality, he'd already taken a couple steps back. She followed his gaze to the trail, where a group of hikers was emerging from the woods.

Daisy turned and began removing her harness. If she'd thought her hands were trembling before . . .

The hikers, a pair of couples from Tennessee, greeted them and made small talk as they began setting up for a climb. Daisy helped Jack pack away their own equipment, not daring to make eye contact with him.

What had she been thinking? Clearly she hadn't. Hope was right about Jack having feelings for her, and she'd have to be dead to be unaware of her own growing attraction. She refused to think it might be anything more.

The hike back to Jack's car was a quiet one. Tension buzzed between them, and awkwardness accompanied them, the proverbial third wheel. He helped her over stumps and boulders, taking her hand a time or two, as he'd done on the way up. Always the gentleman.

But it was different now. That one moment had changed everything. She could no longer ignore the fact that something was happening between them.

When they finally reached the car, he silently loaded the bag into the trunk and started the car.

She checked her watch. "Um, we're running a little late. Would you mind dropping me at Harper's? I'm sure Julia can give me a ride home."

He cleared his throat. "Sure. No problem."

Whereas the trip up had been filled with easy conversation, this one remained deadly quiet except for the Skillet song playing in the background. Were they just going to pretend the almost-kiss had never happened? Maybe that was for the best. Maybe they could just ignore it and go on as friends.

Friends? She didn't go around kissing her friends on the mouth. And that's just what she'd been so eager to do. She turned toward the passenger window, closing her eyes. Why was it so hard to remember that she was no match for Jack? Couldn't he see that? A relationship with him was completely hopeless.

And then there was TJ to consider. Maybe she hadn't met him in person, but she had real feelings for him, and she was pretty sure he had feelings for her. She was also pretty sure he wasn't running around kissing other women.

The trip to Harper's house seemed to take forever. The tension only grew as she provided directions. Finally he pulled into the long gravel drive that led back to the woman's place. Dogs barked in the kennels at their approach, making a ruckus. She was only a few minutes early.

Jack put the car in park. "Listen, Daisy . . . about earlier."

Before he could continue, a car pulled up on Jack's side. Julia waved from inside her rental.

Daisy latched onto the convenient reprieve. "Thanks for the outing, Jack. It was fun." She got out of the car and met Julia around the front.

But instead of leaving, Jack exited the car too and extended his hand to Julia. "Hi, I'm Jack McReady."

"Julia James. Nice to meet you."

"You too. We appreciate your help with the fundraising efforts. The Hope House girls are very grateful, I can tell you."

Julia's blue eyes widened. "Oh, *Pastor* Jack. I feel like I already know you. Daisy has said such wonderful things about you."

Daisy's cheeks warmed, and she felt Jack's eyes on hers.

"Is that a fact?" he said.

"I'd love to attend your church sometime soon; Daisy raves about your messages. But things are a little . . . complicated right now."

"That they are. I've heard wonderful things about you as well. You're a teacher, right? History?"

"Yes, a professor at Wake Forest."

"What time period do you typically teach?"

"Mostly twentieth-century world history, although I've taught a little of everything."

"Ah . . . imperialism, the Holocaust, globalization, the Great Migration . . ."

She chuckled. "All of that and more."

Daisy thought she detected a spark of interest in Julia's eyes. Interest in the topic of conversation, or interest in Jack? For a man who wasn't very "good with women," he sure didn't seem to be having any trouble with her sister.

"Your classes must be fascinating. I envy your students."

Julia laughed. "I'm sure most of them would happily trade places with you."

"That's only because they're too young to appreciate your expertise. I like to study world history from a biblical perspective, considering the book of Revelation, especially."

"I could talk all night about that particular topic."

"Well, as fascinating as that would be," Daisy

said, "I'm afraid Harper's waiting to go over the concert details." She must've sounded sharper than she'd intended, because Jack and Julia turned surprised looks on her.

Daisy softened the outburst with a smile and met Jack's eyes for the first time since their near-kiss. "Jack, thanks again for the ride here and the, um . . . the rock-climbing."

He gave a bewildered smile. "Anytime, Daisy. I had fun."

Julia tossed her mane of hair over her shoulder, drawing Jack's attention. "It was nice to meet you, Jack. Or should I call you Pastor Jack?"

An ache bloomed inside Daisy at the warm smile he gave Julia. "Just Jack, please. I'm not much for titles."

And look at that. In five short minutes Julia had crossed a barrier that had taken Daisy two years.

By the time they said good-bye, Daisy's heart felt as if it had shrunk two sizes.

Jack slipped into his car and started backing down the drive. The dogs in the kennels barked, and a black Lab puppy jumped up on the fence, yapping.

As Daisy and Julia walked up the path toward the house, her sister nudged her. "You never told me he was so good-looking."

Daisy swallowed hard. "He's my pastor. I—I don't think of him that way." *Liar, liar, pants on fire.*

"And he's not married?"

"Nope. Never has been."

"Well, that's a miracle if I ever saw one. What's wrong with him?"

Daisy shot her a look. "Nothing's wrong with him. He's a great guy."

Had she sounded defensive? She didn't dare look Julia in the eye for fear her every emotion was right there to see. She'd finally gotten around to telling Julia about her relationship with TJ, but she hadn't mentioned her growing feelings for Jack.

Listen, Daisy . . . about earlier. What had Jack been about to say?

"Well, if he's interested," Julia said, "maybe we can double date sometime. You know, if you ever bring your relationship with TJ out of cyberspace."

"Sure." Daisy felt that ache bloom inside her chest, bringing actual pain. "Sounds like a great time."

Later that night Daisy tossed a load of clothes into the dryer. She was in a terrible funk. All afternoon she'd kept reviewing Jack and Julia's conversation in her head. She couldn't help but think what a terrific couple the two of them made. They even looked great together. Both of them tall, him with his raven-black hair, her with her mahogany mane.

They'd make beautiful children.

She punched the dryer's On button extra hard and pressed her palm against the ache in her chest. This was ridiculous. Why was she so—dare she think the word—*jealous* of Julia? Daisy had known all along she wasn't right for Jack. Why had watching them connect intellectually hurt so much?

Globalization? The Great Migration? She didn't even know what those things were exactly. And she was pretty sure a book on either topic would put her right to sleep. In comparison, her library of romantic audio books seemed downright fluffy.

She left the laundry room and stood in the middle of her galley kitchen feeling lost. The near-kiss flashed in her mind—the look in Jack's eyes had tormented her all day. Looked like she wasn't the only one who was confused.

Listen, Daisy . . . about earlier.

Somewhere along the way she'd made a wrong turn. She'd begun relying on Jack too much. Had begun spending too much time alone with him. And now she was falling for him. Falling hard. She couldn't deny it anymore.

And then there was TJ. She often found herself thinking of what he'd said throughout the day, and she looked forward to their chats at night. He made her laugh. He made her think. When she was chatting with him, she felt as if her dyslexia didn't define her.

She rubbed her temple. She was falling for TJ too. And, unlike with Jack, there was real potential for that relationship. She needed to nip this thing with Jack in the bud for both of their sakes.

And she suddenly knew exactly what she needed to do next.

She walked into the living room and grabbed her phone off the end table where it was charging. She tapped on the Flutter app and opened a text box. Her heart was a jackhammer in her chest as she spoke the words, watching them form on the screen.

Do you want to meet?

She read the sentence once, checking for errors, then again, making sure she wanted to send it. Then she poised her finger over the screen, took a deep breath, and touched Send.

THIRTY

Do you want to meet?

Jack stared at Daisy's message, his breath suddenly trapped in his lungs. He'd figured this would happen eventually, of course. But he'd thought he'd have more time. Thought he'd find a way of telling Daisy the truth long before this.

He reread her short sentence, frowning at the words.

Why was she asking today, of all days? The same day he'd almost kissed her? If she were interested in Jack at all, she'd be pulling away from TJ, not reaching out for a closer connection to him.

Well, that said plenty, didn't it? Had he completely misread her cues again today? Had he imagined the look of interest in her eyes? The subtle tilt of her body toward him? Had she been about to reject his kiss before those climbers had interrupted them? He couldn't be that obtuse, could he?

Do you want to meet?

Well, if she wasn't interested in Jack, she surely

wouldn't welcome the news that TJ *was* Jack. He sagged against his sofa back.

What a pickle. What had he done?

He looked at Daisy's words on the screen. She'd had her fill of secrets this summer, and who could blame her? She'd been devastated by them, hurt by the people she'd trusted most. His revelation was not going to go in a positive direction, he realized with sudden acuity.

Why hadn't he seen this earlier? There was no happy ending here. There never had been. A hollow spot opened up inside, wide and yawning, filling with dread.

He closed his eyes. *What have I done, God? I've failed her on so many levels. As her friend, as her pastor. I set out to deceive her, never mind that my motive was never to hurt her. I was selfish, and now she'll never trust me again.*

He opened his eyes and fixed them on the laptop screen. Despite the dread, he was going to have to come clean with Daisy—and soon. And "TJ" was going to have to respond to her request quickly, before she started worrying he didn't want to meet her at all.

He set his fingers over the keyboard and began typing.

Daisy, I'd love to meet with you in person. I have so enjoyed our conversations and getting to know you. I'm aware you have a lot on your plate this upcoming week with the concert and Peachfest. How about if we set up a time and place to meet after all that's behind you?

With a heavy heart, he sent the message. Of course that meeting was never going to happen. He couldn't blindside her like that. He was only putting her off long enough to give him a chance to break the news in person. He'd do it the day after the concert. He couldn't drop this bombshell on her until that was over.

He was already dreading it. Already imagining the look of shock that would wash over her face. Quickly followed by a look of betrayal. A vise tightened around his heart. He could hardly stand the thought of disappointing her.

A message came in:

I'm so glad you feel the same way. I live in Copper Creek, and we have a nice little park on the edge of town called Murphy's Park. Are you familiar with it?

He typed back.

I know right where it is.

He waited almost five nerve-wracking minutes for her next message.

If you follow the path from the playground, there's a gazebo near a grove
of oaks, right beside the creek. Meet you
there a week from Monday at 6 pm?

He drew a deep breath and responded.

It's a date.

He hit Send, his heart about to explode in his
chest at the thought of what was coming. Of
what he'd brought on himself. All he could do
was pray this was going to somehow work out.
Because becoming TJ had only made him love
Daisy more than he already had.

THIRTY-ONE

I'll handle garbage detail," Jack said from across the picnic table, his eyes warm and open despite the tension Daisy felt between them. "And I'll round up some volunteers to help."

With the concert only three days away, they'd met at Murphy's Park to go over last-minute details, and they were mostly finished. This project sure had thrown them together a lot. But she hadn't talked to him since their near-kiss Saturday.

"That would be very helpful," Daisy said. "I'll be in charge of cleanup after the concert."

"Sounds like a plan."

Daisy checked her watch. Ava and Millie were meeting her here in a few minutes to shoot hoops on the cement court. Millie wanted to try out for the basketball team at school next year, and Daisy wanted to encourage her efforts.

"Am I keeping you from something?" Jack closed up his notepad.

Part of her wished she could turn back the clock to before that almost-kiss, when things were so compatible between them. But that compatibility was what had led to the almost-kiss.

"Ava and Millie are meeting me here at six thirty. I told Millie I'd shoot hoops with them, but in all honesty it's been years since I even dribbled a ball. Wanna stick around and help me out?" She was eager to put this awkwardness behind them, and maybe some fun—and extra company—would be just the thing.

Jack beamed. "I'd love to. I'm no Kobe Bryant, but I used to play intramurals."

"I can see I'm going to be outranked here."

"Hi, Daisy!"

She caught sight of Millie running across the grassy park, Ava following at a slower pace. It was good to see the little girl smiling.

"Hey, Millie. You know Pastor Jack."

"Hi, Millie," Jack said, holding up his hands. "Pass me the rock."

Millie frowned. "Huh?"

"The basketball. Some people call it— Never mind. Throw it over here."

She passed the ball to him, pushing out from her chest.

"Nice pass. Something tells me you've done this before."

"I've been practicing at recess."

Ava appeared at her sister's side and greeted Jack and Daisy.

"Pastor Jack volunteered to play with us, if that's okay," Daisy said. "Maybe we can play a little two-on-two."

"He's on my team!" Millie said.

Daisy shared a look with Ava. "I think we've been outsmarted."

Almost an hour later Daisy fully realized the truth of her comment. Millie, the little rascal, was far more athletic than Daisy ever dreamed. And Jack made layups like he was born with a basketball in his hands. The two of them conspired and carried out plays like a couple of pros while she and Ava darted around helplessly, missing shots when they finally did manage to get the ball.

"Uncle!" Ava called after Millie put up yet another shot that swished through the hoop. "This is no game, it's a massacre."

"No kidding," Daisy said. "I don't think there's any doubt you're going to make the team this year, young lady."

Millie shrugged modestly. "I guess the practice is paying off."

Daisy eyed Ava. "A little warning would've been nice."

"Hey, I didn't know she'd gotten so good. Last time I played her it was a pretty close game."

Daisy put her hands on her hips, catching her breath as Millie retrieved the ball. The girl might have a learning disability, but she was smart as a whip and athletically gifted besides.

She guessed there were all kinds of ways to be smart. Letters and numbers were only a small part of it. And Daisy realized suddenly that she'd let the voices from her childhood crowd out that truth. She'd given them too much power. She'd learned to cope with her dyslexia, and she had talents and gifts of her own. She was no less worthy than Millie—and Millie was so wonderfully worthy.

She watched as Jack gave Millie double high fives. The girl was obviously going to be just fine.

A moment later he appeared at her side, his head cocked, eyeing her thoughtfully. "You all right? You seem a million miles away."

Her eyes sharpened on his as she gave him an enigmatic smile. "You know what, Jack? I'm going to be just fine."

The next few days flew by in a flurry of activity. Daisy's messages to TJ were sporadic and not live, and even though she was busy, she found herself missing him. She and Jack hadn't spoken, beyond a few texts coordinating the church volunteers for the concert.

She split her time between the flower shop, festival meetings, and phone calls. She confirmed the delivery and setup of staging, Porta Potties, and extra seating for the older folks. Mostly the concert would be standing room only.

It would take place on the large square at the end of town, which would be barricaded, allowing ticket holders only. Harper was handling the barricades and extra security. The church had provided volunteers for the ticket booths and for setup and teardown.

The girls from the Hope House were on board for the evening too. Ava, as Miss Georgia Peach, would have a presence at the concert as well. She'd about fainted dead away when Daisy had asked her to introduce the band. But who better than one of the Hope House residents?

On Wednesday Ava came into the shop alone via the back door. She stopped just inside, where Daisy was arranging a lush bouquet of red roses for Mayor Walters's wife in celebration of their thirty-fifth anniversary.

One look at the girl's face, and Daisy knew something was wrong.

"She has dyslexia." Ava's voice was resolved, but her lower lip trembled.

"Oh, Ava. You got the evaluations back?"

"Yeah. Just today."

Daisy set down the stem and walked over to Ava. "Okay then. Now you know what's going on. She can get the proper help."

Ava's eyes teared up. "I'm so scared for her. What if she never learns to read right? What kind of future will she have?"

Daisy pulled her into an embrace. "She'll read, honey. It's going to be okay. She'll get the right kind of help. You'll be surprised how quickly she progresses now that we know what's going on. I'll tutor her too. You're not in this alone, Ava."

"I don't want to tell her. She'll be so upset that something's wrong."

"It was actually a relief to find out I had dyslexia. Millie already knows something's wrong, sweetheart. Trust me. I can coach you with what to say to her, and I can even be there when you tell her if you want."

"I think I should tell her by myself. But I'll tell her that you have dyslexia too, and maybe she can talk to you about it. She'll probably have questions that I can't answer."

"I'd be happy to talk to her. She'll see that I get by all right."

Ava pulled back, wiping her eyes. "You more than get by, Daisy. You're amazing. I don't know what I'd do without you."

"You're a smart, capable young woman. And Millie will be too, you'll see. We just have to get her through this rough patch."

On the evening of the concert Daisy was a nervous wreck. The stage was all set up, as were the barricades and Porta Potties. The volunteers were busy little bees on the freshly trimmed lawn, setting up extra park benches and trash barrels. A crew worked to finish the lighting.

Daisy straightened out a park bench and double-checked her long to-do list. If anything went wrong, it would be her fault. So many people were counting on her. The Hope House girls, Grainger, Harper and the Peachfest committee, and even Julia. Her sister had arranged this connection, after all.

Harper had made Julia the band's liaison since she was already a friend of Kade's. She was currently making sure the contract's rider was being carried out. The band's requests had been simple: plenty of water and a meal before the concert with a notation of a peanut allergy. Thank God they weren't prima donnas.

The afternoon was a warm eighty-four degrees, but fluffy clouds provided a welcome reprieve from the sun's hot rays, and a refreshing breeze blew in from the east. The smell of freshly mowed grass hung in the air, and Daisy could already smell wonderful aromas wafting over from junk food alley.

She'd forgotten to eat lunch. She looked around at the large stretch of lawn, taking it all in. Her heart squeezed tight as she experienced a moment of gratitude for a community that had come together for a good cause.

This had been a group effort, from the tireless volunteers to the bighearted festival board, to the band that was so generously giving of its time. She was proud to be part of a community that cared as much as Copper Creek.

Her phone vibrated in her pocket, and she glanced at the ID. Julia.

"Hey, how's it going?" Daisy said.

"Running right on schedule. Grainger just arrived on-site, and their roadies are beginning setup."

"Terrific. When is Blue Moon bringing the food?"

"Seven o'clock. I called to confirm. They'll do sound check before supper, have an hour to eat and hydrate, then it'll be showtime. Are you free at the moment? I thought you might want to come back and meet the band."

"I'd love to. Be there in ten." Daisy disconnected the call and shook her head in wonder. How crazy was it that she was getting to meet Kade Patrick and the band in person?

Ten minutes later she was ridiculously nervous as she stuck her hand out to the lead singer. Kade's baby-blue T-shirt made the most of his tanned skin and brought out the color of his eyes. His dark, tousled hair looked as perfectly imperfect as it did on magazine covers.

"I am such a fan." Daisy's heart was beating ridiculously fast. "Thank you so much for doing this. You have no idea how much it means to our community."

His smile was warm and engaging. "Our pleasure, Daisy. I'm glad we could slip in last minute."

"I heard the show sold out in forty-eight hours. That must be some kind of record."

"So I heard. Should be a great night."

"There's already a huge line out front. Do you have everything you need? Is there anything else we can get you?"

"Everything's great. We're not too fussy." He nudged Julia's shoulder. "And Julia's taking great care of us."

"Kade!" one of the crew called. "Which guitar are you opening with?"

"Be right there," Kade called over his shoulder. "I have to take care of this. It was nice to meet you, Daisy."

"Pleasure's all mine." Daisy watched him disappear into the fray of roadies and equipment. "Wow, he seems really nice."

Julia was already checking her list. "He's the real deal. Hey, I should go make sure the rest of the band's all right. Want to meet them now too?"

"I'd love to, but I need to check on the lighting crew. I got a text on my way over. Maybe after the concert?"

"Sounds like a plan."

Five and a half hours later, Daisy paused to take it all in. Darkness had descended on the standing-room-only crowd in the town square. Grainger's music blared through speakers that were mounted to the stage.

The strobe lights zipped haphazardly over the rowdy crowd, capturing blips of palpable excitement. Flashes went off, twinkling like the stars overhead, and the deep thump of the bass reverberated inside her chest.

Getting to this point had been a lot of work. There had been some sound equipment glitches and a bit of a scare when the fire department had contacted her about the square's capacity. But all that had been ironed out, and now she took a moment just to appreciate a job well done by so many people.

"You did good, Daisy," Jack called over the music as he appeared at her side. He was in charge of trash detail tonight and was dressed more casually than she'd ever seen him in a black T-shirt, khaki shorts, and the red ball cap all the volunteers were wearing.

"Thanks. It really did come together. Everyone's having a great time."

"I can't believe how fast those trash barrels are filling up."

"Do you need more volunteers? I can put some of the girls on it."

"No, we've got it covered. At least the garbage is making its way into trash cans. That'll save us a lot of work later." He gave her an affectionate look. "You should be proud of yourself, Daisy. You're really good at this. You put a lot of time into it and it's paying off in spades—and don't you dare sell yourself short."

She laughed. "As if you'd let me. But thank you. It's been really rewarding to see the whole community working together. It'll be even more rewarding to see the Hope House restored to its former glory. I hate seeing it in shambles."

"You won't have to wait much longer. Noah's company is ready to start the renovations as soon as they get the check for materials."

"Pastor Jack," a high-pitched voice called.

Daisy turned to see Leah Sanders approaching, looking much too cute to be on garbage detail, despite the elbow-length gloves.

"Where are the extra garbage bags? We're all out."

"There's more in my trunk." He turned a heart-stopping smile on Daisy. "I'll catch up with you later, Daisy."

"See you, Jack."

Daisy spent the next half hour looking out for trouble in the crowd and filling in wherever the volunteers needed her help. She was picking up trash when Grainger started Daisy's favorite song, a moving ballad called "Fall a Little Deeper."

Daisy worked her way up the sideline toward the front as couples began dancing in place. She'd allow herself to enjoy this one song before she went back to work. Up closer she could see Kade's facial expressions as he crooned about the love of his life. The electric guitarist leaned back, obviously feeling the dynamic riff, and the drummer executed a well-timed fill.

When they reached the first chorus, Daisy swayed in place to the beautiful harmonies. It was so much better in person when she could feel the music humming through her body. She thought of TJ and wished he were with her tonight. He'd enjoy this. They could slow-dance together, and she could stare into his eyes and fall a little deeper.

Soon, she thought, delicious hope swelling inside.

She caught the movement of something red in the corner of her eye and watched Jack tying off a garbage bag. Her heart twisted at the sight of him and the memory of their almost-kiss. She'd found herself reliving that moment more times than she cared to admit. Could she have fallen for two different men at once? Was that even possible?

"Hello, Daisy." Joe Connelly all but shouted as he appeared at her side, holding a monstrous fountain drink.

"Hi, Joe. Having fun?" The attorney and his wife attended her church, though she'd hardly known them before she did the flowers for their daughter's wedding two weeks ago.

"A blast. This is a great concert—I heard this was pretty much your doing."

"Thank you, but I had lots of help. It really came together, and everyone seems to be having a good time. Where's Cheryl?"

"Oh, she's up front, fangirling." He gave her a good-natured smile. "Is that what you kids are calling it these days?"

Daisy laughed. "I think so. I admit I did a little of that myself when I met Kade earlier. How are the newlyweds? Did they have fun in Jamaica?"

"They did. They're here . . . somewhere." He gestured helplessly toward the crowd.

Daisy's eyes swung back to the stage, enjoying the last minute of her favorite song. "They're terrific, aren't they? It's good to know he's a nice guy too. Not to mention very generous."

"Yes, it is. I assume you were able to get that clause added to the contract?"

Her eyes swung to Joe, but his eyes were on the band. How did he know about that clause? When she didn't reply, his gaze turned back to her.

He must've seen the questioning look in her eyes. "Jack had me look over the performance contract. I suggested a small addition—I thought you knew."

Jack had him . . . ? But how did Jack . . . ?

Her eyes caught on a flash of red—Jack's cap. He was putting another bag into a trash barrel about thirty feet away. She frowned, her thoughts spinning in a direction that made dread buzz through her veins.

THIRTY-TWO

D aisy?" Joe set a hand on Daisy's arm. "You all right? You look a little pale."

Daisy heard him as if from far away. Even the music was a dull roar in her ears. "Yeah, I'm—"

She shook her head, unable to go on. Her conversations with TJ were playing back in excruciating detail. She'd confided in him about so many things—about her dyslexia, about how stupid she felt sometimes. It had felt safe because he was on the other side of cyberspace somewhere. She didn't really know him. But she *did* know TJ.

Because TJ was actually Pastor Jack.

Her eyes stung as she found him in the crowd. Disbelief made her insides feel hollow. His gaze swept past her just then and doubled back as he aimed a smile right at her. She stared back, still trying to absorb the blow. The reality. The truth.

His gaze toggled to Joe Connelly, standing beside her, and the smile fell slowly away as his eyes returned to her. She was barely aware of Joe checking his phone and making an excuse. Daisy nodded numbly, then watched as he slipped away into the crowd.

TJ is Jack.

She turned back to him. She could see it now, so clearly. With his ball cap and T-shirt he looked very much the way he did in his profile pictures.

TJ was Jack. How could she not have known?

He'd certainly known who she was. Her pictures were right there on her profile—and unlike his, hers were close-up and looked just like her.

Why had he hidden behind another identity? Why had he lied to her about who he was? He'd not only used another name, he'd never once mentioned being a pastor.

The betrayal was like a punch to her heart. She could hardly breathe. How could he have done something so deceitful? How could he have been so cruel?

The thunderbolt was starting to morph into something less painful, more gratifying. Her body went hot all over, and sweat broke out on the back of her neck.

She wasn't even mollified by the fear washing over Jack's face as he started walking slowly toward her.

But she couldn't talk to him right now. Couldn't even look at him. Blindly, she turned and stepped into the crowd.

Jack couldn't find Daisy anywhere, and she wasn't answering her phone. The square was in chaos, the concert over, and the attendees were trying to get onto the streets where the festival awaited them. He'd been looking for her since she'd fled into the crowd over an hour ago.

He had no doubt she'd put it all together. It was right there on her face. He couldn't erase the image of her pain-filled eyes. He felt so helpless as he watched the realization take hold. First the shock, then the betrayal. Oh, he saw every emotion that had swept through her, and he'd been powerless to stop it. Helpless to comfort her—because he'd been the one to cause it all.

His phone buzzed in his pocket and he grabbed for it, hoping it was Daisy, but his heart shriveled at the name on the screen. Harper.

"Pastor Jack, do you know where Daisy is?"

"No, I've been looking for her."

"There's a ton of media here, including *Entertainment Today*, to video the presentation of the check. Kade's waiting with the mayor, and I need someone to represent the Hope House. I've already tried to reach Lucille Murdock and Daisy, and I'm handling an emergency at junk food alley at the moment. Can you do it?"

Jack caught a glimmer of yellow by the ticket booths and recognized Daisy's form just before she disappeared around the corner.

"I just spotted Daisy. I'll let her know."

"We're in the middle of Main Street under the Peachfest banner. Hurry—the local channels want this on the evening news."

"We'll be right over." Jack hustled the fifty yards to the ticket booth and found Daisy returning a woman's lawn chair—concert contraband. When the woman headed toward the exit, Daisy turned to lock up the temporary booth.

"Daisy, there you are." Jack was breathing hard from his sprint across the lawn. "I've been looking for you everywhere."

"Go away, Jack. I don't—I can't talk to you." She slipped the keys into her pocket and turned away.

Jack took her arm. "I have a lot to say to you, Daisy, but there isn't time for that now."

She jerked her arm away, and her flinty look kicked him right in the gut.

Hopelessness swamped him. "The media's here for the check presentation. They want a representative of the Hope House, but Harper can't get hold of Lucille. They want to know if you'll do it."

The stony look on her face didn't soften. "Harper can do it."

"Harper's hung up with an emergency in junk food alley. She's asking for you."

"I can't do an interview right now, Jack." Her voice trembled with anger. "As you well know, my speaking—I get all tangled up when I'm—my nerves are about shot right now!"

"I know."

The way she faltered with her words, the angry

tears in those green eyes, made his chest squeeze tight. He'd give anything to erase what he'd done. He couldn't do that, but he could do this one thing for her. "Listen, you just do whatever you need to do, and I'll go handle this, all right?"

He didn't think it possible for her face to go harder, but it did. Her lips locked flat together until they went white, and her jaw twitched under the streetlights.

"I don't—I don't want anything from you, Jack." She blinked back the tears. "Where are they?"

"Daisy, just let me do this for you, please. I don't mind—"

She nailed him with a flinty look. "Where are they?"

He'd never seen her like this. Not even when she'd found out about her dad. He'd really done it this time. "They're on Main Street under the banner."

And for the second time tonight, Daisy turned and fled from him.

Daisy was shaking as she got into place on the other end of the gigantic fake check made out to the Hope House. She tried to revel in the amount of zeroes on it, but her palms were sweaty, and her heart was beating a million beats per minute.

The crowd was gathered behind them, held back by a barricade and security. They were screaming like mad for Kade, who occasionally acknowledged their affectionate shouts with friendly waves.

It was hot under the artificial lighting. The mayor's podium was just off to the side, fixed up with more microphones than Daisy had ever seen in one place. The cameramen and photographers faced her and Kade, and already flashes were going off.

"So we'll be live in thirty seconds," someone said. "Mayor Walters, you can take it from there."

Mayor Walters gave a nod. His bald head was sweating under the lights, and his readers slipped down his bulbous nose. He shoved them back into place and took a minute to review his notes.

"You all right, love?" Kade asked from the other end of the check.

Daisy glanced his way. "I-I'm fine. Just a little . . . nervous."

"It'll go quick. The mayor will speak, then there'll be a ton of photos and some of the media will want interviews. Just follow my lead. You'll be fine."

Sure she would be. If only she could swallow past the huge lump in her throat. Or think past the blood roaring in her ears.

Jack . . .

She squeezed her eyes shut. She couldn't think of him right now. She'd need all of her focus to get her through this.

"Here we go," someone said, and one of the cameramen counted off the final few seconds.

Mayor Walters leaned forward and went into motion. "Good evening, folks. I'm Ken Walters, mayor of Copper Creek, Georgia, and tonight we're at our annual Peachfest event. As some of you might have heard, back in April our local girls' home, the Hope House, withstood major damage from a tornado, displacing some of our community's most vulnerable children. Tragically, there was no money for repairs. But a very special band came to the rescue. The popular country band Grainger agreed to a benefit concert that took place this evening.

"I'm pleased to have witnessed that event, and I am so proud of our community for coming together to support this wonderful cause. So thank you to Grainger, to the community of Copper Creek, and to everyone who traveled from across the country to support this worthy cause.

"And now we're all so pleased to witness as Kade Patrick of Grainger presents a check in the amount of twenty-five thousand dollars to the Hope House."

Daisy's smile felt stiff and unnatural as what felt like a hundred flashes went off. She readjusted the sweaty hand gripping the prop and tried to look proud and grateful. But she was trembling with the adrenaline that had been flooding her system for over an hour.

"Thank you all for coming tonight," Mayor Walters said after what seemed like an eternity. He stepped aside, and reporters immediately swarmed her and Kade.

Someone from the Country Music Channel stuck a microphone in Kade's face. "Mr. Patrick, what inspired you to help with this special cause?"

"When we heard what happened to the Hope House, the guys and I were thrilled for the opportunity to support a great cause. The folks here in Copper Creek have really come together to help these girls, and we're honored to be a part of that."

"Do you have a personal connection to Copper Creek?"

"It was sort of a friend-of-a-friend thing. We're all personally connected, though, eh? Through the ties of humanity." He shared a smile with Daisy. "This is Daisy Pendleton—she did all the work to make this event happen tonight."

All eyes swung to her, and Daisy's smile froze on her face. Her stomach turned, and her throat tightened painfully.

"Ms. Pendleton, tell us about the Hope House."

She zeroed in on the reporter's face. On his waxy skin and hungry hazel eyes. Words buzzed through her brain at lightning speed, but nothing found its way to her tongue.

"Ms. Pendleton?"

Daisy blinked. *Come on, say something.* "Um . . . It's a local . . . house for girls who have no one else to take them in."

"Something like a modern-day orphanage," Kade said. "The tornado did a lot of damage back in the spring, and some of the girls were displaced. The money raised tonight will cover repairs to that wing so all the girls can move back home again."

"Ms. Pendleton, how were you able to get Kade Patrick on board with the benefit?"

"Um . . ." Daisy put a hand on her churning stomach. *Oh, please. Not now.* She willed her dinner to stay in place.

She felt heat rise through her, probably turning her ears red. "I—I know someone who knows him. Knew him. Or Kade knows her brother." She winced. She wasn't making any sense!

"A buddy I went to school with contacted me," Kade said. "He told me about the benefit Copper Creek was trying to put together. It so happened we had a short break in our schedule and were able to step in. Thank you all for your questions. I'm sure the mayor can help you with anything else you need." He winked at the camera. "Ms. Pendleton and I need to go cash this check!"

The group chuckled as Kade tugged Daisy across the street. Security stepped in, keeping the crowd at bay. Daisy followed blindly, her breath stuffed in her lungs, her throat aching, her stomach roiling.

She clutched her middle as he led her, with the big check, through a narrow alley and behind a closed boutique. As soon as they reached the Dumpster in the back, Daisy bent over and heaved. The entire contents of her stomach spilled out onto the potholed pavement.

"There you go." Kade set a hand on her back. "Let it all out, love."

Her throat burned, and her eyes filled with tears of strain. She sucked in her breath, clutching her knees. She hadn't thrown up in years, and she had to do it in front of Kade Patrick. She closed her eyes and swallowed convulsively, hoping her stomach was finished rebelling.

"I'm so sorry," she grated over an acid-burned throat. "I can't believe this is happening."

"Hey, don't worry about it. I've seen a lot worse, believe me."

Daisy heard footsteps, pebbles grinding at someone's approach, but she didn't want to know who else had come to witness her humiliation.

"Daisy!" It was Julia's voice, tense with worry. "Daisy, are you all right?"

"I'm fine." Or she would be if she could only crawl into a hole and die.

"Just a little case of the nerves, I think," Kade said. "She was three shades of green back there."

Great. On national TV too. Daisy straightened

and ran her hand over her mouth and nose. Gross.

Julia handed Daisy her water bottle, and Daisy rinsed out her mouth.

When she was finished, Julia wiped at her face with a Kleenex. "Poor baby. Let me take you home."

"I can't. I—I have things to do. I'm in charge of cleanup."

"I'll come back and take over." Julia turned to Kade. "That is, if you guys don't need anything else from me tonight."

"We'll be fine." He set a hand on Daisy's arm. "You'll be all right?"

She tried for a smile. "Yeah, I feel much better now."

"I should take off then. I've got that meet-and-greet. It was nice to meet you, Daisy. Julia, if I don't see you again, take care." He gave Julia a hug good-bye and took off toward the street.

"Come on." Julia grabbed the huge check and put her other arm around Daisy as they started walking. "Are you going to be all right, hon? Did something happen to upset you tonight?"

Daisy gave a wry laugh that came out rough and pathetically sad. "Oh, Julia. You have no idea."

THIRTY-THREE

"Wait," Julia said as she turned onto Daisy's street. "Run that last part by me again."

The night's events had hit Daisy full force once she'd gotten into Julia's rental, and words had been hard to come by. She was a sloppy mess of tears and snot, and her throat still burned. She was pretty sure she wasn't making much sense either.

"TJ is Jack, and Jack is TJ." Daisy closed her eyes against the fresh assault of pain. "They're one and the same. He's been lying to me all this time."

"Pastor Jack is TJ—your online guy?"

"Yes!"

"But . . . he's a pastor," Julia said as she pulled into Daisy's drive and shut off the ignition.

"I know, right?" Daisy sniffled and wiped her face with the soggy tissue. "I've taken the ugly cry to a whole new level."

"Who can blame you? Are you sure about this? How'd you find out?"

She told Julia about TJ offering to pass the performance contract to a friend and about Joe Connelly's comment to her tonight.

"Well, I'll be darned," Julia said.

"I thought I knew him. I trusted him. Why would he do this to me?"

"But how did you *not* know it was him? There were pictures on his profile—you showed them to me."

With trembling fingers Daisy jabbed the Flutter app button and opened Jack's profile. "Sunglasses. Ball cap. A year of facial growth! Is it any wonder I didn't recognize him?"

"Oh." Julia studied the images. "Yeah, I see where you might've missed that. But what about his bio? What did he say about himself?"

"Well, let me just read it to you." Daisy read it off, mocking the carefully worded description of his profession.

"Oh brother," Julia said when Daisy was finished.

"Very clever, Jack. Or TJ, or whoever you are," Daisy mumbled, closing the app and staring out the windshield.

"He actually managed to create his entire profile without even once lying," Julia said.

"But he didn't exactly tell the truth either, did he?"

"No, he did not. TJ . . . the *J* is probably for Jack, right? He must've used his initials."

"I guess so." Here she'd been torn between two men, and they were one and the same. Her prospects had gone from two to zero in a matter of seconds.

"I feel like such an idiot. I told TJ things I've never told anyone. I made myself vulnerable to Jack without even knowing it was him, and that is so not fair. I was falling for TJ, Julia—and he doesn't even exist."

"Oh, but, honey . . ." Julia brushed Daisy's hair off her shoulder. "He does exist."

"Not as far as I'm concerned. Not anymore. I trusted Jack, and he betrayed that trust." Daisy sniffed. "Why would he do this to me, Julia?"

"I don't know. Have you talked to him yet?"

"No. But he knows I know. He saw Joe talking to me, and he could see it on my face. He tried to apologize after the concert, but there wasn't time."

Julia shook her head. "Maybe there's some kind of reasonable explanation."

"What could possibly excuse this kind of deception?"

"I don't know."

"Maybe he's some weirdo who gets his kicks out of deceiving women online. Maybe he's talking to a dozen other women just like me. I'm such an idiot!"

Julia squeezed her hand. "Forgive me, but I have to ask . . . Are you more upset about losing TJ? Or more upset about losing Jack?"

Daisy's heart gave a heavy thump, and she pressed her palm against it. She'd fallen for both of them. That much was obvious now.

"I honestly don't know," she admitted with a heavy sigh.

"Listen . . ." Julia pulled her keys from the ignition. "I'm going to come in with you, all right? I'm not leaving you alone tonight."

As good as that sounded, someone needed to take Daisy's place at cleanup. "That's sweet, Julia, but what about—"

"No buts. I know someone needs to take your place in town, and I have just the right person in mind." She gave Daisy a saucy look, holding out her hand. "Now give me your phone."

Daisy gave her a speculative look as she complied.

Julia touched the screen a few times, and a couple seconds later she spoke into the phone. "No, Jack, this isn't Daisy. It's her sister, Julia. Listen, Daisy needs someone to take over the cleanup crew tonight and— Uh-huh . . . all right."

A smile tilted Daisy's mouth as she mopped up the last of her tears. It felt good to have someone taking care of her. To have a sister on her side.

"She's fine. Yes, she's right here, in fact." Julia listened a few more seconds, then mouthed to Daisy, *Do you want to talk to him?*

Daisy was emphatically shaking her head no before she even finished. Good grief, he was the last person she wanted to talk to right now.

"Now's not a good time, Jack . . . All right. I'll tell her."

Julia hung up the phone, and Daisy held her breath waiting to hear what he'd said.

Julia gave Daisy a sympathetic look. "He sounded awfully hopeful when he answered the phone. He's obviously worried about you. He saw the interview."

Daisy's breath drained from her body. "Great. Why shouldn't he witness my humiliation? The rest of the country did."

"Aw, it wasn't that bad."

Daisy gave her a rueful smile. "Liar."

"He asked me to tell you how sorry he is and said he hoped you'd give him a chance to explain."

"Explain," Daisy huffed. "What possible explanation could there be?"

"I don't know." Julia carelessly tossed her keys into her purse. "But what I do know is that we're going into that house, and we're going to talk or watch a movie or eat a tub of double fudge swirl—if you're up to it—and Pastor Jack will be on trash duty till the sun comes up. Now, let's go have some girl time."

THIRTY-FOUR

The annual Peachfest parade was one of the highlights of the festival, and Daisy couldn't remember a year she'd missed it. So brokenhearted or not, here she was.

She wrapped her arms around her knees, already regretting her decision to attend. It was easy enough to hide in the energetic crowd that lined Main Street, but she'd just as soon be working today.

Julia had gone to fetch some cold drinks from the Mellow Mug, leaving Daisy alone for the first time since yesterday. And all of the hullabaloo only made her feel more alone.

She watched the little girls from Dottie's Dance Studio sashay past, looking darling in their pink sequined costumes. Right behind them was the local VFW's patriotic float. The veterans on board threw candy into the crowd.

Copper Creek High School's marching band passed by next, the trumpets blaring out a rousing rendition of "Louie Louie." Daisy's heart rebelled against the happy tune.

She'd gotten her first call from Jack at eight o'clock this morning. They'd been coming in regularly since then, but she had yet to pick up or listen to his voicemail. He'd also texted her twenty minutes ago, but she hadn't read it. She wasn't ready. She was still too hurt and angry.

"There you are." Hope squeezed in beside Daisy, dropping to the curb, despite the disgruntled looks from her neighbors who'd probably arrived at dawn to claim the prime spot.

"Hey there," Daisy said.

Hope looked like a ray of sunshine in her yellow polka-dotted top. Her brown hair was pulled back into a messy bun, and her wide smile was expertly lined with pink lipstick.

Once the band passed by, she nudged Daisy's shoulder. "I've been trying to call you all morning. The concert was amazing! And twenty-five thousand dollars . . ." Hope's gaze sharpened on Daisy's face. "Wait a minute. You saved the day, you're basically Copper Creek's own Superwoman—shouldn't you look happier?"

Superwoman? Daisy shook her head, hardly seeing the group of Boy Scouts passing by. She was emotionally wrung out. She hadn't fallen asleep until after two o'clock, and it had been a restless sleep, full of strange dreams. Then Julia had gone and dragged her out of bed at the crack of dawn.

"I'll tell you all about it later," Daisy said.

Hope's eyes searched Daisy's. "Tell me now. Did something happen last night?"

"Oh yeah. Something happened." She may as well just get it out there. Hope wasn't going to leave her alone until she did. "You know TJ, the guy I was chatting with on Flutter . . . the one I was falling for?"

"What, did you finally meet him? Is he a first-class jerk? He didn't hurt you, did he?"

"It depends on what you mean by *hurt*. And it turns out I didn't need to meet him—I already knew him." She gave Hope a disgruntled look. "TJ is actually Jack."

Surprise flickered in Hope's eyes. A tenuous smile began forming on her face. "*Pastor* Jack?"

Daisy felt her blood rush to her head. "Don't you dare smile. This isn't some romantic fairy tale, Hope. He lied to me, or might as well have. He pretended to be someone else, and I told him things I haven't told anyone else. Jack—the real Jack—was befriending me and making me like him and trust him, all the while betraying that trust by pretending to be TJ."

Hope winced. "But that . . . that doesn't sound like Pastor Jack at all. So he told you all this last night?"

"Oh no, he didn't do anything as noble as confess. I found out by accident." She shared the same story she'd told Julia the night before. It was becoming a story she'd just like to erase from her memory.

Hope squeezed her hand. "I'm so sorry, Daisy. What did Jack have to say for himself?"

"I don't know. I haven't talked to him since last night. He's been texting and calling, but I'm just not ready yet."

"You'll have to hear him out eventually. Maybe he has a good reason."

Daisy thought of last Friday at the cliff when he'd looked at her with want in his eyes, when his gaze had flickered down to her lips, and a force stronger than the two of them had pulled them together. Her heart gave a wistful squeeze at the memory, and she closed her eyes against the sting of fresh tears.

"I feel so stupid. Why would he do this to me? He played me for a fool." Daisy swallowed hard, but the truth bubbled out anyway. "I think I loved him, Hope."

"Um . . . TJ or Jack?"

Daisy leveled her with a look.

Hope gave her a dry look and lifted a shoulder. "It's a valid question."

Daisy's chest tightened painfully. She thought of TJ and his openness and the way he'd treated her vulnerability so carefully. She thought of the way he made her laugh and the way she was so comfortable chatting with him.

And she thought of Jack and how much she'd admired and respected him. She thought of his endearing awkwardness with women, and his amazing wisdom and patience, and the way he refused to let her sell herself short. She closed her eyes as realization washed over her. She had her answer.

Both of them. She'd loved both of them.

Hopelessness swamped her. What a terrible summer she was having. She swallowed against the tide as all of it came rushing back. She'd found out her dad had a fatal flaw. Her mom wasn't the person Daisy had thought she was. And Jack . . . He wasn't even close to the man she'd built him up to be.

Jack was operating on exactly two and a half hours of sleep, but he had to find Daisy. He thought she'd be at the flower shop this morning after the parade, but only her mom and grandmother were there working. She wasn't answering his calls or texts either, and he couldn't blame her.

He'd walked around most of the afternoon looking for her. He'd gone to her house around suppertime. Had driven by her mom's place, looking for her car. He'd stopped by the motel and knocked on Julia's door. But nobody was there either.

Where could she be? He stopped next to a busy craft booth, the Saturday-night crowd flowing down Main Street. He turned in a tight circle, scanning the crowd for Daisy's blond hair. It was starting to get dark, and he had to try to explain why he'd done what he'd done.

Lord, where is she? There's nothing I can do now but own up to this. I know I can't make it right, but I need to at least explain. I need to ask her forgiveness. Give me the opportunity. And, God . . . she didn't deserve this. Please comfort her right now. Soothe her spirit, and alleviate the pain I've caused.

He'd been whispering similar prayers all day, and he could only hope God had said yes to the second part of the prayer, because so far His answer to the first half had been a resounding no.

The look on her face last night at the concert haunted him, as did her TV interview. He'd seen her face blanch as the cameras had focused on her. Watched her stumble with words as nerves had taken over, and he'd wanted so badly to step in and save her.

But it had been Kade Patrick who'd saved the day. Kade Patrick who'd smoothed things over before rushing her away from the crowd. Jack had tried to follow, but security had held him back, and she'd disappeared soon after that.

Later he'd been relieved to find out Julia was with her, and he'd been more than glad to take over cleanup detail. Penance for his crime, he'd thought. But the penalty hadn't even begun to assuage his guilt.

This had all gone south, he realized, the night

he'd met Daisy at the Mellow Mug to brainstorm about the fundraiser. Rawley had seen them together and dismissed him as "Pastor Jack." Pride had swelled up inside him, and that was when he'd decided to pursue Daisy as TJ.

Good gravy. Deceit, selfishness, and now pride. He was growing quite the list.

Jack had made mistakes before, lots of them—he was human. But he'd never done anything like this. He'd counseled lots of people, though. People who'd made poor, life-altering decisions. People who were dealing with regret and guilt and trying to somehow forgive themselves. He knew all the right words to say to himself. He just couldn't figure out how to make himself believe them.

He'd never known how awful it felt to let down someone you loved. Never known that it planted a physical ache in the center of your chest that refused to be rooted out.

A flash of yellow pulled him from his pity fest. It wasn't Daisy's hair. It was only a shirt, but it was Hope's shirt.

"Hope!" he called as he darted through the crowd toward where she and Brady lingered in front of Zoe's baked-goods booth.

Hope was shifting baby Sam into his daddy's arms when Jack approached.

"Hope," Jack said. "Have you seen Daisy recently?"

She turned a wan smile on him. "Well, hello to you too, Jack."

"Sorry. Hi, you two." He shook Brady's hand before looking back to Hope. "I've been looking for her all day. Do you happen to know where she is?"

"Hey there, Jack." Zoe approached from behind the booth in her Peach Barn apron. "Everything all right?"

"I'm looking for Daisy. Have you seen her?"

"Not since this morning. What's wrong?"

Hope put her hands on her hips and gave Jack a flinty look. "He owes her a big, huge apology."

"Uh-oh." Zoe gave him a patronizing smile. "What'd you do? Can't be that bad."

Jack knew a shame he hadn't felt in years. Not since he'd realized he was a sinner and begged God for salvation.

"Nothing I'm proud of, Zoe," he said.

"She was at the parade this morning," Zoe said as she restocked the pies on the table. "She was with Julia."

Jack scanned the crowd, mostly so he wouldn't have to look into Hope's accusing eyes again. "I've looked everywhere, and she isn't answering my texts. I'm starting to get worried about her."

He forced himself to look at Hope, who was giving him a long, speculative look. "Do you know something? Is she all right? Could you just call and make certain she's okay? She'll answer your call."

Hope's shoulders lifted as she drew a breath, then sank on a long exhale. "She's fine—and she's at the Rusty Nail. But you didn't hear it from me, Jack McReady."

The Rusty Nail was all but deserted, most of Copper Creek preferring instead the novelty of the annual festival. Just a few families gathered around the wooden tables, enjoying the rustic restaurant and piped-in country music.

Jack found Daisy in a shadowed corner, nursing a soda. She was hunched over the table, the newspaper spread out in front of her. An empty salad bowl sat off to the side. He looked at her beautiful face, at her long, graceful neck, at the cascade of blond hair falling over her shoulder like a golden waterfall, and he knew a moment of loss that took his breath away.

Just then she flipped the page and glanced up. Her eyes locked on him and her lips parted.

He approached slowly, his heart going a hundred beats per minute. He hoped against hope he could find the words to heal the damage he'd caused. Not because he wanted her so badly—though he did. But because she hadn't deserved this.

By the time he reached her table, her lips were pressed into a tight line. Her chin was high, and the wary look in her eyes hollowed out a place deep inside him.

"I've been looking for you all day," he said.

"I've been avoiding you all day."

He absorbed the jab. "Fair enough. May I sit down?"

She wavered while his heart hung in the balance. She crossed her arms on the table in front of her, as if she were trying to form a barrier between them.

His chest squeezed tight.

"I guess so," she said.

He pulled out the chair across from her and sank into it, his back loosening from the hours he'd spent on his feet today. But the ache was replaced a dozenfold by the distrustful look on her face.

"Daisy . . ." He swallowed hard against the knot that had formed in his throat. "I need to ask your forgiveness. There aren't words to express how sorry I am for what I did. I wish I could take it all back. The last thing I ever intended to do was hurt you—you have to believe that."

She looked down at the table. A shadow flickered on her jaw.

He wanted to grab her hand, but he knew his touch wouldn't be welcomed. He leaned forward on his elbows, waiting for a response. Anything. He wished she'd yell at him or hit him or something.

Finally she raised her eyes. He met her guarded

gaze and nearly crumbled at the evidence of recent tears. He'd never regretted anything so badly as he did this very minute.

"Why, Jack? *Why?*"

"That's a fair question, and you deserve an honest answer."

"You intentionally deceived me. And you're a *pastor,* Jack."

He shook his head slowly. "Don't put me on a pedestal, Daisy. I don't belong there."

"Clearly."

He winced. All right. He deserved that.

"Were you just going to show up Monday and let me see who you were? Did you think I was going to be happy about this?"

"No . . . no, I knew you'd be upset. When you asked me about meeting in person, I decided I'd tell you before Monday. But I was going to wait until after the concert. I knew you were busy and anxious about it, and I didn't want to—"

"Break my heart?"

His face burned with shame. "What I did was wrong, no matter my motives, and I accept full responsibility. I'm ashamed of what I did, ashamed that I let it go on so long. But what I'm most ashamed of, Daisy . . . is that I hurt the woman I love."

Jack's words pushed the air from Daisy's lungs. The woman he loved? She stared into his eyes.

Vulnerability and fear stared back. "I've been a monumental idiot. And because of that, I'm going to promise you complete honesty from this point on—and that means baring my heart no matter how hard it is."

He cleared his throat, maintaining eye contact. "Daisy . . . I've had feelings for you for quite some time now. I think you're aware there's been something happening between us the last several weeks. But for me it's been going on a lot longer than that."

Daisy couldn't look away from the intensity in his eyes. "How long?"

"A long time. Months." He pulled in a breath. "Over two years."

Two years? She blinked. How could she not have known? She thought back on the times she'd gone into his office and unloaded on him. All the times she'd sought his advice and leaned on him, he'd never given her any reason to believe . . .

"Why didn't you say something, Jack?"

"Honestly?" he said with a rueful laugh. "Daisy, I didn't think I had a snowball's chance with you. You're so . . . beautiful and caring and smart and—"

"Smart," she scoffed. How could he say that when he knew about her dyslexia? When he'd seen her misspellings and typos, seen her verbally flounder in her own mother tongue on camera?

"Yes, smart. Not to mention creative and

talented and amazing. Besides, you only saw me as your pastor—an authority figure of sorts. I was afraid that knowing how I felt would scare you away at best. Or creep you out at worst. I was afraid of losing the friendship we were finally building—it was my only connection to you."

"So you just jumped online and made up a fake person?"

"TJ isn't fake. He's me. But you didn't know that, and it was wrong to hide my real identity. This is not an excuse, just an explanation, but I wanted to get to know you in a different setting. I wanted so badly for you to see me as an ordinary man, Daisy."

"Well . . . mission accomplished."

His eyes squeezed in a grimace.

She felt a prick of guilt. But what he'd done was wrong. He'd made a decision to deceive her every time he'd written her. He'd had plenty of opportunities to come clean, but he hadn't.

Daisy startled as he pushed back his chair and stood. Her heart thudded in her chest at the defeat in his face.

He gave her a sad smile. "I get it, Daisy. I really do. You trusted me, and I let you down. You'll never know how sorry I am for that."

As she watched him walk away, all of her anger drained away, and an aching sadness rose to fill its place.

THIRTY-FIVE

The musty scent of hymnals lingered in the sanctuary, mingling with a hint of old-lady perfume. Daisy worked her way up to her usual pew, smiling at fellow members along the way.

"Good morning, sweet pea," her grandma said as Daisy slid into the pew beside her.

"Good morning, Gram. Where's Mama?"

"She has nursery this morning—it's second Sunday."

"Oh, that's right. I wonder if she needs any help." Anything would be better than staring up at Jack behind the pulpit for an hour. Since his declaration yesterday she'd been a wreck.

"Already checked. She's got it covered."

Daisy sighed. "How was the shop yesterday?"

"Pretty slow. We might close up next year during Peachfest. I didn't see you at the festival last night."

"Oh, I was there. I went home early though."

"You feeling all right? You seem kind of down this morning. After the concert's success, I figured you'd be on cloud nine."

She gave her grandma a weak smile. "Well, the

interview afterward brought me back down to earth with a hard thump."

"Oh, now. It wasn't all that bad. I'm sure you were just excited—anyone would've been."

"The video is all over the Internet. Have you ever seen anyone that tongue-tied? Or that shade of green?"

"Well, I'm sure everyone was too busy looking at that handsome singer to even notice. Twenty-five thousand dollars is nothing to sneeze at, young lady. The Hope House will have the money they need, and the girls will get their home back. That's all that really matters."

"You're right." Never mind that she'd looked stupid in front of the whole country. Pretty much her worst fear.

But that didn't hurt half as much as what Jack had done. She'd replayed his words all night—his declaration of love. She'd tossed and turned, remembering things he'd said and done the past couple of years, trying to view them in light of her new discovery. It was beginning to change her outlook.

Gram nudged her. "So how's it going with that online fellow? Have you met him yet?"

Daisy gave a sad smile. "I'm afraid it's not going too well, Gram." Understatement of the century right there.

"Let you down, did he?"

"You could say that."

Her grandma squeezed her arm, giving Daisy one of those pointed looks she was famous for. "You know, honey . . . sometimes you just have to extend a little grace to people. Not because they deserve it—but because we don't deserve it either."

Daisy bristled a little as the words hit the center of her chest and burrowed deep. Her grandma didn't even know what her "online fellow" had done. She'd be upset too if she knew that her pastor had tried to put one over on Daisy.

Wouldn't she?

But maybe Gram had a point too. Was Daisy really lacking in grace? Was that what Gram was trying to say? Daisy knew she had to forgive others. And, okay, she hadn't really done much of that lately. She hadn't forgiven her dad or her mom, and now she had to add Jack to that list.

The casualties were kind of piling up, if she were honest.

The piano music came to an end, and Daisy watched the stage door for Jack's entrance. But it was the assistant pastor who entered instead and took a seat on the stage. Where was Jack? She looked around but didn't see him anywhere.

The choir director came forward and led the robed choir in a chorus. Their harmonies blended beautifully, their voices echoing through the high-ceilinged sanctuary.

When the song ended, the director led the

congregation in a hymn, and Daisy joined in numbly. When they were finished, the assistant pastor took the pulpit and began a sermon.

Pastor Davies was a good teacher, but Daisy's mind wandered a lot during the next forty-five minutes. Thoughts of Jack and her dad and her mom filled her head . . . along with the disturbing realization that she'd already heard the message she most needed to hear.

Sun shone through the window behind the altar, making the colors in the stained glass vibrant, making the picture come to life. Jack's heart hurt, looking at the image of Jesus on the cross, the thorned crown pressing into His head, droplets of blood flowing down His cheeks.

In the quiet of the empty sanctuary, Jack felt the weight of his sin like a cement block on his chest. He'd already asked God's forgiveness and knew He'd granted it. *As far as the east is from the west, so far has He removed our transgressions from us.*

He'd asked Daisy's forgiveness also. He was pretty sure he hadn't received it, but he'd done all he could. He couldn't turn back time and make a different decision. There was nothing else he could do but wait and hope she found it in her heart to forgive him.

So why the heavy weight? Why the burden of guilt? Maybe this was just the way a man was destined to feel when he hurt the woman he loved.

A shuffle behind him drew his attention. He turned to see Noah coming down the center aisle, still in his Sunday jeans and button-down shirt. His hair looked black as tar in the shadows.

"Forget something?" Jack asked.

"In a manner of speaking." Noah settled in the pew beside him. "What are you doing, sitting here all alone?"

"Just thinking."

"It's so quiet in here. I'm used to all the noise of people and music, the random crying baby."

"I like it like this." Especially when he was indulging in self-reflection.

"I heard how much money the concert raised. That's amazing. Lucille's already called about the renovations, and I've got a crew going over there tomorrow to work up an estimate. They'll have more than enough money, though. Maybe even enough for a few upgrades."

"That's great. An answered prayer."

"We can have it done in four, maybe five weeks, if the weather cooperates."

"Thanks to you. And to Kade Patrick—and Daisy, of course."

Noah gave him a steady look. His amber eyes were darkened to brown in the dim sanctuary. "I heard what happened between you two."

"I figured. Half the town probably knows by now."

"I think we can keep it to our friend group. Jack . . . I'm really sorry. I feel like this whole thing is my fault. It was my idea—I started that profile. You didn't even want to do it. I talked you into it."

"It was my decision, Noah. You didn't hold a gun to my head."

"Still . . . I feel responsible. I want you to know I apologized to Daisy after church today for my part in all this." He squeezed his eyes in a wince. "Man, that look in her eyes . . ."

"Tell me about it." He'd seen that look over and over in his head the last two days. It broke his heart every time.

She'd never again look at him as she used to, her eyes filled with trust and respect. That infectious smile spreading across her face.

There would be no more small talks, no more advising sessions, and certainly no more rock-climbing. He'd been her pastor and her friend, and he'd broken her trust. He didn't even deserve a second chance.

Now there was only regret, and he was finding it to be a bitter companion.

"Thanks for apologizing to Daisy. I do appreciate that."

"Least I could do, considering."

"I wish I'd at least owned up to the whole thing before she found out, you know? I think that hurt her most of all. She's already had such a difficult summer, and what I did just added to her heartache. She trusted me, and I betrayed that trust. I have a feeling she'll never fully get beyond that."

She hadn't yet gotten beyond what her dad and mom had done. She'd probably lost all faith in humanity by now. He could only pray she hadn't lost faith in God. Jack would never forgive himself then.

"Is there anything else I can do?" Noah asked. "I feel like I should, I don't know, send flowers or say a dozen Hail Marys or something."

"That's the church up the street." He gave Noah a weak smile. He didn't blame his friend, but he understood what Noah was feeling. "How about I just say 'I forgive you' and we move on from there, huh, pal?"

Noah's shoulders sank on an exhale. "Those are powerful words. I'm really starting to appreciate them."

"Indeed they are."

They sat in silence for a long moment. The air kicked on, a low hum in the quiet. The pendant chandeliers swayed against the draft of air.

"Where were you today?" Noah asked. "Not that there's anything wrong with Pastor Davies, but it's a rare Sunday you give up the pulpit."

He'd made the decision last night after talking to Daisy. How could he preach to his flock when he'd failed so horribly? He felt unworthy to stand in front of the church this morning. What would they think if they knew what he'd done?

"I just couldn't do it, you know? I feel as if I've let everyone down."

Noah's hand clapped onto his shoulder. "I know just how you feel, buddy. Believe me, I've blown it a time or two myself. But don't beat yourself up over this. And don't forget to give yourself a little of that grace you give so freely to others."

"You know what I'm learning, friend?" Jack gave him a wan smile, the realization dawning even as the words formed on his tongue. "Sometimes it's a lot easier to give than to receive."

THIRTY-SIX

Daisy pulled into the Mellow Mug's parking lot and found an empty space along the building's brick wall. Her mom had texted her after church and asked her to meet there tonight— which was weird because her mom didn't believe in paying more than a dollar for a cup of coffee.

Maybe she'd decided not to sell the house. Or maybe someone had put in an offer. Daisy didn't really care anymore. It was just a house. She'd always have her memories—even though they'd been somewhat sullied by this summer's revelations.

When she entered the coffee shop, the rush of cool air brushed her skin, and the rich smell of roasted beans scented the air. She'd seen her mom's Caprice in the parking lot but didn't see her in the front of the shop.

Daisy stopped at the counter and ordered Darjeeling tea with a splash of milk. She answered a text from Hope as she waited. Her friends were worried about her, but she'd be fine just as soon as she figured out what she was going to do with all these feelings of betrayal. All these disappointments in the people who supposedly loved her.

When her tea was ready, she took the cup and saucer and walked toward the back of the shop. She spotted her mom at a corner gathering place, a sofa and two armchairs. But someone was in the armchair opposite Karen.

Daisy nearly spilled her tea when she recognized the long mahogany hair.

"Julia."

Her sister turned and gave her a wobbly smile. "Hey, Daisy." Julia's eyes were bloodshot, and she'd shredded the tissue in her lap.

Daisy turned a dark look on her mom. "What's going on here, Mama? What are you doing?"

"Settle down, Daisy. I invited Julia here."

For what? Had her mother asked Julia to leave town? To distance herself from Daisy? Had she found yet another way of keeping Julia out of her life? Her heart squeezed painfully at the thought of losing someone else.

Julia squeezed Daisy's hand. "It's okay. Have a seat."

Daisy's legs trembled as she took the other armchair. She set her untouched tea on the coffee table and braced herself for more bad news. She couldn't handle another revelation. Another betrayal. If her mom had done anything to hurt Julia . . .

"Is somebody going to tell me what's going on?"

"Honey, it's okay," her mother said. "I invited

Julia here to apologize. The decision your father and I made to put it all behind us wasn't fair to Julia or you. It was shortsighted and selfish—I know that now. I actually knew it long before now, to be honest, but my life was just too comfortable to risk stirring things up again."

Daisy gave a slight shake of her head and looked at Julia.

"It's true, she apologized," Julia said. "We've been talking for over an hour."

Her mom's eyes misted over. "I regret that your dad never had a chance to know his other daughter. I know he regretted it too, even though we didn't talk about it. We just went on as if it had never happened, but it was there. I saw a look in his eyes sometimes—there was an empty spot in his heart that even Daisy and I couldn't fill. I think he carried that guilt with him the rest of his life."

Daisy was still trying to grasp that her mom had apologized. But she could see remorse in the tightness at the corners of her eyes, in the pinch of her mouth.

"I've accepted your mom's apology," Julia told Daisy, then looked at Karen. "You've been very kind, Mrs. Pendleton. I appreciate your inviting me here."

"Please, call me Karen. And you've been very gracious, Julia."

"On that note . . ." Julia gathered her purse and

empty mug. "I think I'll take off and give you two a chance to talk."

"Thank you for meeting with me," Karen said.

"Of course." Julia gave her a warm smile, then turned to Daisy. "We'll talk soon, okay?"

"I'll call you."

Julia was a few tables away when Karen called out and stopped her. "I hope you'll join Daisy and me for Thursday suppers at my house—until you have to go back home. It's kind of a family tradition."

A beautiful smile bloomed on Julia's lips. "I'd love to, Karen. Thank you. Let me know what I can bring."

Daisy's gaze flew back to her mom's as Julia slipped away. What had just happened? She felt as if she'd been transported to an alternative universe.

Her mother took a leisurely sip of coffee. "Stop looking at me like that. I *am* capable of acknowledging when I'm wrong, you know."

"If you say so."

"Oh pooh. I'm not that stubborn. Besides . . . your grandma got hold of me. She has a way of making me feel like I'm fifteen all over again—and not in a good way."

Daisy's lips twitched. She wondered if Karen knew that she had the very same effect on her daughter.

"I didn't mean for Julia to be here when you

arrived, honey. That must've been quite the shock. I honestly expected she'd be long gone, but she was much kinder than I deserved, and we found so much to talk about."

Her mom set the mug in the saucer and leaned forward, clasping her hands. "And now, honey, I need to ask your forgiveness. The decision your dad and I made all those years ago had a huge impact on you too. We kept your sister from you. I know there's nothing I can do to change the past, but I wish there were. Can you ever forgive me, honey?" Tears trembled on her mother's lashes.

Daisy blinked as her grandma's words played over in her mind. *Sometimes you have to extend a little grace to people. Not because they deserve it—but because we don't deserve it either.*

Her grandma was right. Daisy wasn't perfect either. She'd messed up plenty. Who was to say she wouldn't have done the same thing if she'd been in her mother's shoes? If she'd been betrayed by the husband she loved?

Besides, if Julia could forgive her mom, surely Daisy had it in her to do the same. "Of course I'll forgive you, Mama."

Karen stood as Daisy skirted the table and pulled her mother close. A weight lifted from Daisy's shoulders as her mom's arms came around her.

Karen pulled back and cupped Daisy's face.

"Honey . . . I do hope you'll find it within yourself to forgive your father too. He wasn't a perfect man, but he sure did love his baby girl."

He had loved her. She'd felt that love, and it had helped shape her into the woman she was. She would find the grace to forgive her father because grace brought healing and peace. And all their lives could use a little more of both.

THIRTY-SEVEN

Monday was dragging by at a snail's pace. The store was slow, and Daisy no longer had the concert to keep her busy. Gram had gone home at noon, leaving only Daisy and her mom.

Things were better between them since their chat last night. Better even than they'd been before Daisy had learned about Julia. Not only was the elephant in the room gone, but there was an openness to her mother she'd never experienced before. It was as if acknowledging her part in Julia's abandonment had set her free. It was a beautiful thing to see.

"Oh, honey, that's so lovely. Mrs. Murdock is going to adore it."

"Thanks, Mama."

The girls of the Hope House had ordered the bouquet for the CEO's birthday. The white basket was perfect for the arrangement. Daisy had offset the blue hydrangea with white blooms and tossed in some white delphinium and lemon leaf. Her final embellishments were carefully placed birch twigs that took off in unexpected directions, adding interest and dimension.

Her mom picked up a fallen bloom from the

floor and set it on the table. "I saw the Mitchell Home Improvement truck out at the Hope House on my way in. They're wasting no time getting started."

"The sooner the better. Those girls are eager to be home, I hear. I know Millie is. Ava's on her last nerve and vice versa."

"Sometimes it's best for sisters to just be sisters," Karen said as she retreated to the office.

Daisy thought about all the girls as she arranged the twigs just so. Maybe Daisy's parents weren't perfect, but at least she'd had a mom and dad who'd loved her and taken care of her. That was more than she could say for most of the girls at the Hope House.

In the past twenty-four hours, Daisy had found her heart softening, especially toward her dad. And seeing the new joy her mom had found was all the impetus she'd needed to forgive him. Her grandma had been right. She didn't deserve to receive grace if she couldn't freely give it. So she'd chosen to forgive. She'd chosen freedom.

But then there was Jack. Her feelings for him were more muddled and complicated. The past couple days she'd found herself missing TJ, only to remember there wasn't a TJ. Last week she'd made plans to meet him in person tonight, and Daisy couldn't help but wonder what would've happened if TJ had been real.

But he wasn't.

The bell over the door jingled. Daisy's eyes flew to the entrance, her heart suddenly thumping in anticipation.

But it wasn't Jack, coming to apologize again. It was only Mr. Francis.

"Be right with you," she called. Then she glanced at her mom through the office window and had a better idea. "Mama, can you get that? I'm just finishing this arrangement."

The office chair squeaked as her mother stood. "Of course, honey."

Karen perched her readers on top of her head as she stepped around the debris on the floor, making her way to the front.

Daisy watched from beneath her lashes, going still so she didn't miss anything.

Her mom paused by the register when she spotted Mr. Francis. "Oh. Hello, Dan."

The man's cheeks were pink, outdone only by the red at the tips of his ears.

"Hello, Karen. How are you today?"

"I'm just fine. And you?" Her mom's voice was warm and welcoming.

Mr. Francis blinked his big brown eyes in surprise. "Quite well, thank you."

Karen took a step closer. "I wanted to mention that I stopped by the gallery and took a peek at your work. You have some beautiful pieces on display there."

Daisy didn't think it was possible for his ears to get redder, but they did.

"I— Thank you, Karen. It's really just a hobby."

"Nonsense, you're a very talented artist. I purchased one of the paintings," her mom blurted out, then began fiddling with her apron tie.

"You don't say. Which one, if you don't mind my asking?"

"The one of Pleasant Gap with the red barn in the background. I've always loved barns. My parents were farmers back in the day, and we had an old barn on the property. I loved playing there as a child."

He gave a nod of approval. "That's wonderful. That particular painting is one of my favorites. I would've given it to you, though, if you'd told me you wanted it."

"It was worth every penny. It'll look divine in my new house."

His eyebrows hitched up. "Oh, you're moving?"

"Well, not right away. I have to sell my house first. But a good offer just came in this morning, and I think I'm going to accept it."

"That's wonderful. Where are you looking to move? Not far, I hope."

"Not at all. I'd just like a smaller house, something a little closer to the shop."

"Let me know if I can help. I'm no contractor, but I've done many a repair job over the years. I more or less know what to look for."

"I might take you up on that," Karen said, nearly toppling Daisy from her stool. "I know next to nothing about furnaces and roofing and such. Paul handled all that."

He nodded, a wistful smile on his face. "Judy was the same way. Just say the word, and I'm there."

"That's very kind. Thank you."

An awkward pause ensued. Mr. Francis fiddled with his keys while Karen retied her apron strings.

"So . . . ," her mom said finally. "What can I get you today, Dan? Are you looking for flowers for another still life?"

"Aw." He ducked his head, looking up at her sheepishly. "I think we both know I'm not."

Karen's shoulders rose on a deep inhale. "Right. Well, I'm glad you stopped by. I was hoping I could change my mind on your offer for coffee."

Daisy watched breathlessly as a smile spread across Mr. Francis's face.

"Yes, ma'am. I'd like that very much."

"Wonderful. Are you free Friday afternoon? Say, around four o'clock?"

"I certainly am. Should I pick you up here or at your house?"

"Oh, let's just make it here. It'll be a lot easier for both of us."

Mr. Francis was already backing away, a goofy

grin on his face. "Sounds good, Karen. I'll see you then."

Daisy winced as he backed into one of the displays, nearly toppling a planter and a ceramic dish.

"Oh good heavens." He turned to straighten the items. "I'm so sorry."

Karen dashed forward. "No harm done. I'll take care of it."

Mr. Francis seemed eager for the chance to escape, and he'd apparently forgotten whatever he'd come in for. "Thank you. See you Friday, Karen."

"Good-bye, Dan. Have a wonderful afternoon."

The bells tinkled on his exit, and the happy sound echoed in Daisy's heart.

THIRTY-EIGHT

Dark clouds and nearly 90 percent humidity had chased everyone away from Murphy's Park on Monday night. Jack leaned forward on the wooden gazebo steps, his elbows digging into his knees. Behind him the creek rippled by, and overhead leaves brushed together under the warm breeze. Branches clapped rhythmically as if mocking his monumentally stupid idea of coming here tonight.

His deep breath stretched the achy muscles of his chest. This wasn't how it was supposed to go.

It wasn't that he expected Daisy to show up after everything that had transpired. In fact, he thought, looking at his watch for the tenth time in as many minutes, she'd already stood him up. No, he'd only come to torture himself a bit. To remind himself why you shouldn't lie to the woman you love. It never turned out well.

He couldn't get Daisy out of his mind. He prayed for her continually, that God would heal her heart. That He would soothe her hurt. *He heals the brokenhearted and binds up their wounds.* Jack knew the words were true. Not only because it was Scripture, but because he'd seen it play out in his own life. In the lives of those around him.

He prayed Daisy would find it in her heart to forgive him. Not because he expected a second chance, but because he didn't want her carrying the burden of unforgiveness. He'd seen too many others turn bitter and cynical. He couldn't bear to see that happen to her.

He thought of the stupid app that had drawn him into all this. He pulled his phone from his pocket and opened it. It was time to delete his profile once and for all. Close this chapter of his life. His bio appeared, along with the vague pictures that bore little resemblance to him in his everyday life.

His eyes automatically drifted to the envelope icon, a little hope still tucked away in his heart. It drained away at the absence of a waiting message. Resolutely, he clicked on Settings, then on Delete Profile. A message prompted him: *Are you sure?*

Oh yes. His lips curled wryly. He was sure. He touched the Yes button. *Your profile has been deleted,* it said. He pocketed his phone, feeling miserable all over again.

A red squirrel nattered from the base of an ancient oak tree, then scampered across the grass, stopping a dozen feet away. Its beady little rodent eyes stared at him unflinchingly while its bushy tail twitched. The animal stood, hunching on its backside, and began chirping at Jack.

Jack scowled at the critter. "Get in line, buddy."

With a final wave of its tail, the squirrel scampered up the nearest tree. Jack watched it go higher and higher until it disappeared into a nest of leaves and twigs.

Jack scanned the canopy overhead, noticing for the first time that the leaves were turned over, exposing their bottom sides. That usually meant—

A dollop of rain hit him right in the forehead, and he blinked. A second landed on his nose, followed by another on the back of his hand.

"Great. It figures."

A steady rain began falling, and he stood with a sigh, remembering the long walk back through the park to his car. He was going to be drenched by the time he got there.

He'd taken a few steps and was about to pick up his speed when he saw a flash of red up the path. He zeroed in on the petite figure. On the blond hair and the green eyes staring back at him.

"Daisy," he whispered. He had stopped walking, he realized, and so had she. Of their own volition his legs started working again, closing the gap between them.

And then she was walking too. Running, in fact.

Daisy couldn't take her eyes off Jack even as she ran toward him. She'd seen him sitting there from a distance, looking so forlorn, and her heart had broken at the sight.

She didn't know if he'd even show up tonight, and she was so late she didn't think he'd still be here even if he had. But here he was, rushing toward her, love shining in his eyes.

When she reached him, she threw her arms around him and held him tight. He felt so good against her. She turned her face into his chest and breathed deeply of his familiar scent. How could she miss so badly something she'd never even had?

"Daisy," he whispered, wonder in his voice. "You came."

She wrapped one hand around the hard curve of his bicep and palmed the back of his neck with her other.

"I can't believe you're here." He pulled her tighter, as if he might never let her go, and set his cheek against the top of her head. "I didn't expect you to show up. Am I dreaming? Don't wake me up."

The rain had turned into a steady patter, but he shielded her from the worst of it.

"You're getting soaked," she said.

"I don't care. Just let me hold you. I'm so sorry, Daisy. I've been so full of regret I can hardly stand myself."

She pulled away and set her fingers on his lips. "Stop. It's okay. I know you didn't mean to hurt me."

He started to respond, but she pressed her fingers more firmly against his lips. "You don't have to apologize any more. I understand why you did what you did. And you were right. I put you on a pedestal, just like I did my dad. And that's not fair to either of us. It only set us both up for a fall."

He took her wrist and pulled her fingers from his lips. "I was wrong, and I let you down."

"Noah told me what happened with the Flutter app. Why didn't you tell me he set it all up?"

"I didn't want to make excuses. It was ultimately my decision, not his."

She loved that he took full responsibility. She looked deeply into his eyes and wondered if he knew how sexy that particular trait was.

She'd reviewed her chats with TJ in her mind all weekend. Everything he'd said. It was all so Jack. In retrospect, she wondered how she hadn't seen it. "I was falling for him, you know . . . TJ."

Uncertainty flickered in his eyes, and the corners of his mouth drooped. "Oh. I see."

She squeezed his hand and fell headlong into

his deep brown eyes. "I was falling for you too, Jack."

He closed his eyes briefly. "That must've been very confusing."

She gave a wry laugh. "I'll admit I was feeling pretty torn."

"I'm so sorry, Daisy. Can you ever forgive me?"

She smiled at him—because in giving grace, she received hope and joy. "I already have, Jack."

His exhalation stirred the hair at her temple. "Thank you." He brushed her knuckles with his lips. "It's humbling to be on this side of the fence. I can't say I like it, but I sure do appreciate your forgiving spirit. And I feel like we need to talk about something else, Daisy—get it out in the open. You admitted things on Flutter that you never divulged to me directly. I realize that was a serious breach of trust."

"My dyslexia, you mean. It's been a real insecurity in the past, I'll admit. But I've been coming to grips with all that. Working with Millie has helped me see things a little differently."

"Your dyslexia is just a small part of you. But it's part of what made you who you are—and I happen to love who you are, Daisy Pendleton."

She blinked against the sting in her eyes. He had a way of making her feel okay. She remembered the way TJ had responded to her admission so tenderly, so carefully. That was Jack. All Jack.

"I was afraid it would change how you looked at me, Jack. That's why I never told you. I only told TJ because . . . well, because his friendship didn't matter to me at that point as much as yours did. And when he confessed his own insecurities, it made me feel it was safe to admit my own."

He brushed a thumb across her cheek. "Those insecurities are real, Daisy. I still feel like that gangly, awkward boy sometimes. And I always want you to feel safe with me. There's nothing you can tell me about yourself that'll make me stop loving you."

Her chest squeezed tight, and her throat constricted. That sounded so wonderful. How did he always know exactly what she needed to hear?

"I want to believe that," she said.

"It's true." His gaze sharpened on hers as he gently palmed her face. "If you give me a chance, I'll prove it to you."

Oh, that deep voice. It scraped right across her heart, like a match against a striking surface, lighting a fire inside her. "I'd like that very much."

She could drown in those deep brown eyes. They stared back at her with such affection. Such love. She could hardly believe she inspired those things in him.

His gaze fell to her lips, locking there for a long moment, and her breath caught in her lungs.

Then he leaned forward and brushed her lips.

The kiss was sweet, unhurried, and measured, like Jack himself.

When he returned for seconds, she gladly yielded to him. Her hands trembled as she pressed them against the warmth of his chest. The woodsy scent of him filled her lungs, making her incapable of coherent thought.

He cupped her cheeks, his fingers threading into her hair. She lost herself in his kiss, in his reverent touch, until the world around them closed in. Until it was only the two of them, his love like a protective cocoon around them.

That's what Jack did to her. He'd worked his way into her heart and made her forget all her self-doubt. All her shortcomings. He believed in her. Saw the best in her, and that filled her with hope and confidence. He was so good for her. She hoped she was just as good for him.

When he eased away, he set his forehead against hers, his eyes still closed. "My heart's beating so fast right now."

She gave a breathy sigh, feeling the truth of his words against her palm. "Mine too."

He opened his eyes, his gaze locking on hers. "We're getting soaked."

"I couldn't care less."

"Me neither." He drew away, still touching her face. His hair was wet now, his lashes spiky over his hooded eyes.

Raindrops trickled down Daisy's cheeks like

tears of joy. She remembered his position in the church, and her own inadequacies tweaked at her conscience.

"Are you sure about this, Jack? I never saw myself with a pastor, and the last thing I'd want to do is hinder your ministry in any way."

"I have no doubt you'll be an asset to my ministry, Daisy. And I hope to be your biggest supporter."

That sounded perfect. Just what she needed to hear. She swallowed hard and searched his eyes for a long moment. "I guess I've been a little worried you might . . . get bored with me."

"Daisy . . ." Jack breathed the word. He gently swept away the raindrops, his touch as soft as a whisper. "I wish you could climb inside my head right now and know all the wonderful things I think about you. Then you'd know I could never get bored with you, and you'd see why I love you so very much."

Her eyes burned with unshed tears. "I love you too, Jack," she said, meaning it with all her heart.

His eyes searched hers, and he must've found what he was looking for because he closed the distance between them. He took her lips in a lingering kiss. The kind she could happily live with for the rest of her life.

When he eased away, his eyes locked on hers. "Oh, Daisy . . . I really didn't expect a second chance, but I'm so grateful for it. You've made me one happy man, you know that?"

The adoring way he looked at her made it easy to believe every word he said. Especially the good ones. She could still hardly grasp that he'd cared for her for so long. That he'd waited so patiently for her. That he loved her so deeply.

"I can't believe this is happening," she said.

"And if I have anything to say about it, it's going to keep happening for a very, very long time."

Something told her that being loved by Jack would be a very special thing. She didn't need to doubt it. It was all right there in his reverent kiss, his tender touch, and his soulful eyes.

"I like the sound of that," she said.

EPILOGUE

The morning of Saturday, July 13, dawned sunny and bright. The clear blue sky was a striking contrast with the Blue Ridge Mountains, which stood sentinel behind the majestic Hope House.

The property was buzzing with people as Daisy made her way across the sloped lawn, where a crowd had already gathered. The smell of freshly cut grass and the sweet scent of lilacs lingered in the air.

The renovations were complete on the sprawling old mansion, and the damaged wing of the house now looked as good as new—better even. There'd been money left over, and the crisp white paint and shingled roof made the place look almost brand new.

It felt good to know she'd had a small part in the project. One look at the girls' smiling faces was all the reward she needed. Daisy joined her mom and Julia at the back of the crowd, greeting them both with hugs.

Julia had decided to stay in Copper Creek until summer's end. She'd been joining them for Thursday supper the past several weeks. It was a little awkward at first. But Karen had been gracious and happy to feed Julia's curiosity about her dad. They'd recounted story after story and watched home videos until late at night. They'd all laughed and cried as Julia slowly learned about the man who'd been her father.

"Here we go," Karen whispered. "It's about to begin."

The residents and staff were gathered behind the ribbon with Mayor Walters. Three news crews were set up opposite them, and filming was now under way. Mayor Walters was speaking into a microphone, and Lucille stood nearby, waiting to chime in on behalf of the Hope House.

Daisy was glad to be safely behind the scenes, right where she belonged.

An arm slipped around her from behind, and a gentle kiss landed on her temple. "Sorry I'm late," a voice whispered.

She turned a smile on Jack as a shiver of pleasure ran through her. Would she ever get used to his kiss? She hoped not.

"It's okay," she said. "I'm glad you made it."

He took her hand as they listened to the mayor elaborate on the renovations. Daisy couldn't help but remember the ribbon cuttings her dad had presided over as mayor. Daddy had been a better speaker than Mayor Walters, more charismatic and entertaining. Mayor Walters tended to pontificate in a monotone.

After ten long minutes Jack leaned close. "Please tell me I'm not this boring."

"Not even close." She winked at him. "Besides, you're much nicer to look at."

She loved the way his eyes smiled just before his lips. They'd spent a lot of time together the past several weeks. Sometimes he took her out to eat or rock-climbing, and sometimes they met at Murphy's Park. It had become their favorite place. They walked the trails and swung in the swings like children. Once Jack had pushed her on the merry-go-round until she was so dizzy she was ready to fall off. Most of all they just talked. She loved talking with Jack.

The news that they were dating had spread quickly through the church and the rest of the community. Daisy was relieved that the casserole brigade had ceased its relentless pursuit. If anyone was going to cook for Jack, it was going to be her.

Jack was still a little self-conscious about their age difference—it was kind of cute. And no one seemed to think she was an awful match for him. Daisy was beginning to see that it had all been in her head. She wasn't unfit to be a pastor's wife—if things should wind up going that direction.

Jack had been right. She was already ministering to people and meeting their needs as a part of her own job. Being a pastor's wife wouldn't be so different. And now that she was learning to give herself a little grace, she didn't have to dread being in the spotlight either. She wasn't perfect, and she was learning to be okay with that.

When Mayor Walters finally finished his monologue, Lucille said a few words. She thanked the festival committee, Mitchell Home Improvement, Daisy, all the volunteers, and especially Kade Patrick for donating the profits from the concert.

When she finished, the mayor held the scissors up to the ribbon, pausing long enough for the photographers to capture the moment. Then, in a grand gesture, he snipped the ribbon. The crowd applauded wildly. The girls of Hope House high-fived each other. Daisy couldn't stop smiling.

A few moments later the group broke up, some moving on to the refreshments spread out on picnic tables and others heading to the house for the grand tour. Many of the girls came over to hug Daisy and tell her thank you.

She was smiling as she and Jack meandered across the lawn, finding Noah and Josephine by the refreshment table, Nicolas napping nearby in his stroller.

Jack put out his hand and greeted Noah with a shoulder bump. "Nice job on the renovations, buddy. I can't wait to see the inside."

Noah grinned, surveying the home's exterior. "It turned out pretty good."

Josephine curled into her husband's side, her

blond tresses a beautiful contrast to Noah's dark hair. "He's being modest. It's fabulous. Wait'll you see it."

"We're taking a tour when the line dies down," Daisy said. "The girls seem thrilled."

"They sure do," Jack said. "How's business, Josephine? I keep meaning to come by for a trim, but something always comes up."

"It's going great. In fact, we've been so busy I had to hire a new stylist last week. She's really good too."

Hope and Brady glided up to the group, and there were greetings all around.

Daisy reached for Sammy, who was in Brady's arms, and the toddler came to her, grinning his adorable toothy grin. "How's my boy, huh? Auntie Daisy has missed you." She turned a look on Brady and Hope. "Your mommy and daddy don't bring you around on Saturday nights any-more."

Brady curled an arm around Hope, giving his wife an amorous look. "It's called date night. You'll understand one day."

Daisy hoped so.

They talked about the renovations for a while, the men breaking off from the women as the girls caught up with each other, talking kids and work.

Soon Cruz and Zoe joined them, little Gracie in tow. She was her mom's mini-me with her adorable auburn curls and freckled nose.

Daisy hugged Zoe and gushed over Gracie in her green sundress. "I'm glad you guys could make it. I know you're busy right now." Peachfest kicked off peach season, and Cruz was busy with the harvest while Zoe managed the Peach Barn.

"We wouldn't miss it for the world," Zoe said. "Noah, the renovations look spectacular. We just finished up the tour."

"Thanks. My crew did a great job. They donated their time, you know."

"Wow, that's cool of them," Cruz said. "We're proud of you too, Daisy. It's amazing the way you pulled all this off."

"Thank you. Everybody really came together. It was a community effort."

Jack squeezed her hand. "The line's died down. You ready for that tour?"

"Absolutely." She gave Sammy a kiss on the cheek and handed him off to Hope. "We'll see you guys later tonight."

Ava and Millie led their group through the new wing, proudly pointing out every detail. Millie had been working hard the past five weeks on her reading. She was still going to be held back a year, but she was heartened by the progress her new tools had brought her.

It was obvious from her beaming grin that the little girl was happy to be back in the home with her friends. It was better for both of them when

Ava was free to just be her big sister, not her parent.

The smell of raw lumber and fresh paint blended with the tang of excitement. The girls had gotten new furniture and bedding as well, as those things had been ruined in the storm.

"You should be very proud of yourself," Jack said after the tour as he walked Daisy, hand in hand, to her car. "You did a good thing here, Daisy."

"The girls seem happy, don't they? So excited to show off their new things. It does the heart good."

He squeezed her hand, his eyes piercing hers. "*You* do *my* heart good."

Daisy couldn't stop the smile that lifted her lips as she turned at her car door, facing Jack. He said the nicest things. And he said them often. "Right back atcha, Jack McReady."

He leaned toward her, setting his palm against her car, trapping her there. His eyes slowly scanned her face with a flicker of male appreciation.

"Don't forget we have a date tonight," he said.

Her blood hummed at the way he looked at her. "As if I would. Are you sure I can't bring something?"

"I've got it covered."

"Of course you do." Jack was extremely capable. One of his many good qualities.

"I'll pick you up at seven."

"I'll be ready."

He set a kiss on her lips and stepped back, helping her into the car. When she looked in her rearview mirror a few seconds later, he was still staring after her, a contented smile on his face.

Daisy twirled in front of the mirror, her baby-blue sundress swirling about her legs. Since the weather this week had been so mild, Jack had suggested a picnic in the park tonight. She'd never actually had a picnic date, but it sounded wonderfully simple and romantic. They were joining their friends later at the Rusty Nail, so she paired the dress with her favorite dancing shoes.

Jack was right on time, looking handsome in a button-down shirt and his ever-present khakis. His jaw was freshly shaven, and the scent of his cologne drew her close enough for a brief kiss.

"You look beautiful," he said as he drew away, his eyes clinging to hers. "I like your dress."

"Thank you. It's new." She ran her fingers through his soft hair. It was one of her new favorite things, the feel of his hair. "Looks like you finally had time for that trim. It looks good."

"Josephine worked me in today. Are you ready?"

"Should I grab a tablecloth or a quilt or something?"

"Nope. I've got it."

When they arrived, the park was dotted with children enjoying the last rays of the day. Jack found a secluded grassy spot in a grove of trees. The canopy of oak leaves shaded them from the evening sun, and the fragrant evergreens screened out the rest of the world.

Once they were seated on the thick quilt, he unpacked a variety of foods he'd picked up from local businesses. Loaded potato salad from Bentley's Deli, fresh fruit from the Peach Barn, fried chicken and mashed potatoes from the diner, and raspberry cheesecake from the Blue Moon Grill.

"Sorry it's not homemade. But trust me, it's better this way."

"Are you kidding? You brought all my favorites. You're the best boyfriend ever."

The smile she earned warmed her to her toes.

Conversation flowed as they shared their supper. She raved over the food and was so full she had to force herself to split a slice of cheesecake with him.

She told him the latest about her mom and Mr. Francis. As of last night the couple had become exclusive. Daisy had never seen her mom like this, brimming with the hope of new love, sweetly uncertain, and breathtakingly beautiful. She had a good feeling about those two.

Just as she had a good feeling about herself and Jack. She'd never been with anyone like him. She'd fallen so deeply in love with him. It was crazy how quickly her feelings of friendship had shifted into more. Much more. She looked forward to being with him. When something happened, he was the first person she wanted to tell. He was confident and handsome, yet boyishly uncertain of himself sometimes. And so carefully forthcoming, helping to build back her trust in him.

Oh, she wasn't blind to his faults. He tended to waffle over decisions a little too long. He hardly knew the meaning of the word *relax,* and he was definitely too hard on himself. But she could relate to that one easily enough. And all of those things made Jack who he was. She accepted the good with the bad—just as he did—and understood they were both works in progress.

"What are you smiling about over there?" he asked.

The empty plates were stacked beside them, and the sun's light was now swathing the horizon in hues of pink and purple as it set.

"Just thinking about us."

One eyebrow lifted, obscured by a thatch of hair the breeze had blown over his forehead. "Good thoughts, I hope."

She leaned her weight on the arm closest to him, nudging his side. "Hence the smile."

He dropped a slow kiss on her mouth, then

stared into her eyes for a long, sweet moment. "Go for a walk with me?" he said softly.

"I'd love to." They packed the leftovers into the basket and folded up the quilt. "Should we take it to the car?"

"We'll get it on the way back. No one will bother it." He took her hand, and they set off on the paved path that meandered through the woods and along the creek.

She loved it back here. It was so peaceful. The breeze ruffled the leaves, and somewhere nearby a squirrel scrabbled through the carpet of leaves. In the distance the muted laughter of children pierced the air. The earthy smell of decaying leaves and wood mingled with the wonderful, familiar scent of Jack.

She snuggled up to his side. "We never run out of things to talk about. I love spending time with you. Have I mentioned that lately?"

He tugged her tight against him. "Right back atcha, Daisy Pendleton. I still can't believe you're my girl. I'm the most blessed man alive."

He dropped a kiss on her lips, their steps slowing as the kiss continued. She was too busy to notice the white twinkle lights on the gazebo until they were right up on it. It had become one of their favorite places. They'd spent hours talking here.

"Ooh, look. It's so pretty. They must've decorated it for the Fourth of July." The town decorated the gazebo in red and green lights for Christmas, but Daisy was partial to the white ones.

Jack took her hand, and they walked up the wooden steps. She started toward the bench seat, but Jack turned to face her, taking both her hands. There was an enigmatic look on his face she'd never seen before.

She blinked up at him, her heart stuttering.

"The town didn't decorate the gazebo, Daisy," he said in that deep, smoky voice. Then he slowly dropped to one knee. "I did."

Daisy sucked in a breath, her eyes searching Jack's. Her heart galloped in her chest, her lungs struggling to keep pace.

"I know it might seem quick," he said. "But I've never been more certain of anything in my life. I fell for you a long time ago, Daisy. You drew me in with your infectious grin and your easy laughter. You held me captive with your adorably contrite confessions and your tendency to overshare."

A breathy laugh slipped out. Jack had made a confession of his own recently: he'd been utterly charmed during their counseling sessions. She'd had no idea.

He squeezed her hands. "But it was the way you always think of others that stole my heart— and, okay, the way you laugh at my corny jokes didn't hurt either."

"Oh, Jack."

"I love the way you love me—and I love *you,* Daisy." He pressed a gentle kiss to her knuckles, holding her gaze steady. "So very much."

He let go of her hands and reached down, lifting up a small jewelry box.

Daisy's heart felt as if it might beat right out of her chest. She pressed a palm against it as if to hold it in place.

Jack opened the lid, and a brilliant diamond gleamed back at her. A somber look came over his features, those brown eyes looking at her with so much love she could hardly stand it.

"Daisy Jane Pendleton . . . would you do me the honor of becoming my wife?"

She swallowed hard against the emotion swelling her throat. "Yes. Oh, Jack, yes, of course I will."

His lovely mouth bloomed in a wide smile. He removed the ring from its velvet nest and slid it onto her finger.

"It's beautiful. It's perfect." She met his gaze. "I love you so much."

His shoulders sank on an exhale. "I was really hoping you'd say that."

She was still laughing at his obvious relief as he stood and pulled her close. His arms roped around her waist, his hands coming to rest on the small of her back.

He brushed her lips with his once. Twice. There

was so much in this kiss. Love and affection and adoration. She soaked it all in, yielded to it, giving back with equal fervor. She wanted to spend the rest of her life in his arms.

When they parted, her eyes drifted to the hand pressed to his shoulder. To the diamond glimmering on her finger.

"Do you like it?" he asked uncertainly. "If you'd prefer something else . . ."

"No. It's perfect," she said, falling into his beautiful brown eyes. It was so beautiful. *He* was so beautiful, inside and out. And he was all hers. "Absolutely perfect."

ACKNOWLEDGMENTS

Writing a book is a team effort, and I'm so grateful for the fabulous fiction team at HarperCollins Christian Publishing, led by publisher Amanda Bostic: Matt Bray, Kim Carlton, Allison Carter, Paul Fisher, Kristen Golden, Kayleigh Hines, Jodi Hughes, Becky Monds, and Kristen Ingebretson.

Thanks especially to my editor, Kim Carlton, for her insight and inspiration. I'm infinitely grateful to editor L. B. Norton, who saves me from countless errors and always makes me look so much better than I am.

Author Colleen Coble is my first reader. Thank you, friend! Writing wouldn't be nearly as much fun without you!

I'm grateful to my agent, Karen Solem, who's able to somehow make sense of the legal garble of contracts and, even more amazing, help me understand it.

Kevin, my husband of twenty-nine years, has been a wonderful support. Thank you, honey! I'm so glad to be doing life with you. To my kiddos, Justin and Hannah, Chad, and Trevor: You make life an adventure! Love you all!

Lastly, thank you, friend, for letting me share this story with you. I wouldn't be doing this without you! I enjoy connecting with friends on my Facebook page, www.facebook.com/author denisehunter. Please pop over and say hello. Visit my website at the link www.DeniseHunter Books.com or just drop me a note at Deniseahunter @comcast.net. I'd love to hear from you!

DISCUSSION QUESTIONS

1. Which character did you most connect with? Why? How did you feel about having a pastor for a hero? How did Jack's occupation affect your impressions of him?

2. Daisy had a lot of bad dates from the dating app before she connected with TJ. Have you ever joined a dating site? Do you think this is a good way to meet potential mates?

3. Daisy felt as if her dyslexia defined her in some ways. Have you ever felt defined by something—a job, a relationship, an event, a mistake?

4. When the story opened, Jack had been feeling unrequited love for quite some time. Have you ever experienced this? How did you cope? How did it turn out? Do you think God ever feels this way about humankind?

5. Daisy found herself in the position of having to offer grace to others and herself. Have

you found yourself in a similar situation? Do you find it harder to give grace to others or yourself?

6. Daisy realized that she'd put her parents and Jack on pedestals. Have you ever done likewise? Discuss the problems that can result.

7. What would you have done if you'd been in the situation Daisy's mom had found herself in years ago? Do you think you'd have been able to save your marriage? Do you think you would have welcomed Julia into your life? Why or why not?

8. Daisy's father sinned, and it caused a ripple of consequences for those around him. Have you experienced anything similar? Discuss.

9. Jack reminded Daisy, "There's only one who'll never let you down." Do you believe that? Have you experienced this in your own life?

10. How did God bring something good out of something bad in each of these situations: Daisy's dad's infidelity, Daisy's dyslexia, the damage to Hope House?

ABOUT THE AUTHOR

Denise Hunter is the internationally published bestselling author of more than thirty books, including *A December Bride* and *The Convenient Groom*, which have been adapted into original Hallmark Channel movies. She has won the Holt Medallion Award, the Reader's Choice Award, the Carol Award, and the Foreword Book of the Year Award and is a RITA finalist. When Denise isn't orchestrating love lives on the written page, she enjoys traveling with her family, drinking green tea, and playing drums. Denise makes her home in Indiana, where she and her husband are currently enjoying an empty nest.

DeniseHunterBooks.com
Facebook: Denise Hunter
Twitter: @DeniseAHunter

| Books are produced in the United States using U.S.-based materials | Books are printed using a revolutionary new process called THINKtech™ that lowers energy usage by 70% and increases overall quality | Books are durable and flexible because of Smyth-sewing | Paper is sourced using environmentally responsible foresting methods and the paper is acid-free |

Center Point Large Print
600 Brooks Road / PO Box 1
Thorndike, ME 04986-0001 USA

(207) 568-3717

US & Canada:
1 800 929-9108
www.centerpointlargeprint.com